Forever, Alabama

Forever, Alabama

A novel

Susan Sands

TULE
PUBLISHING

Dear Reader,

If you're reading this, it means you've gotten hold of my third novel! Thank you! It's been a tough one to finish and I appreciate your taking the time to read it.

This past year has been a handful for many reasons. I won't touch politics, but I will tell you that while I wrote this story, I had quite a few personal struggles within my own life that made my journey as a writer more difficult.

Special thanks to my mentor and dear friend, Karen White, for your advice and support. I can't believe you still answer my calls! To my writer friends and critique partners: You are my base when things get crazy and it all blows up. Thanks to Christy Hayes, Laura Alford, Laura Butler and Tracy Solheim for the writer's retreats and your friendship. Thanks to Sharlene Moore for the many fantastic graphics. A special gratitude to Andrea Brown for taking my headshots. You make me pretty.

Thanks to Jennifer Tarpley for being a character in my book!

Special gratitude to the Tule team: Jane, Sinclair, Meghan, Lindsey, and Michelle. You are the most professional, kind, and efficient group of ladies, and I'm debt for your patience when things got hairy.

As always, to my parents, my husband, and my children: I love you all and couldn't do this writing thing without you.

Chapter One

EVERYBODY, WHO KNEW him, loved Ben Laroux—especially the female population of Ministry, Alabama and surrounding counties. Ben had to admit that'd been a pretty accurate statement in his experience—right up 'til now.

It made no sense. Still uncertain how his few interactions with Sabine O'Connor had gone so badly, Ben tried to catch up to her before she stalked out the door. She'd shaken his hand with formal politeness but obvious disdain earlier, then she'd dismissed him completely.

The woman was magnificent, with black hair, pale skin, and the lightest blue eyes he'd ever seen; they were nearly silver. He watched as she stopped short just before exiting the building, madly digging through her purse.

"Looking for something?" he asked.

He might have been just a bit too close for comfort—her comfort.

Her head snapped up, and she nailed him with a level stare. "Let me guess; you found my phone?" The sounds of country music and laughter made it difficult to have a normal conversation.

"Now, why would you think I had your phone?"

"Because you're grinning at me in a smirky, satisfied way, while I'm obviously panicking and searching for it."

"I might have it," he admitted.

She placed a hand on her hip and asked, "So, what will it take to get it back, and for you to leave me on my way?"

"Have dinner with me." Well, she'd asked, hadn't she?

She narrowed her eyes at him. "Okay. Give me your business card, and I'll call you." She nearly yelled to be heard above the din of music and laughter.

She'd probably toss his card into the trash on her way out. "How about I enter your number on my phone and I'll call you to schedule?"

"Are you planning to stalk me?" It sounded like a bit of a challenge.

"Nah, I just want to figure out why you're such a Ben-hater. I'm intrigued. If I fail to change your opinion of me, I'll leave you alone. Scout's honor." He held up the international Boy Scout hand gesture.

She rolled her eyes in unmistakable doubt of his scouting background.

"You seem so certain you know my character."

"It's not so hard to figure out," she said.

The certainty in her ice-blue eyes bothered him. Seriously, he'd not done anything to her, or anyone else he could think of that warranted this edgy hostility.

Did he detect a whiff of bourbon along with her Coco Chanel? "Can I offer you a ride home, or call you a cab?" His upbringing forbade him leaving a woman stranded at a bar without a ride.

She shook her head. "I'd planned to ride home with—a friend, but they didn't show, so I'm going to call a cab."

"Wait, somebody stood you up?" He tried to keep the shock from showing in his expression.

"What? Of course not." She smiled then, apparently realizing how incredibly nasty her tone and demeanor had been toward him. "It was a—misunderstanding."

"I'd be happy to drive you."

"No, thank you."

"I'll wait here with you for the cab." She didn't seem like the type to get behind the wheel after shooting whiskey, but he'd hang around just to be sure.

"Fine."

He figured she realized by now the uselessness of arguing with him after their brief time spent together.

So, they stood just outside in silence as she waited for her ride.

"Nice night," Ben observed.

"Uh huh."

"I want you to know that I appreciate what you've done for my family," he said, and meant it.

She was a family therapist and had played a big part in

helping his brother-in-law, Grey, and Grey's daughter, Samantha, deal with some incredibly nasty stuff last year when they'd come back to town. But he'd not spent any real time with her, personally.

"You're welcome."

More silence. *Alrighty, then.*

The cab arrived just as the silence was wearing awkwardly thin. Ben cleared his throat. "It's been my pleasure." He grinned. "Looking forward to dinner," he said as he opened the car door and tucked her into the backseat.

He couldn't tell through the window if that was a wave or not. Ben decided to remain optimistic for now.

Perhaps he should write her off as unfriendly, or simply uninterested and trying to make her point but, in his experience, people didn't go out of their way to be snippy and rude unless they had a reason. Really, something was up with this gal. It was odd, because his family members thought the world of her.

Why had she singled him out for such raw treatment? Who hated Ben Laroux? Go figure.

≫≫≪≪

BEN LAROUX WAS a handsome dog, no offense to the mostly sweet and cuddly four-legged creatures she'd met thus far. She'd met him briefly through her clients, the Laroux family, whom she thought highly of, and considered friends.

But he was one of *those* men. All charm and manners and

white, straight teeth—like a wolf. She was all done with that kind of misrepresentation. They always started out just fine, until their phony representative took off for the hills, and left the real guy behind. Then, the handsome façade and invisible personality warts became evident. In her case, warts would have been a far preferable flaw than what she'd ended up with. She'd married her frog, who'd ended up a snake—a poisonous one.

Sabine hadn't missed the adoring glances of women and greetings from nearly everyone around during the brief time she'd been in Ben Laroux's company. He was evidently very popular. Small-town high school football quarterback popular. He was also very intent on her reaction to him. Like he hadn't ever met anyone who'd displayed an unfavorable response to him. He'd clearly been confused by her lack of adoration and approval.

The cab pulled up to her small house, and she took a moment to make certain no one was around—no cars parked outside or just down the street. A lamp shone through the curtains inside the cottage.

Sabine so rarely went out these days; her social life was almost nonexistent.

She paid the driver and went to work unlocking the three dead bolts. The porch light startled her.

"Hey, honey, did you have a good time?" Her mother's lightly aging features were highlighted in the soft glow.

"Hey, Momma, you should be in bed."

"I couldn't sleep. It's just like when you were a teenager."

Sabine stepped inside and dead-bolted the locks. "I'm not a kid anymore," Sabine reminded her mother.

"Obviously." Her mother held her at arm's length. "Nobody could accuse you of being a child. You are a beautiful woman and I'm so proud of you."

Sabine smiled at her mother, her sweet, loving mother, who'd been through far more than any person should at the age of fifty-five. She hardly looked a day over forty-five, and no one believed they were mother and daughter.

Sabine hugged her mom and checked the back door, leaving the lamp on in the living room, as was her habit. The house had three bedrooms. Just enough for Sabine, her mother, and her sister, Rachel, whenever she turned up for an occasional visit.

As Sabine washed her face and brushed her teeth, her mind wandered back to the scene at the bar with Ben Laroux. As if she would have dinner with him.

The lower the profile she kept here in this sweet Southern town, the better.

The very last thing she needed was to bring anyone else into their small, comfortable life. Things had finally settled down into a peaceful routine.

Climbing under the covers and settling in with her trusty laptop, Sabine googled Ben Laroux. Though she had no interest in him as a potential date, he certainly was an interesting case study. If he did indeed plan to stalk her, she would be ready. Sabine knew who he was, but after their interaction this evening, admittedly, her interest had been further piqued.

The results were astonishing. There were thousands of hits upon simply entering his first and last name. He was a local attorney and philanthropist. He was also linked socially, to what must be, nearly every gorgeous woman in the state of Alabama, according to the images section of Google.

No wonder he seemed so surprised that she wasn't interested. But she *had* known who he was the instant he'd introduced himself. In fact, besides meeting him at the Laroux home briefly a couple times, she'd been hearing incredible stories about Ben Laroux for awhile now.

A smile played about Sabine's lips. After reading more about him, she better understood what a well-deserved trouncing of his ego she'd accomplished.

»»»«««

AS BEFORE, WHEN he'd been in her presence, even a brief period, his world had tipped slightly, and it unnerved him. Nobody tipped *his* world, at least not in a very long time. He'd planned to wait a few days before calling, but he saw her contemptuous ice-blue eyes every time he closed his.

Ben dialed Sabine's number while he sat at his desk in his office, files piled all around. He'd shut the door, so he wasn't disturbed. The line rang several times, then a pleasant and professional voice came on the line stating that Dr. Sabine

O'Connor wasn't available at present, and to kindly leave a message and she would return his call. Even her husky voice message caused an uncomfortable tightening in the zippered area of his jeans.

He ended the connection without leaving a message, unsure exactly what to say.

As he pondered the many possibilities, the blaring of his AC/DC Highway to Hell ringtone nearly made him drop the thing. "Ben Laroux."

"Oh, it's you. I didn't recognize the number." She must have done a call-back.

"I'm flattered that you haven't hung up yet, Dr. O'Connor."

"Don't be. I guess you want to have dinner." She sighed into the phone.

"Sounds like you'd rather catch an incurable disease. But dinner was why I called. Wouldn't want you to think I had no follow-through." He didn't want to squander what would likely be his only opportunity to figure out what her deal was.

"Fine."

"I'm sorry?" He nearly fell out of his chair.

"I'll have dinner with you." Her tone was grudging, but he supposed he'd bullied her just a little.

"Glad to hear it, though don't sound so enthusiastic."

She ignored that. "I'm done here for the day, so I guess we could grab something quick. I'm starving, and you've assured me you're not the lowest sort—" She stopped, as if unsure how to proceed.

Ben smelled her defeat at his hands and grabbed the lead. "Where are you? I know a little place—"

"*I* know a place." She snatched control back and held onto it as if to keep him in check. She was only about five minutes away from his office and gave him directions where she wanted to meet.

"Yes, ma'am."

>>><<<

FIFTEEN MINUTES LATER, seated with slabs of ribs and giant mugs of root beer, Ben was grinning ear-to-ear. "I like your place."

Sabine held up her finger while she slugged her root beer, set it down with a clunk, then daintily dabbed at her lips with a napkin. He'd half-expected her to swipe her mouth with the back of her hand based on the gusto of her attack on the frosted mug.

"Thirsty?" He cocked up an eyebrow in question.

"It's been one of those days." She didn't elaborate, only dove into the full slab of baby backs with an equal measure of enthusiasm.

This stunning creature ate ribs like a truck driver. He waited for the belch that never emerged. Still stunning, he decided. He'd only have been more impressed had that root beer been an actual draft beer. But she was driving.

"So tell me about your practice." He was dying to know more about this woman who obviously could hardly stomach him, but had grudgingly agreed to share a meal—ribs at that.

"I'm a clinical family therapist. You know, people with real problems—addiction, abuse, marriages in trouble."

He raised his eyebrows. "Sounds like heavy stuff."

"Some of it is very heavy. But, I've got several patients who treat therapy like a nail appointment and use it to complain about pet peeves and gossip." Sabine's expression became guarded. "I shouldn't have said that."

"No, I find it fascinating. I've got clients who do the same thing. They use litigation to annoy their neighbors. If they don't like the color the neighbor painted the barn, then how better to irritate than to threaten a lawsuit against the barn's owner? It's not meant to pursue, just a well-placed letter from an attorney's office. But it forces the barn owner to gain legal representation and spend time and money to defend the threat. See? We do have something in common." He grinned, pleased with himself for finding common ground.

She nodded, reluctantly. "I can see that both our professions require a lot of time, energy, and paperwork and, when clients make light of our efforts for petty gains, it can be very frustrating, though I do realize those are the ones often in the most pain and crying out for attention."

"Exactly. So, I'm wondering why I haven't seen you around more, this being such a small town?" Sure, he'd known she lived here, but he rarely, if ever, saw her out and about.

"My office is tiny, and I work alone—no partners. I don't get out much." She shrugged.

"I would imagine it takes a lot of compassion and kindness to counsel those with such deep human conditions. The ones who come to you for the real reasons."

"So, I guess you're wondering why, if I'm such a kind and compassionate person, I didn't treat you more fairly when we met?" She teed it up for him.

And he swung away. "An explanation would be nice."

Finally, she pushed away the nearly-clean platter and noted her surroundings, as if she'd only just become aware of them. The crowd consisted mostly of men, a few with dates, but none who compared to her in looks, class, or anything within the ballpark. He recognized several of them—most of them. A few had nodded. She hadn't seemed to notice.

"It's a little slow this evening," she said.

He knew it was because this place was a favorite of his too.

"Come here often?" he asked, wondering if she was formulating a reason for her former rudeness or had decided not to fill him in.

"Often enough to know it's a little slow."

The waiter had recognized her and addressed her as 'Doc.' But he'd also slapped Ben on the back and called him by his first name.

"So, *are* you going to tell me why you treat me like I slithered out from under a maggot-covered rock?" He'd been dying to get to the bottom of her response to their initial introduction.

"It has little to do with you, personally." Then, her posture relaxed and a small smile formed on her lips. "I know this surprises you, but I'm not interested in your type."

"My type?"

"You're too good looking—"

"Thanks—" Ben cut her off and grinned.

She held up a hand. "I mean, women say yes all the time to you, don't they?"

He made a face. "Not sure I want to hear this."

"You're so confident everyone will fall at your feet and adore you. You expect attention as your due, while the rest of us have to earn respect to gain notice."

"Do you honestly think, with your looks, that you have to do anything but enter a room to get attention? That's a bit hypocritical of you."

"I work hard to gain respect, despite my physical appearance, and despite that I'm a woman. I often don't get taken seriously because of how I look. People assume I'm successful because of my looks. So, it's different."

He could only stare. "Why did you agree to have dinner in the first place?"

"Because I was rude to you and you didn't deserve it. I appreciated your bringing my phone back, though if I'd been less-fortunate-looking, I wonder if you'd have bothered. Maybe lost and found would have worked just fine."

He ignored the comment because he didn't want to analyze the truth of her words. But he'd seen her softening, the shame at her behavior toward him. "Well, I guess I should be honored that you even stooped so low as to meet me." The way her mind worked bugged the crap out of him.

"You're intentionally taking this the wrong way. I've been completely honest with you." She seemed to be struggling with herself not to be rude, but unable to dig out of it.

"Honest? Your assumptions about my character, without even knowing me, and your pretty pathetic stab at minding your manners have been entertaining. Irritating, but entertaining."

She lowered her head. "I'm sorry. Your reputation precedes you. I must admit to being somewhat—no—*very*—biased against you."

He frowned. "Has someone been talking trash about me?"

Her face turned bright red. "I—I really can't say." She picked up her purse from the unoccupied chair and stood. "Thank you for dinner—and for returning my phone. I appreciate both. Can we part ways now?"

He waved off her attempt to settle half the bill and paid the check. They made their way out to the lot where they'd parked a few spaces apart. He climbed in the cab of his truck, shaking his head with wonder at her prejudice against him.

Ben started the truck and waved a hand as Sabine zipped past in her tiny, red sports car. He thought he could let it go. But damn if he didn't mumble and curse all the way home.

Chapter Two

S ABINE'S DECISION TO have dinner with Ben Laroux likely had shocked her more than him. She'd had no intention to see him again for dinner or otherwise.

Truth was, Sabine had come to mostly unfavorable conclusions about Ben Laroux's character in an entirely rational way. He was a favorite topic of her female patients. Either they claimed incurable heartbreak after a short and passionate affair with him, wanted to regale her with his, um, considerable charm and skills as a lover, or they'd just plain crushed on him since high school. It was nauseating, really. She wondered if he understood his part in these women's inability to let him go completely.

Of course, it wasn't her place to counsel him. Unless he asked. But could she help? Or would she lecture him on his serial dating habits and leading women on? His happy oblivion was almost entertaining to watch, really.

After that night, Sabine was successfully able to put him out of her mind, except, of course, when she had to listen to those who continued extolling his virtues on a weekly basis.

Besides patients, Sabine had managed to keep her social footprint pretty small here, just outside Ministry.

Her clients, on the other hand, kept her posted on the town's goings-on as it pertained to their lives. She had several patients with serious issues, as she'd told Ben. But she also counseled those who used therapy as their weekly spotlight for "let's talk about me."

Of course, Sabine didn't judge, and eagerly waited for the opportunity to give constructive advice. If anything serious was revealed, she was there at the ready with real help. And she wanted to help.

The phone on her desk rang, startling Sabine out of her musings. She picked up the receiver.

"Honey, I'm planning on making a shrimp gumbo tonight. Sound good?"

Sabine's thoughts were broken by her mother's plans for dinner. "Perfect. Do you want me to run by the store to pick up anything on my way home?"

"I went earlier, but forgot the rice. Grab a bag, if you don't mind. Long grain—not Uncle Ben's, okay?" It was a huge step for her mother to venture out on her own these days, and Sabine was thrilled for the progress.

"Of course. I'll be leaving here soon." They hung up.

As she locked the exterior office door, Sabine caught sight of a black sedan disappearing around the corner. Had that been a fleur-de-lis decal on the back fender? Her heart nearly dropped to her toes.

Since Sabine and her mother had left—*fled* might be a better term—Louisiana a year and a half ago and changed their last names, they remained cautious. Hopefully, this was her paranoia working overtime.

⫸⫷

BEN COULDN'T BELIEVE he stood facing Sabine O'Connor in Judge Haney's chambers. He'd just gotten the memo that the expert witness had been injured in a car accident, and Dr. O'Connor was to replace him. She wore a cranberry-colored suit, just short of all the way red. Her lipstick matched the color and his eyes were drawn to her very full lips.

They'd had to admit to the judge knowing one another. Ben tried hard to focus on the judge's questions instead of her lips.

"What exactly is the nature of your relationship with Miz O'Connor?" The elderly Judge Haney eyed Ben through his thick spectacles as if Ben'd been caught stealing candy.

"It's *Dr.* O'Connor, Judge Haney. She's got a PhD."

"Is that so?" The judge's bushy gray eyebrows shot up in a high V.

"Yes. I returned her cell phone at a bar, and we had dinner together one time. We've not had contact since." Oh, that sounded ever-so-simple. Ben could smell her perfume, a light jasmine scent that he'd remembered for days after their last encounter.

17

The old judge turned his rheumy eyes toward Sabine. "Do you concur with Mr. Laroux's statement, *Dr. O'Connor?*"

"Yes, Your Honor," she answered, not sparing Ben a glance.

"So, to be clear, there's no personal relationship ongoing between the two of you?" The judge asked again, just as Ben dragged his gaze away from Sabine.

He hoped he could keep it together when the time came for cross-examination. What in the world was it about her that got him so cranked up?

"No, sir." They answered in unison.

Judge Haney motioned to the district attorney. "Do you have any objection to Dr. O'Connor testifying as an expert witness in this case?"

The DA shook his head. "No sir."

"The matter is settled then, and the trial will resume with a forty-eight-hour delay for Miz—uh—*Doctuh* O'Connor to familiarize herself with the case."

Ben let out a breath. He'd prepared his cross-examination for the witness without realizing it was to be Sabine. She was testifying on behalf of the prosecution and he represented the defendant.

As they left the judge's chambers, neither chanced a glance or conversation. Of course, they'd been completely honest, but he resisted the niggling of guilt that there was still something between them—at least on his end. This was based on his physical response to being within a few feet of her again.

He would definitely keep his distance in the courtroom, lest he embarrass himself for everyone to notice. But the next time they faced off would be in his domain, so she'd better be prepared. And she'd be under oath.

When the trial resumed, no matter the outcome of these proceedings, there wouldn't be any winners here. It was a wrongful death suit involving a terminally ill child brought to the emergency room with complications from treatment.

The issue was with the ER doctor on staff and how the delay of a request for test results had affected the efficiency of care during a particularly busy time in the hospital. Sabine's testimony related to the stress level and decision-making ability of the physician and if he could be held liable for the child's delay in treatment.

Ben's client was the physician on call that night. The only way to handle this kind of case was with the utmost compassion for the family who'd lost their child too soon. No winners here.

❧❧❧❧❧

TWO DAYS LATER, Sabine answered the questions calmly and competently. She stated facts and supplemented her testimony with well-documented sleep-deprivation and behavioral studies to support her responses.

Her testimony was only a small part of this complicated

puzzle. The most relevant information would come from the timeline that night, and how quickly the child was sent through triage, tests performed, processed, and the call made for treatment. A single person's mental status under stressful conditions could hardly tell the entire story.

Sabine had tried to explain this to the prosecutor, but he'd been deliberate in pushing forward with this line of questioning. All she could do was be truthful and protect the facts and her reputation in the process.

Ben fired away at her, asking pertinent and direct questions. He didn't succeed in stumping her, yet neither did the prosecutor prove his point succinctly either. In her point of view, she'd been a waste of time and money as a paid witness, even though she'd done precisely as asked.

It had ended in a draw. But Sabine could say, grudgingly, that Ben Laroux was an excellent attorney.

Damn, she didn't want him to deserve any merit at all. It still didn't make him a good person—no matter how Google expounded his charitable works. Any man who did with as many women what those women said he did wasn't worth real estate in her brain, even for a moment.

She climbed into her car, started the engine, locked the doors and proceeded to read a couple of texts that had come in while she'd been in court. Sabine was so intent on a message from her sister that she shrieked loudly and came off her seat at least a foot at the tap on the driver's side window.

Mortified, she rolled it down a crack to face Mr. GQ

lawyer, lover of all the women. "Did I scare you?"

"No, I just won the lottery. I was excited."

He grinned at her obvious lie. "Great job in there. The prosecutor made an ass of himself."

"That was his fault. He didn't ask the right questions to sway things to his advantage. I won't put my reputation at risk for his case, no matter how empathetic I am toward the family."

"You're for real aren't you?" He appeared surprised.

"If you mean that I can't be intimidated, then, yes." She'd dodged her share of corruption within her own family, and she didn't ever want to mar her professional life by lying or cheating to get ahead.

"So, do you want to have lunch?" He grinned.

"Are you kidding? We swore to the county judge that we have no connection to one another."

"Your testimony is over."

"Yes, but if anyone sees us together during the rest of this trial, it'll appear we're in cahoots. Especially after the prosecutor's debacle today."

"Is cahoots a legal term? I'm unfamiliar." He tapped his temple as if puzzled.

"You're the attorney. You know how foolish that would be."

"So shoot me." He slid her a lopsided lady-killing grin.

"Nice try, slick." How could she let her guard down with this one for even a half a second? She couldn't. "Sorry, I've got to go call my sister. See you around." This was the truth.

"Okay, I can take a hint. I guess we'll see each other again when you come to your senses and call me."

"Don't count on it. Take care." Sabine meaningfully slid her gearshift into reverse, causing him to take a quick step backward. Wise move.

She threw up a quick wave, clicked the button for the window to close automatically and didn't glance his way again, leaving him standing next to an empty parking spot.

What was it about him that made every bitch hormone in her commence z-snapping whenever he got within fifty feet? Well, besides the *stuff* she knew about him? That stuff made her want to run in the other direction as fast and far as possible—or climb him and beg him to show her how that worked.

Of course, it was only because of the *stuff* she'd been privy to lately during her sessions. In fact, it was as if there was some sort of bragging rights affiliated with having been linked with him romantically in this town. Like a contest of sorts.

Sabine had no idea how true any of the, uh, information her clients felt the need to share with her was. But they made certain she knew.

Shaking her head, Sabine pulled into her small drive. Somehow, she'd made it across town without noticing her charming surroundings, damn the man.

Maybe she was using him as distraction to avoid calling

Rachel. Her sister's communications could mean there was a problem, or not at all. Rachel was a talented freelance photographer who'd figured out that the best way to distance herself from the family was indeed distance. Sabine had no idea where her sister was at the moment.

Rachel's text asking her to call might be simply just a check-in. But Sabine had a sixth sense when it came to her siblings, and, right now, she had a lead weight sitting in the pit of her stomach that didn't bode well.

As Sabine got out of the car, she noticed something odd. Well, two things, actually. A truck was parked in front of her house—a slightly familiar one—though she couldn't place it right off. The other was rarer and strange. It was the rich sound of her mother's laughter from the backyard.

Sabine stood beside her car, almost unable to move. It was a sound from her past. One that brought back warm and wonderful flashbacks from her childhood. The one before all the bad things happened.

Sabine inhaled the aroma of freshly-cut grass mixed in the evening air. Another reminder of happy times. Who was in her backyard with Mom? Making her laugh? Instead of heading toward the front door, Sabine took the small cobbled pathway around the side of the cottage.

Unlatching the gate, she tried not to appear sneaky in her approach. "Mom?" Sabine called out.

"Sabine? We're over here." Her mother's voice held a note of excitement and something else she'd not heard in—

maybe never.

The mystery was quickly solved the moment she rounded the back corner. Norman Harrison was the truck's owner. That made sense as to why it seemed familiar. "Hi, Norman. What a surprise." Sabine smiled at the older man.

Norman's handsome, weather-beaten face cracked into a huge grin. Instead of shaking her hand or a polite nod, he closed the gap between them and gathered her up into a great big bear hug. "How the heck are you, Sabine? It's been too long."

Sabine'd nearly forgotten how warm a few of the true friends she'd made since she'd been here were. "I had no idea you knew my mother."

Mom piped in, "We've run into each other a few times at the nursery. Today, I tried to carry a bag of mulch—" They looked at one another and burst out laughing again. It was then that Sabine noticed her mother's filthy clothing. Her mother rarely wore dirt.

"Oh, looks like you took on a little too much." But Mom didn't appear self-conscious.

"Norman was kind enough to offer his truck for delivery services."

"It was my pleasure, Eliza."

Eliza? Nobody but her dad had ever called her mother Eliza. Mom was Elizabeth.

"How's Grey?" Sabine asked Norman about his son.

"Oh, he's just fine. Busy, you know. Cammie, Samantha,

and the new house are keeping him hopping—not to mention the Preservation Society contract."

Norman Harrison's son, Grey, was a historical architect and former client whose ten-year-old daughter still came to see her as a patient on a regular basis. The child lost her mother two years ago in a single car drunk-driving accident. Samantha was making good progress, but her abandonment issues still created some alienation between her and Grey's new wife, Cammie.

Cammie was Ben Laroux's twin sister. Small towns; go figure. Everybody was related or connected somehow.

So, the connection between Sabine and Norman, her mother's new friend, was that of a recent happy ending with a client and his family. At least she knew Norman wasn't an old gold-digger.

"Well, thanks for bailing her out," Sabine said.

"Of course." Norman bowed slightly. He was clearly smitten. "I'll look forward to seeing the fruits of your efforts later this spring." He grinned at Mom.

She blushed. "I like to wear gloves, an apron and kneel on an ergonomic cushion while I plant annuals in prepared flowerbeds or pots. This is just for the top dressing on my annuals. I do it a little at a time. No heavy stuff for me. I'm a lightweight." Something was definitely happening between the two of them.

"Mom, I love the flowers you plant around here. They make everything brighter." Sabine wanted Mom to feel good about her contributions to their home.

Norman looked around the tiny yard; there were various planters ready to pot with annuals, flower beds, weeded, some with flats of young plants beside them. "This is a nice space. Spring is the most fun for planting."

Sabine loved the yard, with its large old oak tree in the rear that provided shade in the evening. The patio overhang from the roof was screened and would allow them to sit outdoors without mosquitoes being a pain in the summer. The gas grill sat off to the side, and if history repeated, promised to be as well-used as last year.

The two of them normally got on well together. They were comfortable here. It was a very different setting than the enormous Garden District house/mansion in New Orleans where she grew up, but change was good most of the time. She hoped her mother felt the same.

"Norman, you'll have to join us for dinner one day soon. Sabine is a wonderful cook. She doesn't tell anyone, but she's almost as good as me."

"She lies. No one is as good as her," Sabine said, hoping to reestablish their earlier relaxed and pleasant atmosphere.

"I would be honored to join you ladies for dinner. Looking forward to it."

"Thanks again, Norman. I'll walk you out and we can exchange numbers," Mom said.

Sabine waved as they started toward the gate. Wow. One never knew what the day might bring.

Her phone buzzed at that moment. Rachel. She'd forgotten to call. "Hey, Rach, what's up?"

"It's about damn time you pick up! I've been trying to get ahold of you, or haven't you noticed?"

"Sorry, I was in court and just got home. Mom had a *man* here with her when I arrived."

"A *man?* Like a man who fixed something?"

"Nope. One who followed her home from the nursery to carry her mulch and flex for her."

"You're kidding, right?" Rachel's shocked tone was understandable.

"No. He's a client's father. Nice guy. Helped her home in his truck with some soil for her flower beds."

"Mom has flower beds? You've got to be joking. Soil? What's happening in Alabama? Next you'll be telling me she's wearing a pair of overalls and listening to country music." Rachel expressed her disbelief over their very well-dressed city mother's digging in the dirt.

"So, what's going on? You've obviously got something to tell me."

"Yeah. Just giving you a heads-up that James might be in your area. He called a few days ago asking questions. Of course, I didn't spill any information, but you know how resourceful he is."

Sabine was quiet for a moment. Yes, their half-brother could be very tricky.

"Sabine? You okay?"

"Yeah. I think I saw someone sitting in a car outside my office before. It could have been him."

"Watch your back. I don't think he'll cause any real trouble, but I think Dad might've put him onto keeping an eye on the two of you. The parole hearing is coming up soon, according to James."

"Damn. I thought we'd have more time." Sabine wasn't ready to face this. "Rachel, do you know when the hearing is scheduled?" Sabine's pulse beat faster.

Rachel sighed. "I don't think there's a date posted yet, at least not one that's listed on the website," Rachel said. "Yes, I've been checking." Rachel's relationship with their father was still in a rough place.

Rachel hadn't spent any real time with them to settle into a routine or become accustomed to a new family structure without their father in it. Of course, Sabine had lived with Richard when everything had hit the fan, so they hadn't all lived together for several years anyway. But it certainly would be nice for the three of them to have some relaxed bonding time together.

Sabine heard the thread of sorrow in Rachel's voice. "It's been nearly two years. I wish you would consider taking some jobs closer to us. We keep a bedroom for you here."

"Should I tell Mom about James and the parole hearing?" Sabine bit her lip, hoping to figure out a way to save Mom from further stress relating to her dad.

"Not yet. She may not have to be upset by any of this.

We're not sure when it will be yet, so give it a little time."

"Where are you, Rach?"

"I'm down at Oak Alley Plantation shooting a wedding. It pays the bills. I'll try to make it over there soon."

"Take care of yourself, Sis. You're a little too close to home for my comfort."

"Hey, don't worry about me. You look after our mother and keep the strange men away." Sabine smiled at that absurd comment as she hung up. Their parents had been estranged for nearly five years. Dad's incarceration for obstruction of justice and civil rights violations, and whatever else, had finally made it possible for Mom to obtain a divorce two years ago. It was the final break she'd so desperately needed from the man she'd loved with her heart and soul, but who'd taken everything from her—mostly her trust.

Chapter Three

C OWS. BEN WOULD like to say he couldn't believe this was happening. But it wasn't the first time the Millers and the Johnsons had battled over the Miller's bovine herd breaking loose, trampling, and devouring Mrs. Johnson's precious vegetable and flower garden. No, wait, the message Ben'd just listened to, if directly quoted was more like, "Those damned cows from Miller's land busted through again and shit all over the front yard, ate the flowers, and ruined all the new rows we just planted! I want to file a lawsuit, Ben, do you hear me?"

Loud and clear. But these folks were neighbors and had been for going on thirty years. The Johnsons actually didn't want to start a war, so it was up to Ben to figure out a way to keep the peace when tempers invariably flared. Of course, the time and effort would yield no income for Ben. Just another good deed to maintain the balance. Ben handled both the Miller and Johnson family's wills and estate business, though. So, it was sensible to keep everyone happy.

Jerking at the necktie he'd worn in court for the last

eight hours, Ben decided that if he was to face the angry neighbors, better to be comfortable while doing so. He changed from loafers into glove-soft, well-worn boots— better to dodge any remnants from the well-fed cows. They weren't dubbed shit-kickers for nothing.

He wished he had a pair of jeans to change into, but he'd not planned on mucking around today, so he'd make do with what he had.

His cell phone rang as he was heading out. "Hello?"

"Hey there, handsome."

"Oh, hi, Celine."

"I'm feeling a little lonely. You off work yet?"

"Sorry, no can do. I've got to take care of some business off Highway 9."

"How about tomorrow?" she pressed.

Should he tell her she'd used up her share of dates? How did one do that without coming off sounding like a pure ass? "Well, the thing is—" He would skirt the issue if possible.

"Are you blowing me off, Ben Laroux?" she asked.

The two of them hadn't been serious and she'd never seemed the jealous type, but she deserved an honest answer, he supposed. "Well, you see, Celine, I've decided to limit my dating—"

"Limit your dating?" She sounded more curious than angry, which was a good sign.

"I don't want to hurt anyone's feelings, so, I'm sticking with a two-date rule for now, since I'm so busy."

Laughter. "So, I've used up my time, huh? Good luck with that, honey. If you think you can outrun the women in this town by making rules to keep them away, really, good luck."

She hung up, still snickering. What was so hilarious? He was working to make his life more manageable and maintain pleasant relationships. On the bright side, she hadn't yelled at him for refusing to see her. She could've at least pretended to be a little more upset, though. More likely, she'd pass along the info at the next Bunco group—or better yet, post it on all the social media outlets via the worldwide web.

Could be his newly instated status would make its way around town via Celine and her friends faster than any electronic postings could, thereby saving him the painful task of breaking it to every potentially interested young woman in and around the county. His sisters made great fun of his brilliant plan to streamline his busy schedule by cutting down on the social aspect of his week.

Truly, it made perfect sense. It wasn't like he was hurting anyone. He simply wasn't involved enough with any one person at present for this decision to cause a problem.

Pulling up at Johnny Miller's barn, Ben sighed and got 6ut of his truck. Looked like the cows were back home safe and sound, based on the dozens of rather enormous, bored sets of eyes that regarded him as he made his way across the fenced enclosure and into the dark recess of the huge red structure.

"Johnny? You in here?" Ben called.

It smelled of dried hay, manure, and leather. Horses shifted, in at least a half dozen stalls, snickering softly.

"Ben? That you?" Johnny emerged from the small office at the rear of the place.

The two men shook hands. Johnny's were far more rough and weathered than Ben's. Not that Ben was soft—far from it. He had his own land, just outside of town, with a few acres, where he kept a couple horses and a small barn adjacent to his house. Ben simply didn't put as much time into working with his hands outdoors. Far less than he'd like, that was for certain.

"Heard the cows got loose again," Ben said. No point beating around the bush.

"Yup. Got 'em back in pretty quick-like though." Johnny worked the wad of chewing tobacco in his left cheek. He turned after he spoke and spit at the base of one of the horses' stalls.

"You know old man Johnson's hot, and ready to file suit against you this time?"

"Yup. His missus got a bee in her bonnet 'bout them flowers."

"If I were you, I'd buy her some new flats of annuals, have one of your guys go over and install them, and while he's at it, remove all traces that your cows paid a visit. And apologize."

"Yup. Already figured I'd handle it. Gonna fix the rows

for the garden too."

"Give a call to George and let him know before he heads over to the police station to file a report, why don't you? I'll go on over and try and smooth things over with Mrs. Johnson."

"You was always good with the ladies, Ben. Didn't matter how old they was." Johnny laughed, a rusty sound. and spit a dark stream of tobacco juice just to the side of Ben's left foot.

"You gotta keep your fences in good shape and make sure it doesn't happen again. I can't keep mediating between the two of you."

"Aw, come on, Ben. Mediatin's your job, now, ain't it?" Another rusty laugh followed Ben out to his truck.

One of these days he wouldn't be everyone's boy. What would happen if he just left them alone to handle this themselves? There would likely be several sides of beef in dispute as to whose freezer they should belong.

Ben cranked up and headed across the road hoping to heck the Millers' daughter wasn't visiting on this fine day. They'd, uh, had a few pleasant encounters a few years back, and Cissy-Mae had recently suggested they pick up where they'd left off—even though she'd gotten married last summer at Evangeline House.

He really didn't think she was serious, but it made him quite uncomfortable whenever he ran into her around town.

Thankfully, she wasn't at her parents' house just then,

but neither were Mr. and Mrs. Johnson. He'd give a call later and speak with them. Hopefully, that would suffice, and this disturbance would cool down and work itself out.

Now, he just wanted to go home to a TV dinner, a cold beer, muck his barn stalls, and watch the local news before bed. Surely it wasn't too much to ask.

His cell phone buzzed. He groaned and checked the caller ID. It was his oldest sister, Maeve. Apparently, his fantasy evening was about to be blown.

He turned in the direction of her house as they spoke. He was needed. Again.

"Ben, what in the world would we do without you?" his sister Maeve asked after an hour-long tutoring session. Her daughter Lucy had a pre-algebra test and was struggling with the concepts.

"Thanks, Uncle Ben." Lucy was almost eleven, and swore he was the only person who could help her understand the idea of solving for x.

"You're gonna rule that test tomorrow. Text me afterward and let me know how you did, okay?"

"Thanks!" They both chimed.

Ben again climbed into the cab of his pickup and headed toward home. This time he turned off his phone. He was dog-tired.

No wonder he didn't have time for a social life. He barely had time to get through a normal day.

"I JUST CAN'T stop thinking about him, you know? He's just soooo sexy. And he does this thing with his mouth—"

"Cissy, I don't think going into detail about an ex-lover's technique is going to help you move forward in a healthy marriage." Sabine was ready to crawl out of her skin. If she was forced to listen to Ben Laroux's prowess as a lover in detail again, she might just toss this girl out of her office.

"I'm sorry, Dr. O'Connor. I love my husband, I do, but I don't know how to get Ben out of my head. I'm ashamed to admit that I tried to get him to sleep with me since I married Scott." The girl lowered her head in humiliation.

"Have you admitted this to your husband?"

"No! Of course not. It would kill Scott to know that sometimes I think of someone else when we make love. But it's not all the time, just when I—"

Cissy stopped, apparently too embarrassed to complete her thought.

"It's not that uncommon to have fantasies during love-making. But it's true; he likely wouldn't want to know they're about a former boyfriend or lover." Sabine considered herself a consummate professional and, as such, she sought to help this girl improve the quality of her marriage.

But, damn. Why did it seem to be Ben Laroux these women fantasized about?

"But what can I *do*?" Cissy seemed truly regretful about her disloyalty to dear, sweet Scott, God love him.

"First, even if you want to have relations again with Ben

or anyone, don't put your marriage at risk by propositioning another man. Not if you want to stay married. Second, ask yourself why you are having a hard time letting go of Ben."

Cissy screwed up her cute little bow-shaped mouth and lolled her head around in real contemplation of that for a moment. "I think it's because he's so nice. I mean, sexy too, but he's really sweet."

"You can't stop thinking about him because he's nice?" That was unexpected.

"He was always such a gentleman; not just when we had sex, but after—even when he didn't want to date anymore. I never felt used or cheap. And we weren't, like, in love. I kind of chased him and made sure he knew I was available."

"I see. So, you weren't in a serious relationship with Ben, and since he was such a nice guy, nothing particularly unpleasant ever went on during your times together?" Figures; he used her but didn't make her feel used. Brilliant way to get what he wanted without a fuss.

"Yes, exactly. We only had good times. So, when I think about him, it makes me feel happy."

"You realize that marriage to anyone, even someone who's super nice wouldn't always be like that. I mean, ordinary happens to everyone after the new wears off any relationship." Sabine hoped to help Cissy understand that her light, unemotional encounter with Ben had been a bit of a fantasy, or break from the reality of her daily marriage grind.

"I guess. It was just such fun. Marriage is hard, you know. Harder than I thought it would be. Ben was such fun. And nice."

Cissy hung her head, guilt over her feelings weighing on her.

"It's okay, Cissy. But you can do more for your marriage besides just give in to monotony and boredom."

Cissy's head came up. "What do you mean?"

They discussed Cissy and Scott's daily routine and decided she and Scott were in a rut. Not only in their daily lives, but with meals, lack of a social calendar, and declining sex life. Sabine assured Cissy that these things were perfectly normal within the first year of marriage, but that it took a concentrated effort to make positive change.

The difference in Cissy's demeanor when she left the office was tremendous. "I can't thank you enough, Dr. O'Connor. I'm so excited to shake things up with Scott."

"Make sure you let him know what you're up to and that you're doing it for both of your sakes. If you hit him with too many unexpected changes at once, he might get unnerved and think something strange is going on."

"Are you kiddin' me? He'd never in a million years think anything was weird between us. He thinks I walk on water." Cissy flashed a grin. "I've never given him a hint that I'm anything but tickled pink to be his wife."

Somehow, Sabine believed that to be true. "Still, go easy. Many men can be creatures of habit, and rely on their comfort and routine. You don't want to throw him for a loop."

Cissy gave Sabine the two thumbs-up sign as she walked out, not mentioning Ben Laroux again.

Sabine sighed. Despite her distraction with Ben when she came in today, Cissy seemed refocused now, and hopefully would devote her time and attention to her new husband moving forward.

Looking at the clock on the wall, Sabine realized it was nearly five o'clock. Her stomach growled. She'd worked through lunch, taking an "emergency" patient who'd come to a life-altering decision to quit her job to join the peace corps in a flash of clarity during the night. Sabine convinced her to hold off on announcing this to her boss until they'd had a few more sessions to hammer out the whys of this sudden conviction.

Sabine sometimes felt like her head would explode, so full of information was she. Stuff she couldn't share—with anyone. It was as if she walked around with the town's secrets in her head, afraid to bump into anyone. *Because she knew.*

As she locked up, Sabine decided that maybe she should schedule a few days off. At present, there wasn't anyone on the verge of suicide so far as she could tell, which was a relief, because she couldn't always say this.

THE ANNUAL MINISTRY Arts Festival was in full swing. As small and Southern as the town was, it boasted a deep love of music and visual art. The town square had been roped off, allowing residents and visitors to meander through the brick streets of the most picturesque part of town. Ministry history was steeped in Civil War culture and the downtown area boasted countless gorgeous historic buildings and homes from that era.

There was a militant preservation society here that virtuously maintained any structure that predated 1900. It made for a picture-perfect town and a perfect choice for Sabine and Elizabeth. They loved the South and couldn't have borne leaving for a colder climate. Plus, they'd chosen Alabama for a reason.

It was a lovely, sunny April evening. Her mother was adamant they get out of the house and enjoy the day together. Now that she was here, Sabine had to admit it was an inspired plan. Truly, they didn't get out nearly enough. And there wasn't any point in hiding forever.

Stopping to study a canvas of the French Quarter by a local artist, Sabine was struck by a wave of homesickness.

"Honey, are you alright?"

"The Quarter seems so alive in this painting. I'd forgotten how much I miss home sometimes."

Mom sighed. "Me too. Someday, maybe we can go back to stay. But I like it here too, you know? I'm glad I can finally say that. It was so hard to be away from New Orleans at first."

Sabine grinned back at her mother. "I know what you mean. We're going to try harder to make this our home—at least while we're here. It's been long enough."

They complimented the artist before moving on. "Personally, sweetheart, I think you should call Richard and work on settling things."

Sabine tensed. "I don't think so, Mom." She hadn't given Richard much thought lately.

He was one of those "things" she'd done her best to sweep out of her immediate consciousness. She now pictured his too-handsome face, dark hair, perma-tan, and straight, white teeth. No wonder his constituents loved him. He had such charisma. She'd been drawn to him, just as they were. He'd once been the love of her life. But she didn't have all the information then.

"You can't move forward until you get him on board with a divorce."

"I'm not even sure how to approach him."

"I think you should call him up and give him the boot—permanently." Her petite mother stood before her, hands on hips.

"Uh—why don't we have a look at the floral arrangements?"

"Nice try, darling. But I think you should give some serious consideration to making that call."

She nodded. "I'll consider it." Hopefully, that would buy

her some time without her mother fussing about the subject.

"That's all I ask." They began moving toward the flower arrangements.

"What about you? Are you considering dating again?" Sabine asked.

"Oh, I'm considering it," her mother replied.

This honestly surprised Sabine after the hell her mom had been through. "What about Dad?"

"What about him?" her mother snapped.

"I mean, are you going to see him and try and at least talk about what happened—tell him how what he did made you feel?" Sabine felt like she had to try.

"No. If I never see his lying, cheating, and manipulating ass again, I'll rest in peace." Her face was pure granite.

"I don't doubt it, but I think you might be able to move forward a little easier if you could put the past squarely behind you."

"Honey, I'm your mother, not your patient. Please don't *therapy* me."

"Okay. Sorry." Sabine understood how Mom felt about her trying to analyze her feelings, and about her father.

Jean-Claude Prudhomme deserved nothing from her former wife—except maybe a Taser to his testicles. But he was the reason they were here in Alabama—to be nearby—even if her mother wouldn't see him.

As they continued to meander through the crowds, Sabine looked up from reading a text and noticed she was on a collision course with a pair of her patients. It was inappropriate for her to make their connection public knowledge. So she deftly avoided Judith Jameson and Sadie Beaumont.

"Yoo-hoo, Dr. O'Connor!" Crap. Judith was a pain in the butt on a good day. Professionally speaking, of course. "Hey there, Sabine. You've met Sadie Beaumont, our former mayor, Tad Beaumont's lovely ex-wife, haven't you?" Sure, she had, but Sabine took Sadie's cue and acted like she hadn't. "Sadie, Dr. O'Connor is my *therapist*. You know, we talk about things. She's helped me get in touch with my feelings."

"So nice to meet you, Dr. O'Connor," Sadie said with only a slight twitch and a great show of even, white teeth.

"You should try therapy, Sadie. Might help you work out some of *your* issues." Judith Jameson lifted her eyebrows. *If you know what I mean.*

Sadie shot Judith a foul look, which Judith missed, and mumbled a polite goodbye as they moved on, arm-in-arm.

Sadie had more real issues than most people in this town put together. Thankfully, she'd sought counseling for the right reasons. Sadie was making fantastic progress after what her shithead of a husband had done to her life and their daughter's. Thankfully, the former mayor had moved out of the state and had been *persuaded* to remain gone. Sabine didn't have all the details on that deal, but knew for certain it was best for Sadie and Sarah Jane.

"Friends of yours?" Her mother's laugh was partly

amused but mostly horrified.

"Can't discuss those two."

"Oh, I get it. Patients."

Sabine remained silent.

"Must be hard carrying the secrets of half the town and not having anyone to share the burden with."

"Kinda sucks sometimes." Sabine laughed it off.

As she looked around, she recognized several faces. On the exterior, they laughed with family and friends, enjoying the day. But in the hour a week she spent with them, far more was revealed; either about their true nature or disturbing events within their pasts or current lives—sometimes both.

No wonder, when folks ran into her outside the sanctum of her office, it was often uncomfortable, downright awkward, or they ignored her altogether. Of course, Sabine told them how to handle this kind of meeting, when or if it happened, however they saw fit. But a small irrational part of her still felt rejected on those occasions. Maybe because she put so much effort, time, and emotion into her work.

It made no sense, but then, maybe it did, just a little. Her professional side totally got it, but her squishy insides, the part that craved connection and friendship with others thought it totally sucked.

"The mother in me hates that word still." Her mom sighed. "But I guess they all know you know and deep down wonder if you're going to tell someone."

"Let's just say; some people don't want our association known in public. The ones who are dealing with their problems don't want anyone to know they come to see me professionally. Today's society dictates that everyone have a picture-perfect life; think, Facebook. Lots of smiling snap-shots. I do understand."

"I'm so proud of you, sweetheart. I always knew you'd find a way to do something with your sharp brain and serious nature."

"Are you saying I'm a nerd?"

"Of course not. I'm saying you were always a serious and thoughtful child who was smart as a tack. I wish you could find a way to have more fun though now that you're an adult. You seemed to miss out on your share growing up."

"I had fun. I just didn't have the same kind of running, screaming, crazy fun other kids seemed to have."

"What was fun to you as a child? I can't seem to remember you enjoying much outside of reading and playing with your cats." Her mother's expression was reflective, and maybe a little sad.

"Well, that sounds rather pathetic, Mother. You paint me as an eighty-year-old spinster." It had been rather pathetic. A shy, quiet child, Sabine had adored her books and cats. Her younger brother had been a nuisance who'd mercilessly terrorized the household as a toddler. It had been easier to withdraw into her room and her reading.

"Rachel was such a social butterfly from the moment she

took her first dance class." A small smile played on her mother's lips.

"Then it was an art lesson, photography class, theatre group, and on and on. She couldn't wait to leave home and do something else." Rachel was somewhat attention-challenged, in Sabine's professional opinion. She didn't stay with one thing very long.

"She had wide interests. It was a challenge to keep her appetite for new things fed. I couldn't stand to hear how bored she was when she was stuck at home. I'm sure you never once said that to me."

"I don't remember ever being bored." But she'd been compelled to remain home near her mother and was often frustrated with her siblings for making so much noise.

"Two wonderful daughters who are such different people," her mother murmured.

"Hello, ladies." Sabine nearly jumped out of her skin at the sound of Ben Laroux's deep voice.

She hadn't seen him approach and was completely unprepared to see him again. Before she could drum up a cool smile, her mother, always on her social toes, replied politely with interest, "Oh, hello. I'm Elizabeth Prud—O'Connor." Mom extended her hand to Ben, who shook it with a slight bow toward her mother.

"Sabine, you look lovely this afternoon, so nice to run into both of you." He fixed her with his signature grin.

She was feeling a bit flushed from the humidity. Perhaps

a less weighty blouse would have been a wiser choice. "Hello, Ben. Good to see you." Best to not alert her mother to the scent of discord.

"Hey there, Ben!" A small gaggle of ladies passed and tootled at him.

"Ladies." He nodded a greeting.

"We've got tickets to the concert. I guess we'll catch you later," Sabine said.

"So nice to meet you, young Ben." Mom nodded toward Ben.

"I'm heading that direction. May I escort you?" Damn. She wasn't getting away so easily.

Just then, Ben was nearly taken down by two young girls around the ages of nine or ten as they flew at him, threatening to tackle him to the ground. She recognized one as his niece, and her current patient, Samantha Harrison.

"Whoa, wild things! Are you trying to kill old Uncle Ben?" The image on a box of rice of a graying, balding black man made Sabine snicker.

Samantha saw Sabine then and beamed. "Hi, Sabine."

"Hi there, Sam." They hugged, now a comfortable habit between the two. That had taken a while. "Do you remember my cousin, Lucy?" Grey, Samantha's dad, approached with his new wife, Cammie, who was also Ben's twin.

"I sure do." Sabine shook Lucy's hand.

"Hey, Sabine." They all exchanged friendly greetings. Sabine introduced her mother to everyone.

"Oh, you're Norman's son. I can't wait to tell him we met." Click. The puzzle pieces came together for her mother.

"You know Dad?" Grey asked.

"We've run into one another a time or two at the nursery. He brought home my mulch the other day in his truck. Nice man."

Grey's eyebrows went up, but he only said, "Well, I'm glad he could help such a lovely lady."

"Just as charming as your dad." Mom kind of giggled as she said it.

Grey and Cammie exchanged a look.

Ben appeared a little off-kilter with all this laughter and friendship among them.

Sabine saw what was happening here. She wasn't included in the easy-going banter.

Sabine said, "Nice to see everyone; sorry we've got to run. We're heading over to the concert." A Beatles cover band was performing, and her mother was pretty excited about it.

"We're meeting my dad at the gate for the same concert in a few minutes. He's been looking forward to it," Grey said.

"Since there's no reserved seating, we should all sit together," her mother suggested.

Thanks, Mom. Well, who could argue with that?

"Sounds like fun," Ben agreed, sending her a satisfied smirk. He really enjoyed getting under her skin, damn his sexy ass in those jeans. She only wished she hadn't heard quite so much about it in such detail from so many.

>>>>>><<<<<

AS DARK DESCENDED, the stars moseyed out and music surrounded them. It was one of the most enjoyable evenings in Ben's recent memory. His mother, her new husband, and three other sisters joined them, along with a couple of brothers-in-law and a few more nieces and nephews of assorted ages. It didn't hurt that he'd commandeered the seat right next to Sabine and kept getting a whiff of her clean, slightly floral scent with nearly every breath. What was that? Gardenia?

She seemed to relax and enjoy the music. It was the most laid-back he'd seen her since they'd met; a sweet smile curved her lips as she tapped her foot a little and swayed to the beat. He even noticed her singing a little under her breath.

His family, on the other hand, was talking, laughing, and singing loudly. There *might* have been a bit of alcohol consumption as well. His sisters were a party all their own when one got them together.

At least they didn't seem to bother Sabine. Sabine's mother, Elizabeth fit right in with the rest of the group, enjoying a great time with Grey's father as well. Hmmm, guess one never knew.

Ben wondered if Sabine would agree to go out with him again. Not that they'd actually been on a date. The dinner didn't count. That had been more like a battle of wills. He glanced over at her. She truly was beautiful; far more than just surface attractiveness. It took depths to absorb other people's hurt and pain and turn it around to something positive. Maybe that was why she always seemed so serious. He'd caught a glimpse of something unfathomable when he'd questioned her in court. It had piqued his curiosity, stirred him up.

Of course, the fact that she hadn't thrown herself at him the moment they'd met was pretty darn appealing as well, he could admit. It was a tad disappointing too. What did one do with such a serious woman? He'd not had a lot of experience with such, except maybe his twin, Cammie. But she was his sister, after all. Quite a different situation.

Oh, and his ex-fiancée, whom he'd banned from his thoughts, permanently. She'd been serious, but clearly not the one for him. End of story.

As the concert wrapped up, they made their way to the parking area. He insisted on seeing Sabine and her mother to her car, since it was so late at night. As the only male in the family of five females, he'd been the man of the house since his father died. He'd barely been old enough to drive at the time. But even at such a young age, he'd been taught to take care for the safety of his mother and sisters.

He would no more have allowed them to walk alone to their car than he would any of his four sisters, his nieces, or his mother. It simply wasn't acceptable.

"Really, there's no need. We're perfectly fine," Sabine had protested.

"I insist. My dad wouldn't approve. And he taught me the same."

"Your father was a good man, son," Elizabeth O'Connor said.

His father, Justin Laroux, *had* been a good man, and a great dad. Ben only hoped he could someday be half the man his father was for their family. The very memory of their father's death on Lake Burton as his children stood watching could still bring them all to tears.

Ben shook it off. Not certain how he'd gotten to that file in his memory, he shut Sabine's driver's door after saying goodnight. Something about her caused him to feel things. Normally, women were mostly lighthearted, good fun. That was the way he preferred it. Less complicated. There wasn't anything uncomplicated about Sabine O'Connor.

As he rejoined his own family in the parking area, the party still in progress outside his sister Jo Jo's minivan, he felt thankful for such a soft place to land. Of course, these sisters of his rarely showed their soft sides the way they all needled him and each other. But they were a strong and loving group, the kind of circle he was lucky to have. With Ben's many opportunities for companionship, he worried he might end up alone.

He was living proof that one could feel lonely while with others.

Chapter Four

～～

S ABINE'S HEAD ACHED. Determined, she tried her hardest to attend while Judith Jameson gesticulated wildly, describing the largeness and ugliness of her sister Jamie's new derby hat—and how she, Judith, had endeavored to persuade Jamie she simply shouldn't don the heinous headwear beyond her backyard, much less out in public for the upcoming and socially visible pre-Kentucky Derby steeplechase party at the local fairgrounds.

"Sabine, I told her that *I* wouldn't be caught dead in that ugly piece of crap. But would she listen? Heck, no."

"I know you're only trying to look out for Jamie, but she's got the right to wear what she likes, and you must understand that it's no reflection on you." Sabine honestly couldn't believe her extensive education had led her to this moment.

"Well, of course I'm worried about my own reputation, honey! She oughta care what I think and not put me in such a terrible position." Judith's jaw suddenly dropped as if she'd been zapped by sudden enlightenment. "Do you think she's doing this to me on *purpose?*"

The horror in the woman's voice caused Sabine to stifle a grin, so dramatic and narcissistic her statement.

Sabine had counseled a few true, real narcissists, but only at the behest of spouses threatening to take half—narcissists required money to buy things to impress—the courts, or one or two who simply felt the need to pontificate for an hour at a time, thereby getting a special, goodly dose of themselves. Fortunately, she saw some real signs of humanity in Judith, so she'd hang onto her as a patient for now.

"Judith, as your therapist"—Judith loved that word "—I feel it's important for you to take a large step back from this very small issue as it relates to the bigger picture here."

Judith's head swiveled and her eyes locked on to Sabine's. "Are you saying I'm making too much of this?"

Sabine mentally suited up for her reply. "Honestly, yes. Getting bogged down in a hat issue, while it feels like a big deal now, isn't something you want to let hurt your relationship with Jamie. She's your sister. Let her wear the ugly hat if she loves it."

Judith set her mouth in a grim line. She obviously wasn't used to anyone arguing with her, certainly no one having the last word. "Fine. But I can't pretend to like it."

"Just make sure you're not giving her a hard time about the hat for a different reason."

"I'm sure I don't know what you mean." Judith took offense.

"I'd like for you to think about your relationship with your sister; listen closely to how you speak to one another this week. Try and understand your motivations for why you criticize her so often."

"I don't—"

Sabine held up her hand and spoke gently. "I'm only asking you to pay closer attention to how the two of you interact."

"Fine. We do tend to argue and fuss quite a bit. And she gets her feelings hurt pretty regularly." An admission of any kind proved she wasn't a bona fide narcissist.

"Judith, remember what I said about *getting one's feelings hurt?* It's a passive-aggressive term. Chances are, someone has the responsibility of hurting another's feelings. So, if you hurt Jamie's feelings, please tell her that you're sorry *you* hurt her feelings not that she got them hurt."

"Alright, fine. Can I tell her to work on not being so sensitive?"

"Having good, honest discussions is always healthy. Good work today. I'll see you next week." She walked Judith to the door.

Digging in her purse, Sabine found one of her migraine tablets. The headache had intensified throughout the session with Judith, but this particular headache began earlier in the day, and was proving to be quite a doozy.

A noise outside the door caused Sabine to freeze, glass of water midair. She'd locked the door to her office, as Judith was her last patient of the day. All she had left was to transcribe notes in a few remaining charts before heading home.

The sound hadn't been a knock, but it had startled her and it *was* just outside the front door. Moving from her inner office to the side window, she pulled back the corner of the closed blind in the reception area just a crack. Trees and the usual street traffic. But she hadn't quite made it to the front door yet.

There it was again, the noise. *Bump!* Sabine's hands trembled. Should she fling open the front door? Or just dial 911? Taking a deep breath, Sabine unbolted and pulled the handle hard.

She stifled a scream as something cold and wet fall on her ankles and feet before she saw anything—oh, flowers. A very large, colorful flower arrangement was tipped over and in danger of dismemberment. The wind must have rocked the glass container against the wood creating the weird sound that'd so freaked her out.

Carefully, Sabine bent down and tried her best to right the gorgeous bouquet. Who in the world would have sent such an extravagant gift? Maybe it was a mistake. Why didn't they ring the bell? Was someone watching her right now?

She gathered up the flowers and hurried inside. Thoughts like that led to bad places. Paranoid places where good sense and reason held no stake in reality.

There must be a card amidst the chaos she'd made of the arrangement. Yes, there it was. *It was so nice to see you again.*

Dinner soon? Ben L.

Well, that was nice. But what exactly was his agenda? Just dinner? With a guy who'd recently instated a two-date rule to keep things fair for the women in town? How could she? What if her patients saw them together? They would assume she'd ratted them out.

No. A real live date with Ben Laroux could never happen. Total conflict of interest—mainly hers. After the things she'd been told. It would be worse than an oncologist who specialized in lung cancer taking up smoking two packs a day—nuts.

But good manners dictated that she thank him for the flowers, so before she lost her nerve, she dialed his number, still programed in her phone from their first encounter.

⟫⟫⟪⟪

BEN WAS PULLING into his drive when the phone rang. He saw the number pop up and smiled. "Hello there."

"Hi. It's Sabine O'Conner."

"I don't know anyone else named Sabine, so you can drop the last name."

"Oh. Well, I wanted to thank you for the flowers. They're beautiful."

"You're welcome."

"About dinner—"

He didn't let her finish. "Can I pick you up tomorrow around seven?"

"Well, I'm not sure that's such a good idea."

"It's a great idea. I had a nice time at the concert the other night and thought maybe you didn't hate me so much anymore."

"I don't hate you, but—"

"Great; see you tomorrow at seven. Text me your address, if you don't mind."

"O-okay."

Ha. She'd tried to wiggle out of going out with him, but he'd worn her down. Not sure again why it was so important for her to like him, Ben rode on his wave of accomplishment the remainder of the evening. Thankfully, it was a quiet one with no cows, emergency math tutoring, or needy women calling, except Sabine. And he'd been happy to receive her call.

He'd checked his mailbox at the end of the dirt drive as he'd pulled in, throwing everything on the passenger's seat of the truck. Now that he'd eaten a frozen dinner, popped the top on a longneck, and was properly stretched out on his sofa, a soft, oversized work of leather perfection, Ben sorted through the enormous stack of bills, sales circulars, and various other non-urgent wastes of trees.

He'd just about made it to the bottom of the stack, picking out the keepers, when a thick envelope with "IMPORTANT" stamped in red on the front with the return address of the Office of the Governor of the Great State of Alabama. Governor Ted Grumby had promised to keep an eye on Ben last they'd met.

Governor Grumby had taken a shine to Ben and suggested he make a run for the state house of representatives. Ben hadn't given it much thought beyond a few pieces of legislation he'd personally like to see passed that would decrease unnecessary red tape for local businesses and streamline permitting for licensing filed through the state tax commissioner's office.

If he considered it, there were a dozen or more things on his mind with regards to improving the way the state commissions did business with its counties and municipalities. As an attorney, he dealt with the minutia almost daily and had to admit he'd repeatedly come across such flaws in the system that it made him want to enact change for his own professional, as well as personal, reasons.

But a life in the political spotlight on a large stage didn't sound very appealing. He liked being his own man a little too much. He'd seen too many other honest men and women with good intentions fall into the politician trap. Too many favors exchanged and owed, both ways, and too much power. Very few emerged resembling the person they'd been going in. Ben preferred his life as it was.

As Ben opened the envelope, his stomach hit the floor. This was altogether something different. He'd been preliminarily appointed to the governor's special task force. Holy shit. He'd seen a call come through from Birmingham and let it go to voice mail yesterday when he was speaking with a client; and he'd left the office without remembering to listen to the missed message. The governor, if he remembered correctly, didn't believe in cell phones. He was rather old school. He left voice messages on answering machines and still used snail mail.

Ben guessed the appointment paperwork was sent to his home address to allow for privacy. Anything from the governor's office was cause for speculation within the office. The gossip would've been a nightmare.

This wasn't good news because he really couldn't say no. The time. The stress. The responsibility. Crap. He was already trying to pull back a little and make life less crazy.

Turning back to the paperwork, he noticed a lengthy list of in-depth and personal questions he'd have to answer. Very personal, as in all the people he'd had "meaningful" intimate relationships with. Surely they didn't mean everyone he'd slept with. He could honestly say, on his part, that anything truly meaningful could be narrowed down to only one. And he made a habit of not discussing her. No one did—they didn't dare—out of respect for him.

It was kind of like that in his family. All his siblings, even his mother, they'd recently found out, had one person in their past that'd done a number on them. Cammie had found forever love with her obliterator, Grey, but that had ended as a good thing, since they were now together and living out their happily-ever-after. Emma had recently found her true love with Matthew, despite former mayor and ex-boyfriend, Tad Beaumont's, best efforts to keep her from ever dating again. His mother and her first love, Howard, had recently married, years after his father's passing. They were all still struggling a little with that one—especially since the revelation that Maeve, his oldest sister, was Howard's daughter.

They were pretty much a "one and done" family. Ben was nearly thirty years old and still just as single as he'd been his last year in law school. The year of heartbreak.

He'd not allowed Lisa to sneak into his thoughts in such a long time. A picture of her shining, long blonde hair and laughing, pale green eyes attacked his consciousness before he could put up the bulletproof emotional barrier.

She'd been the world to him—his soul mate, confidante, lover, and best friend. They'd shared everything—eventually even his roommate and lifelong buddy, Steve. In one fell swoop, Ben had lost both his best friends at once. And Steve and Lisa still had each other, along with a couple of adorable pale green-eyed, darling children.

But the town had chosen Ben. *Cheaters never prospered.* He thought he remembered that from a kids movie he'd watched. From then on, he'd been the town favorite. Steve and Lisa had been completely shunned wherever they went. Everyone learned about her perfidy and his dissing of a bro.

The blackballing in town had become so awful for the couple, they'd eventually moved a couple counties away, closer to Birmingham. But both still had family and close ties to their hometown, so, they invariably came here to visit on occasion. Now, Lisa and Steve could bring their children to visit grandparents and such without open hostility anymore, so far as Ben knew.

Ben realized much later that Steve and Lisa had tried to avoid one another, tried to deny their feelings. He'd even forgiven them, as much as he could, but the trust thing, well, that'd left a mark. The big, nasty kind of emotional gash he hoped someday to overcome. So far, he hadn't found anyone else who'd scratched the surface of his deeper emotions.

Ben had moved about Ministry without mentions or re-minders of Lisa from the townsfolk or from his family. Because they'd chosen *him*, it was swept right under the rug, never to be dredged up again, preventing his embarrassment and pain. Of course, his sisters tried, occasionally, to discuss the matter, but that never went well or got them very far. So, he hadn't heard anyone mention her in the last few years.

Ben filled out the remaining invasive paperwork for Governor Grumby, knowing they'd already have done an initial background check. The information he provided would direct them to the individuals necessary for character assessment interviews.

Life was about to get a whole lot more interesting around here.

"DAD SAYS IT'S time for a visit from his favorite daughter."

Sabine's cell phone rang at seven o'clock the next morning, just as she'd left the house and was on her way to the office. It was Friday, the day of her date with Ben.

"Hello to you too, James. It's been a while." *How did you get this number? Where are you calling from?*

"Cut the big sister crap, Sabine. You're the one who ran out on your family." Classic James.

She took a deep breath and tried to calm her rapid heartbeat. "I didn't run out on anyone. Dad's in prison. Mom's with me. Rachel doesn't live at home anymore."

"What about your husband? Your home is in New Orleans."

"My home is wherever I want to live in this free country, last I checked."

"Don't get smart, nerd girl."

"Charming, James. Just as I remember you—a runt and a bully." Why was she taunting him? Because she despised her own brother, that was why.

"Dad wants to see you."

"Is it about the parole hearing?" In truth, she was shaking from head to toe.

"No, it's because you're his favorite." He snorted. "Of course it's about the hearing."

"Uh huh. Right. Tell him I'll come, but I'm not sure about Mom."

"That's between him and your mom. Oh, and he's pissed that you changed your names."

"He'll have to get over it or stay pissed." She was becoming angry now.

"Call the prison and let them know you're coming," he said.

"Tell our father I will meet with him but he needs to leave Mom out of this and not try and contact her." He knew what that meant.

"Yeah. I understand. I'll let the old man know." She heard a click on the other end.

She hated her own brother. The family therapist her mother had hired for the "James victims" had a motto for such folks. "Can't change 'em, fix 'em or treat 'em. Just gotta cut 'em loose." James had no conscience. This Sabine knew well. He'd been a terror when Dad had brought him into the family at age three. Dad demanded her mother raise him as her own son.

James was her father's bastard, son of a New Orleans social climber who'd overdosed on cocaine. Had their father allowed any discipline of the toddler, he might have turned out differently. Narcissistic sociopaths were created by neglect at a young age or true overindulgence. James had been neglected before his mother died and grossly overindulged after. He hadn't stood a chance.

Her mother had agreed to take James in because she'd had no choice, had even tried to love him. After all, he was a blameless child. But James refused to be nurtured. He was a scary, angry and violent boy who wouldn't be reined in.

Except when it came to their father. James understood innately where his bread was buttered. Dad saw only his adorable male protégée in James, and the son he'd never had within his own marriage. And James could fool their father, manipulate, and make Dad believe in his loyalty.

The rest of the family, including the long-term staff knew differently. They all were forced to suffer James Prudhomme, the crowned prince of New Orleans. Really, he was just a thug in nice clothing. He was educated, charming, and far too handsome. A lot like their father.

By the time Sabine reached her office, she'd calmed a little. This was bound to happen at some point. It was a bit of a relief. She looked forward to her father's parole hearing, and his release. Not because she wanted him back in their lives, but because he might realize Mom had moved on. Then, he would do the same.

Sabine glanced up at the clock on the wall. In thirteen minutes, she would counsel another person on how to handle their life's problems. Considering her screwed up family and background—what a fraud she was.

But she'd always believed most therapists became such to try and figure out their own lives. It'd certainly been a large part of her career motivation.

>>><<<

BEN'S DAY HADN'T exactly gone as planned. Fortunately, he'd not been scheduled for court, but had taken depositions in a pit-bull attack case. Another terrible situation where the animal had been raised as a killer from puppyhood. These dogs were never going to improve their reputations if humans continued using them as terrorists.

Seeing the wounds from the bites on the ten-year-old boy and hearing him recount the horror in detail left Ben agitated and bothered the rest of the day. He couldn't help think how he would feel had it been one of his nieces or nephew who'd been the victim.

He was still anticipating the evening ahead with Sabine as his reward for such a crappy day. The governor called his office and asked to be put through. His ever-efficient assistant, Chase, had rushed in, excited. "You'll *never* guess who's on line one for you." Chase was clearly leaping in his loafers to tell Ben the caller's name.

"I'll bite; who's on the line?"

"It's none other than the governor of our state." Chase nearly squealed.

"Ah, okay. Thanks, Chase." Ben had expected someone from the governor's office might call soon, so Ben had answered, half-excited, half-dreading the conversation. There would be no going back.

"Governor Grumby, it's an honor. What can I do for you?"

"Son, you know damn well what you can do. You can get that paperwork back to me ASAP. I want you on the special task force." The governor boomed through the earpiece.

"Yes, sir. I filled everything out and sent it registered mail this morning. You should have it by tomorrow, Monday at the latest."

"Excellent, son. So, you accept the appointment?"

"Yes, sir. I'd be honored."

"Good. After we get all the hassle and paperwork sorted out, we'll make the official announcement. No skeletons in the closet, I take it?"

"None that I'm aware of, sir."

"Just checking. 'Cause, we don't like skeletons—or surprises. Gotta check with all your people, just to make sure you're as solid as we know you are."

"Yes, sir. I understand. My fiancée ran off with my best friend in law school. That's as scandalous as it gets." Now why did he say that?

"Ouch! So long as she wasn't a Russian spy, we don't have a problem. Heh. Heh. No ties to corruption?" the governor asked, serious now.

"None that I'm aware of." He could honestly say this.

"You'll do just fine, boy. Just fine." Governor Grumby chuckled.

Ben squirmed in his office chair uncomfortably. He sensed he'd just become somebody else's boy. Not the best feeling. "So, can you tell me what this task force is going to focus on?"

"Sure. It's a clean-up crew for waste and corruption. I

only want the squeaky clean folks on this one. Can't have anyone accusing my team of being in anyone's pockets."

After they'd hung up, Ben noticed the buzz outside his office door. Handling this might be tricky. Best to keep a lid on the appointment until everything was official. Time for a little bait and switch.

"So, Ben, what did Grumpy Grumby want with you?" George, one of the three partners asked quietly.

"Just checking in. You know, I sent that letter to his office last month with the suggested legislation changes to the House. Somebody passed it along to the governor. He wanted to discuss it."

"Must have really ticked him off." This came as a smirk from Jeff, his backstabbing colleague, who was gunning for partner. They really should get rid of him. That kind of over-competitiveness was bad for business and company morale. His uncle was senior partner, unfortunately.

"Just a discussion. He had a few questions for me." Ben shot them his best grin and turned back toward his office. Hopefully, that would quell speculation for the moment.

"What was that about? I don't want to overstep, but, sir, you *have* to tell me if I'm going to be out of a job." Chase came in after the others.

"Don't worry, Chase. I trust that you'll keep this between us for now." Chase nodded. Ben explained about the task force, knowing his secret was safe with Chase.

His firm had four partners; he was the youngest of the

four. Two were old enough to be his father and one was just five years older than him. They employed two associates who, if they played their cards right, would make partner within the next two years at the rate the firm was growing. Each partner had an administrative assistant. They had a couple clerks and an intern. Babin, Bach, Smith & Laroux was a medium-sized firm on the move.

Right now, he needed to get a move on so he wouldn't be late for his date with Sabine.

He'd set up something special and hoped she would like it.

Chapter Five

⚮

SABINE DIDN'T MENTION her brother's phone call earlier this morning. There wasn't any need to upset her mother just yet. When the time came to make the trip to the detention facility, Sabine would fill her mom in. Of course, she couldn't leave her mom here alone, or she wouldn't subject her to traveling back to Louisiana, and all that entailed.

But here, she had no backup. What if Mom needed something? What if she had a panic attack like she used to? No. Sabine couldn't risk it.

Sabine attempted to put all thoughts about the males in her family aside as she readied herself for this evening.

"You look amazing," her mother said.

"Thanks, Mom, but this isn't really a date."

"What would you call dinner with a handsome young man who is picking you up from your house and taking you out?"

"I'm not sure what to call it, but I know I'm not comfortable dating Ben," Sabine said, realizing how ridiculous she sounded.

"Then why are going out with him?" Her mother was an intuitive woman, even though she'd been quite obtuse for many years within her own marriage.

"Because he didn't really give me much choice."

"You're going so you don't hurt his feelings?"

"Maybe. I'm not sure." And she wasn't.

"Well, if you figure it out, it might be fair to let him know."

"You've got a point," Sabine conceded as she heard the crunching of tires on the gravel of the drive. "He's here. Don't forget to lock up and set the alarm." Sabine had installed a state-of-the-art security system with cameras, monitoring, the works—the kind she could check from her smart phone at any given time.

"Got it. I'm fine. And I've got my Smith and Wesson should anyone breach Fort Knox," said her former high society mother who was a crack shot with the small .32 caliber revolver she kept handy, especially while Sabine was out of the house.

"Just don't shoot anybody that doesn't need shooting."

Her mother chuckled. "Don't you want to let the boy come inside to fetch you? You'll seem eager if you meet him on the front step."

"It's okay. He knows I'm not too eager," Sabine laughed as she shut the door behind her.

She stepped out onto the small front porch to see Ben

approaching with a bouquet of daisies. "Are those for me?"

"Yup. Do you want to go inside and put them in water?"

"Sure." She smiled at his decidedly old-fashioned thoughtfulness. "Thanks. They're lovely."

After she'd dashed inside and endured her mother's oohs and aahs over her blooms, she returned to where Ben was sitting in a wooden rocker on the porch.

"All set?" He was wearing a sport jacket over a pair of dark jeans with a pair of cowboy boots.

She nodded and climbed into his truck while he held the door and offered her his hand as assistance.

She'd decided on a lightweight printed sundress, mostly yellow, and flat ballet slippers. High heels weren't her thing, mostly because they were terribly uncomfortable. After her somewhat formal upbringing, Sabine reveled in her more casual wardrobe. Of course, she dressed more professionally for work, but always comfortable.

"You look gorgeous." His blue eyes were framed by thick black lashes. Had she ever noticed his eyes? They were just part of the impressive Ben package. To pick it apart might be overwhelming to a mere mortal woman.

His compliment made her blush. It shouldn't have. Men had complimented her over the years, but it had hardly fazed her. Ben's words flustered Sabine.

"Thanks. I wasn't sure where we were going, so I figured I'd be okay in this." She sounded like a first-class goober.

"Since the verdict hasn't been reached in the trial you

testified against my client in, I thought maybe we'd best not be seen in public."

"Oh, thanks for thinking of it. I'm usually the worry wart about that kind of thing."

"So, I came up with an alternative." At her suspicious expression, he laughed. "No, we're not going to my place, well, not exactly."

"What's the plan, then?"

"You'll have to trust me."

Trust him? Trust Ben Laroux. She nearly laughed out loud at the notion. If he had any notion of the things she'd heard about him over the past two years, he'd be mortified. Of course, all of that was communicated through strict doctor/patient confidentiality. He could never know her prejudices against him. What a bizarre situation.

"Hmmm. Not sure I'm ready for trust," Sabine said with a smile, almost kidding. But she did trust him, or at least she did in this instance.

"I'm convinced you'll be happy with the compromise between going out to a fancy restaurant and dining at home. Just give me a chance."

Just give him a chance. "I'm curious." That pretty much summed it up for now.

A few minutes later, he pulled into the drive at his family's mansion/event-planning business, the Evangeline House. Sabine had been here before on a couple of occasions. He'd grown up here, and his mother still lived in the house.

Everyone in three counties knew about this place. The event planning business was legend for hosting weddings and nearly every other kind of party or event.

"Are we getting married?" she joked.

"Do you want to?" he asked, deadpan.

"No, but I am hungry."

"Whew. Okay, because I hadn't planned a wedding, only dinner."

"This isn't a restaurant, is it?"

"Not for most people."

"Not sure what you mean."

He came around and opened her car door, true Southern gentleman-style, then led her up the steps of the front porch that extended the entire length of the plantation home. Ben opened the heavy front door without knocking or ringing the doorbell, motioning for her to precede him.

The place was gorgeous, like stepping back in time—in the most Southern and charming way. Sabine almost expected to see grand corseted ladies appear with ball gowns and yards of lace and ribbons. Instead, his mother and sister entered the room, wearing jeans and a black T-shirt emblazoned with Evangeline House logos.

"Hey there, Sabine. So glad you could come tonight. We've set you up in the library. Grey's just finished the remodel work and it's all set for dinner. Ben, show her the way. The wine and appetizers are already set up." Cammie, Ben's twin sister had obviously put her chef's skills to work for their evening's pleasure.

"Oh, that sounds nice. Thanks, Cammie."

"Thanks, Sis." He kissed her on the cheek.

"So nice to see you again, Sabine," Maureen Laroux, Ben's mother shook Sabine's hand. "You two enjoy your dinner. Please let us know if you need anything—and give a shout if this scamp gets out of line." Maureen's eyes twinkled, obviously adoring her son.

"Thank you both so much. Something smells delicious."

"Hope you're not allergic to seafood. Surf and turf coming up in a bit," Cammie announced and headed back toward what Sabine assumed was the direction of the good smells.

Ben led her to the library. It had been turned into a library dining room. Sabine had seen this new trend in decorating magazines where entire rooms had walls of shelves filled with books lining the walls and, in the center, a large dining table.

The bookshelves in this gorgeous place were floor to ceiling, stained a deep mahogany, and filled with thousands of what looked like ancient, but well-preserved leather-bound tomes. Sabine sighed. All those lovely books.

Every space not covered by bookshelves was paneled and stained. The floors were wide-planked maple and the rug was so incredible, and obviously antique that she was afraid to walk on it, much less take the chance of dropping seafood on it that wouldn't smell so wonderful tomorrow.

The dining table was a carved masterpiece from history as well. "They expect us to eat in here?" Sabine was mortified.

She had grown up in a similar style, but they'd not been allowed to eat anywhere but the kitchen except on Christmas and Thanksgiving in the formal family dining room.

"It's a dining room. People eat in here all the time."

"Should be a crime."

"Don't worry. It's all good." He pulled out a chair and she sat.

She had to admit; his manners were excellent.

"So, Sabine, where did you grow up?" he asked while they sipped wine by candlelight.

Sabine was charmed by her surroundings and by this handsome man who'd planned such a perfect evening. "New Orleans," she answered before thinking better of it.

Crap. She hadn't meant to let that slip, but she was lulled by the soft, background piano music and ambient lighting.

"I'm surprised I didn't pick up on the accent."

"Probably because I lived uptown my whole life. Most people with the stronger New Orleans drawl live in the outlying areas—Metairie, Kenner, and over on the Westbank and North Shore."

"I had no idea it was different depending on what part of town you were from."

"My N'awlins bursts out every now and then, when I get

angry or excited. Same with my mother."

"Kind of like my redneck drawl."

She smiled. Her lack of an accent was something of an anomaly. But she'd worked hard to drop what was left of it too. Less questions from the locals that way.

The stuffed oysters were delicious. "Mmm. I haven't had these since we left."

"How long have you been in Ministry?" Crap. He was going ahead with the full-on medical history.

"About two years." She didn't elaborate.

"Do you have any other siblings?"

"I have a sister and a half-brother." She tried to answer briefly, to put an end to the questions, but he continued.

"Oh. Where do they live?"

"My sister is a freelance photographer and moves around with her job a lot, and my brother lives in New Orleans." There.

"What line of work is your brother in?" Geez.

He's a nasty little piece of shit who's involved with lowlife scumbags that do God-knows-what. And I have no idea how he actually makes a living besides his stupid trust fund. "He's just graduated recently from Tulane. He and I aren't that close. He's eight years younger than me."

"What about your father?"

In jail for jury tampering and collusion. "Dead. Um, I mean he passed away a few years ago from a sudden heart attack."

What could have possessed her to say such a thing? She'd never been a liar. But he was getting a little too close for comfort with his line of questioning. Plus, he'd never have a chance to know more about her past, so no point in bringing up all that awful baggage.

"So sorry. I lost my dad when I was in high school. I don't think it's something any of us ever recovered from completely." His voice took on a husky tone. He obviously hadn't noticed her discomfort regarding her family.

She was a horrible fraud. "I know what you mean." She knew about what had happened to their father because of some of the therapy she'd done with other family members—Grey and Samantha, in particular.

"Excuse us." Cammie and Maureen eased into the room, quickly removing the remnants of their first course, replacing the silverware and resetting the table with fresh wine and glasses. The lobster tails were broiled and drizzled with some sort of lemon caper sauce. Accompanying the lobster was a perfect petite filet. Obviously, Ben had informed his sister of her carnivorous appetite.

"This looks amazing. Thank you again for such a lovely evening. Your house is incredible."

"Well, it's not every day brother Ben here asks us for a favor. We're usually the ones who rely on him. We're happy to do it for both of you. Goodness knows you've helped my family in ways I can never repay. We'll scoot out now and let you have some privacy while you eat. Ring the bell if you need anything else." Cammie and Grey were very open about his and Samantha's therapy sessions.

Ben grinned at his sister. "Thanks."

"You have a really great family," Sabine said; and she meant it.

The interactions she'd had with Cammie and Grey had been very honest and positive. There was a deep love between the couple that Sabine couldn't help but envy just a little. They'd been through hell and come out the other side.

"They're all batshit crazy, but it works for us." He smiled at her then, a genuinely relaxed and contented expression, one that felt miles apart from the surface-beautiful, suave womanizer whose exploits she'd been hearing about for so long.

He seemed like a nice guy having a nice time. And Sabine responded to that in a very basic way.

They chatted for a while about Ben's childhood, his sisters, and their kids. It seemed he tutored math, taught everyone to ride bicycles, and could be relied upon day or night to pick up someone from school, the airport, or take them to the emergency room for stitches. He was quite bonded to his family. Something Sabine could hardly comprehend.

Besides the thing with all the women, he seemed like such a great guy. But that was a very big thing.

AFTER DINNER, BEN suggested they walk around the grounds of the house. It was a nice evening. He tucked her arm inside his. It was an old-fashioned, romantic gesture, which made Sabine feel shy and very girly. But she didn't resist. He was warm and smelled like soap and man.

She hadn't been close to a man in any kind of intimate way in such a long time. An unhealthily long time, which made this whole situation uncomfortable. Two and a half glasses of wine were more than she normally drank at a time and she was feeling a little buzzy just now.

They came upon a wicker swing, hung from a huge oak in the garden behind the house. "I can't imagine how nice it must be having your childhood home so close." Sabine's childhood home had been a haven, until it wasn't.

"I can't imagine things any other way. This place has been our home since we were born." Ben took her hand and tugged her down toward the swing.

Once they were sitting, he didn't let go of her hand, and was now stroking the inside of her wrist with his thumb as the swing gently creaked to and fro on its chains.

She wondered how much action this swing had seen in its day. No, she didn't want to know. The hard facts about Ben and her foolish attraction toward him were fighting a mighty war right this second. The last thing Sabine needed was to jump from the smart ship to the sinking one with all the women of the county who'd been struck down with the "*Do-Me-Ben*" disease.

When he leaned in close, she inhaled his clean, soap-scented, manly smell. Before she could come up with a denial, he kissed her. His lips, so warm, so sexy, were firm, but not exactly demanding.

She heard a sigh. Was that her? When his strong arms encircled her back, she pressed closer. He groaned. She tingled in the parts that hadn't had attention in far too long. She couldn't catch her breath—or get close enough. *Oh, God.* Was there room on this swing—

He pulled back first. "Uh—maybe we should—" He sounded like he'd been running sprints.

Sabine realized at that moment that she was straddling his thighs. *She was on his lap.* And he was sporting quite the erection. "I'm sorry. So sorry. I—don't usually. I mean, I'm not—"

He laughed softly. "No explanation needed."

Sabine was mortified. She'd found her way back to her own side of the swing, and quickly pulled her dress back down her legs.

But she was still exceptionally turned-on by that kiss. "I feel like I need to explain. It's just—that it's been a really long time since—since I've been with a man, or even kissed anyone. I guess, I wasn't expecting my own reaction."

"Wow. And I thought it was just me you couldn't resist. I guess I could have been anyone." Ben ran a hand through his shiny brown hair.

"Yes. I guess. I mean, I don't know. I just haven't dated,

or been so intimately close to anyone that my response surprised me."

"Sounds like maybe you're past due," Ben said, then rose from the swing, and held out a hand to her. It was the gesture of a gentleman.

She took his hand and stood. "Thanks for understanding."

"Sure."

"You're really not a bad guy."

He stared at her for a second. "I never thought I was. Not sure why you did either." He shook his head and led her back across the yard to the house.

That hadn't come out right, and she wasn't quite sure how to apologize without explaining where her information came from.

While Ben checked his phone in the other room, Sabine ducked her head into the kitchen to thank Cammie and Miss Maureen for providing such a lovely evening.

"Oh, honey, don't mention it. It was our pleasure," Maureen replied.

"Plus, it's fun watching Ben pine after you like this. That hasn't happened in years. Not since Lisa—oops."

"Lisa?" Sabine was curious.

Ben came in at that moment. "What's going on in here?"

"Oh, you're in trouble, now," Maureen said.

"Uh, nothing. Sabine was thanking us for this evening."

Ben narrowed his eyes. "I do hope you ladies aren't

speaking out of turn about things best left unspoken."

Cammie shot him a feigned look of pure innocence.

"Right." But, as uncomfortable as the situation could have become, Ben obviously decided to let the matter drop without causing a scene. "Thanks for everything." He waved a hand in the air.

Sabine chimed in. "Goodnight. Everything was delicious."

⋙⋘

HE LED HER around to the passenger's side and helped her into his four-wheel-drive truck. It wasn't especially high like some of the red-neck mobiles Sabine had seen around town, but it had larger-than-normal tires, in her opinion. Of course, Ministry wasn't a big city, and there were abundant rough terrain and unpaved roads to warrant the adjustment to an automobile. Who was she kidding? New Orleans was so full of potholes, an off-road vehicle was nearly required to navigate the streets, depending on which political district one was traveling through at the time.

Every district used its tax money how the elected official deemed. Instead of the state handling the road repair, the districts each took care of their little length of highways and roads. So, bizarrely, in the metro New Orleans area, Sabine could drive from one end of the parish to the other and encounter three different standards of road conditions.

Once they'd gotten onto the road, he asked, "So, how

much did my sister tell you?"

"About what?" Sabine was pretty certain she knew to what he referred, but chose to let him reveal as much or as little about his past as he chose.

He barked a short laugh. "Nice therapist move. I'm talking about my ex-girlfriend, Lisa. I heard Cammie mention her name."

"She said the name Lisa and inferred that you haven't been involved emotionally with anyone since. At least I think that was what she meant. It was something to that effect."

He nodded. "That's about right. I've dated plenty, but haven't really experienced a connection with a woman since Lisa."

Sabine looked away, afraid he would read something into her expression. Judgment maybe? Or knowledge of the stories she'd been told by women. Just being with him made her a liar by default. She had to hold back the things she knew even though it was necessary.

"What?" he asked.

"Nothing. You know the two of us can never work, right?" Sabine asked.

"I didn't propose for real, you know," he said, jokingly.

"Yeah, I got that. But I mean it. There are things I know about you—or things I've been told that cloud my judgment toward you." She could tell him certain things without being specific.

"What does that mean?"

"Women. They talk. A lot. To me. I can't tell you who, or what they've said, but because I'm human, it affects my opinion."

"That's just fantastic." He pulled into her driveway and came to an abrupt halt.

She turned to face him squarely. "I didn't ask them about you. But it's something I can't ignore."

"You know, Sabine, I can't defend myself against the words of the women of Ministry, Alabama. Or your low opinion of me. Whatever they've said, you can believe parts of it. Their versions of it. It's your choice which parts to believe. I know who I've been intimate with, and the circumstances. I've never behaved in an underhanded manner with a woman, or done anything reprehensible. I don't lie or cheat. I've not been unkind to anyone. I *have* been forced to break it off when more was demanded than I was willing to give at the time, and because it wasn't fair to lead someone on—"

"I—" He held up a hand when she tried to speak.

"Please let me finish," he said. "Ask these women if they've been wronged by me—besides the fact that I ended things when someone got too serious. I never even led anyone to believe I wanted long-term. Everyone in town knows about Lisa, and what happened. It's like they've been in a competition to be the one to heal my heart."

Sabine sighed. "I can't discuss their end of it, but I'm sorry you were hurt. I know how that feels."

Her stomach knotted up when he took her hand. "Sabine, despite what you've heard, I'm not a bad person. But you're going to have to come to that conclusion on your own."

"I don't think you're a bad person, or I wouldn't have spent time with you." She wrinkled her nose. "But *all* those women."

He shrugged, his shoulders relaxing. "I assumed we're going back a few years. Like from middle school? I can't change the past, but it sounds like I'm on the receiving end of a situation where I can't fairly defend myself."

She laughed, despite the gravity of their discussion. "I believe that's a pretty accurate statement."

He leaned over and kissed her cheek. "Well, I had a fun evening." Then he whispered in her ear, "And I especially enjoyed your climbing on my lap."

Every womanly part of her perked right back up in that instant. "Okay, well, gotta go now. Thanks for dinner." She hopped out of his big truck like a scared bunny, not giving him time to get out and come around to her side.

She headed through the front door of her house and waved a quick goodbye before triple dead bolting the door at lightning speed. Sabine was leaning against the back of the door, her breath coming in quick gasps, as if she'd sprinted home from Evangeline House, instead of bounding inside from the truck.

"Darling, what is it? What's wrong?" Her mother's voice

held alarm.

Sabine realized her mistake then. And laughed. "Oh. It's nothing. I-I just got home from dinner and was locking up."

Mom narrowed her eyes and took in her appearance.

Sabine realized that her cheeks must be flushed, and well, there was the heavy breathing. "Did that boy try something?"

"What? No. He didn't *try* anything. Of course not." She laughed, what to her own ears sounded like a nervous little thready laugh.

"So, tell me what's got you all upset about?"

"I'm not—" Sabine realized her mother had her number. "Okay, fine. He kissed me. And I nearly came unglued."

Her mother's face split into a great, gleeful grin. "Well, now. It's about time somebody unglued you."

"I don't think so. He's not the one I want to do the ungluing, believe me."

"Well, why in the world not? That young man is—is, well, he's *hot* is what. If I was thirty or so years younger, he'd be my choice." Mom wiggled her eyebrows.

Sabine couldn't help but laugh. "Mom, you crack me up. Speaking of hot; have you heard from Norman?"

Her mother shook her finger at Sabine. "Sorry, young lady. I'm not quite ready to discuss Norman just yet. I'll say that we are considering having dinner together, and that's all."

"Fair enough. I understand how hard it is to get out there again," Sabine said.

"You really should do something about your situation. I mean, you can't go on like this forever."

"What do you suggest? My hands are tied until Richard agrees to a divorce." Her marital status wasn't something Sabine discussed.

In fact, her mother and father were the only living souls in Alabama who knew she was married. Unless her bastard half-brother was still in the state. He knew. And he'd get a kick out of telling everyone she knew if her father allowed it. Her sister knew. The state of Louisiana knew. But she'd changed her name, so nobody here had a clue she was the state senator's estranged wife. In fact, she was fortunate no one had made the connection yet, especially Ben.

She'd changed her hair. It had made a huge difference in her appearance. But really, Sabine was living on borrowed time, waiting for the other shoe to drop. She and Richard had come to a tenuous agreement. But Richard's patience wouldn't last.

"He can't hold you prisoner, Sabine." Her mother's voice was hard now.

"Can't he? How long did Daddy hold you prisoner? How many years did it take to escape him? I'm just thankful not to live with him anymore."

Her mother's eyes teared. "That's all true. And I thank God every day that I'm free. Even if I'm hiding out in Alabama to stay that way."

Sabine hugged her mother. "We're going to figure a way

out of this for good. Don't worry. We know too much for them to try and force us to do anything. It's not worth it to them to rock the boat right now with Dad's parole hearing coming up."

Sabine could have smacked herself for the slip-up. Mom didn't know about the hearing.

"When?" Her mother had gone completely still.

"Soon. He wants me to come to the prison for a visit."

"Do you really think he'll get out the first go-round?" Mom asked.

"I don't know. We're fortunate he's incarcerated, for now, here in Alabama. It cuts down on the likelihood of any of his political connections being an issue." It was very likely her father would be released on parole.

His were insidious, but not violent, crimes. He was transferred to the minimum security federal "camp" in Alabama for that reason. Plus, he was an influential, high-profile political figure.

"I don't think his being in Alabama will help one bit. Don't underestimate the reach of your father's political arm. He has connections *everywhere*." Her mother whispered the last word for effect.

"I know he does, but he's out of the loop now. He got caught and convicted. Those connections likely don't want to associate with that kind of failure."

Her mother's mood visibly brightened at that idea, and she nodded. "That could be somewhat true. Nobody likes a loser."

"Mom, you deserve happiness more than anyone I know. You've already paid your life's penance up front and in-full, or there's something really wrong with karma. You should be free and clear from here on out."

"You're running a close second, my dear. I'm looking forward to a day when the two of us can pursue our own permanent happiness without the past shadowing our steps wherever we go."

"But, let's make an agreement to live our lives as fully as possible in the meantime, okay?" Sabine wanted that for her mom more than anything.

"Okay, therapist lady. I will, if you will." Her mom hugged her tight.

Sabine stood from where they were sitting on the sofa and stretched. "I'm heading to bed. I have an early patient in the morning."

"I'll double check that everything is locked up tight."

"Thanks, Mom."

Chapter Six

"THERE'S THE MAN of the hour." Jeff slithered up next to Ben and slapped him on the back, a wide, fake grin on his face.

The half dozen or so employees who'd come in early applauded. What the hell was going on?

"Look at his face. He hasn't seen it yet." Jeff grabbed a copy of the local newspaper and held it up in front of Ben's face.

Local Attorney, Ben Laroux, Named to Governor's Special Task Force.

"You sly dog. Way to work yourself into Gumby's good graces with that legislation." If Jeff's envy were any more obvious, he'd be physically turning a bright shade of green any moment.

"Thanks." Ben addressed the expectant group of coworkers surrounding them. "I didn't want to mention it until everything was official."

George, one of the senior partners, moved forward to shake Ben's hand. "We're proud of you, son. Your appointment reflects well on the firm. Puts us on the map. We might be in a small town, but our reputation precedes us when our people make themselves known in state politics. Well done."

"Yeah. Well done." Jeff sneered as George walked away.

Ben had meant to address Jeff's disrespect for a while now. It was directed at Ben only, for some unknown reason. And it seemed that no one else noticed or paid attention. "Hey, Jeff, could you step into my office for a moment, please?"

"Now, how could I refuse?" Jeff simpered.

Ben motioned for Jeff to take a seat once they were inside Ben's office.

"So, Jeff, I'm not sure where your attitude is coming from where I'm concerned. I've ignored it so far, but it seems you're working to get it noticed."

Jeff smirked. "Who, me? I'm just the nephew of the senior partner."

"And you think that makes it appropriate for you to act like an asshole toward me?"

"I think it makes you unable to do dick about it."

Ben didn't know what this stemmed from. "What the hell is your problem with me?"

Jeff's expression was filled with unadulterated hate. "I'm engaged to Hailey Choate."

Ben frowned at the name, trying to make a connection. Just as the mental picture of a lovely blonde entered Ben's mind, Jeff launched himself out of his chair and across Ben's desk. The punch was intended to land squarely across Ben's nose, but Ben moved more quickly than Jeff anticipated and only caught a glancing blow to the jaw. Jeff lost his balance, and his momentum carried him over and into a heap on the other side of the desk.

The commotion couldn't have been a quiet one, because several coworkers came rushing in.

"Ben—what the hell?" George demanded. From his vantage point, Ben could only imagine how the scene must appear.

"He threw a punch, and I tried to avoid it." Ben rubbed his jaw.

Jeff was untangling himself from his position on the floor amidst the items on and behind Ben's desk, including the shredder, printer, and the pen set he'd gotten as a gift last Christmas from his assistant.

"You son-of-a-bitch. You don't even remember Hailey. What kind of bastard are you?" Jeff was poised to throw another punch.

By then, everyone was staring through his office door. *Hailey.* Of course he remembered. They'd gone out two or three times. But he'd called her by the nickname of Hales. Dinner, dancing, and yes, they'd slept together. It had been casual and fun. Two adults doing adult things with full consent. Ben didn't remember her being the clingy type or even asking for more than a lighthearted dating relationship. In fact, he couldn't exactly remember how they'd left off. They'd gone out not terribly long after he and Lisa had broken up. Oh.

"You used her. I'll bet you have no idea what happened to her after you threw her away, do you?"

Ben was stunned. "What are you talking about? I didn't throw anyone away."

"She was pregnant. With your baby."

Ben sat down in his office chair, because his legs threatened to collapse. *Pregnant?*

"What the hell are you talking about, Jeff?"

"Oh, don't worry; she miscarried. No responsibility on your end. But now she carries the baggage of losing your baby around in our relationship. So, you wonder why I don't like you? Now you know." Jeff kicked Ben's trash can out of the way and stormed out of the office, his peers parting like the Red Sea.

Ben stared at them, and they stared back. In his almost thirty years, he'd never been at such a complete loss for words.

Greg announced, "Okay, people. Show's over. This is personal business." Then he cleared his throat loudly, held up his hand, and everyone stilled. "I expect that none of this will leave the office. Your contracts include an airtight confidentiality clause that encompasses all office happenings.

This incident applies. If I get wind of a gossip leak from within, you're out."

He shut the door and stayed inside. "I'm assuming you knew nothing about this."

Ben, still stunned, shook his head. "Nothing."

"Well, there's obviously no legal issue here. But you and Jeff need to figure out some kind of working relationship moving forward."

"George, I've dated women, but I'm always careful. I can't even imagine how this happened. And she and I were in a casual relationship, so I would have been extra cautious."

"Son, birth control fails, no matter how careful we are. Ask my wife. Condoms break and pills are forgotten, or they fail. Nothing is a hundred percent. You're fifty percent of the process, so you can't ever blame the other person, no matter what they tell you. Always hold up your half of the bargain."

"I always have. That's why I don't understand this."

"Maybe you should consider only having sex with someone you don't mind having a baby with from now on. It might keep you on the right track, and it would certainly prevent any further liabilities such as this—emotional or litigious."

Ben might as well have been a horny fourteen-year-old boy, sitting in front of his dad, squirming through his first lecture on how not behave with young ladies, such was his humiliation. George was the grandfather of six, so Ben judged him to be in his mid-to-late fifties. George Bach had served as mentor and friend since he'd come to work at Babin, Bach, & Smith, now Babin, Bach, Smith & Laroux.

"It was a long time ago—several years. Just after my breakup with a long-term girlfriend. I've since been far more discerning with regards to my behavior with women," Ben said.

And he had been. His limiting the number of dates with the same person had mostly been about taking the third date decision to have sex out of the equation. In his experience, women were often willing to go the next level by the third date, mostly because they believed there was a chance of a developing relationship.

"I'm just saying that it might be time to start looking at dating as a more permanent situation instead of a good time and quick fix. Every time I see you out in public, you've got a different woman on your arm."

Ben flushed. "I don't sleep with every woman I escort to a party, George. And I don't date the same woman more than twice, as a rule. They don't have expectations that way. It isn't fair to lead anyone on."

George grimaced. "Son, that's cold. But, I get it; you're not interested in getting serious. Somebody must've hurt you pretty badly along the way."

Ben didn't like this sharing. "I don't discuss my personal life if I can help it."

George held up his hands. "My wife has a therapist. Maybe you should consider it. Might help you work out your demons. She swears by her. Doctor O'Connor, I think is her name. Maybe I'll share her name with Jeff and his fiancée. Sounds like she might need to speak to someone."

"I would prefer you didn't, since I know Dr. O'Connor personally."

"Her too, huh? You do get around." George shook his head.

⁕⁕⁕⁕⁕

SABINE HAD GIVEN each patient her full and complete attention, along with the very best advice and feedback possible without losing herself in their problems today. It wasn't terribly hard in some cases, when the "problems" weren't much deeper than choosing a seat on the board on the Junior League when one's friend was passed over for the position. Keeping a professional distance continued to be an issue when the patients were children suffering from abuse, or women who were trying to figure out whether to leave their husbands, or not.

She and Mom were leaving after Sabine got off work to travel the two hours' distance to the Montgomery Federal Prison Camp on the other side of Montgomery.

"I don't understand why you couldn't just go by yourself," Mom said. Her displeasure over being strong-armed into taking this trip was obvious.

"Because I couldn't focus knowing you were home alone. Plus, you need to face Dad. It's way past time."

"I faced him for twenty-seven years, thank you very much. Every day and night."

"You know what I mean. I'm talking about since you left."

"I'm not afraid of him."

"That's easy to say. We're all a little afraid of him, Mom. He can be a pretty scary guy." Dad hadn't ever been abusive to any of them, but he had an edge of icy authority about him that booked no argument. He'd rarely shown that side of himself to his family, but when he'd put his foot down about something, they'd known not to argue the point further.

"What can he do to me that he hasn't already done?"

"He can make things harder for us to move on beyond his imprisonment. If we go and talk with him, maybe he'll believe we've done as he's asked."

"I don't want to capitulate and bow down to him."

"I know; me neither. But you can face him. Tell him how you feel. Don't call him names, though. It won't help anything, okay?"

"I can't believe you would ask that kind of restraint of me." Mom's expression was fierce as she stared out the car's windshield.

"I know he deserves every name in the book, but having an honest conversation really would be helpful for you both. And it won't incite him to do anything rash."

"Fine. But it doesn't keep me from wishing for him to

get exactly what he deserves. Like someone throwing him naked on an anthill with peanut butter on his genitals. You know, real justice."

Sabine nodded and laughed as she exited the interstate. "Wow, that's a powerful visual. And while I know that would give everyone he's hurt some real visceral satisfaction, I look forward to the day that we can both just wake up every morning without a cloud hanging over our heads."

Dad had used his position as district attorney of New Orleans to manipulate politics and people. It had taken years for the right people to catch on, or maybe it had just taken that long for them to build an airtight case against him. He'd tampered with juries, influenced witnesses, and used his political connections to sway outcomes of trials. Sabine didn't understand his motivations, but believed him to be a misguided vigilante.

Dad had often ranted about criminals getting away with murder, human trafficking, and some of the most heinous crimes imaginable. He said the system was slow and broken, and that the worst of the thugs too often got off on technicalities. He'd figured out his own elaborate system to make sure that wasn't the case during his time in office.

Unfortunately for him, the feds hadn't agreed with his methods.

Sabine pulled into the parking lot of the budget hotel where they had reservations. It was a chain, but she knew it to be clean and recently updated from her first visit last year.

Last year, her mother had refused to see her dad. She'd remained in the hotel room when Sabine had gone to the prison.

➤➤➤◄◄◄

BEN COULDN'T SLEEP. How had Hailey Choate gotten pregnant? Why hadn't she told him? How must that have affected her emotionally? He'd convinced himself he was so chivalrous and fair with all the women he'd dated. Maybe he'd been fooling everyone. The town had treated him with such respect, a respect he'd believed was well-earned.

What if he was every bit the selfish bastard Sabine believed? Clearly, he'd hurt people with his emotional unavailability. But to impregnate a young woman who'd miscarried his child was far too much for him to ignore. He bore real responsibility in that.

He picked up his cell phone and dialed Jeff's number.

Jeff answered in a gruff voice. Ben had obviously woken him. "What the hell do you want, Laroux?"

"I want to meet with Hailey."

"Fuck off." The line went dead.

Well, maybe tomorrow would be a better time to approach this issue.

Ben had an inexplicable urge to see Sabine. To speak with her about this. She had inside info that he didn't. It bothered him deeply to think his perception of himself was profoundly distorted.

He doubted she would appreciate a two a.m. phone call.

So, Ben grabbed the handy notepad he kept on his bed-side table to jot down ideas for making his cases in court when inspiration struck after hours. He made a list. Of women. It began with his high school girlfriends and prom dates, then college. He skipped the two-and-a-half Lisa years. As he flipped to the third page, a sick sensation began in the pit of Ben's stomach.

No, he hadn't slept with them all, not even half, but how many of them had been emotionally invested that he'd blown off with his casual insensitivity?

He always used a condom, besides with Lisa, and that had taken at least a year, at her insistence. No, he didn't have any diseases, of that he was certain, due to his annual check-ups.

How had he not seen what he'd become? Yes, his sisters gave him a hard time about the number of women he'd dated over the years. But he'd dismissed it as the usual harassment.

He needed to speak with Hailey. Perhaps he should go down his list and make amends. Like the program for addicts. Face his shortcomings, take responsibility, and ask for forgiveness. A daunting task. But he had to know how many women he'd hurt, and the possible impact it might have had on their lives. Obviously, Hailey's life had been affected.

And those women in therapy. How many were legit?

Or was his opinion of himself way overblown? Might he just be the egotistical ass Sabine had suggested? Perhaps there was a middle ground. Sabine held the key here; he was certain.

>>>><<<<

SABINE'S HEART WAS beating fast, so she could only imagine how her mother's emotions were faring. A casual observer wouldn't be able to notice Mom's discomfort at a glance. She wore a fitted jacket in medium blue, with a white blouse beneath, paired with hammered silver jewelry. Her warm brown, medium-length bob haircut was shot through with only a few gray strands. Her nails were impeccably done in deep coral. She appeared cool, neat, and calm, and utterly beautiful as always. Her stress carried all on the inside. She'd had years of practice at maintaining her outer composure as a politician's wife.

They waited at what reminded Sabine of a cafeteria lunchroom table with its navy plastic seated chairs with shiny metal legs.

The parole hearing was coming up soon and she assumed her father wanted her to speak up as family on his behalf. She knew him so well.

Jean-Claude Prudhomme was escorted into the room without handcuffs or shackles. He sauntered in wearing tennis shoes with Velcro and a simple gray sweat suit. His graying beard was neatly trimmed, as was his head of curly, thick salt and pepper hair. He had deep laugh lines at the corner of his eyes and around his mouth. His snapping, pale blue eyes were Sabine's exact color. He was an incredibly handsome man. That alone had gotten him far in life.

"Ah, two of my favorite ladies." A genuine smile lit his face upon seeing them.

Sabine rose and greeted him with a light kiss on both cheeks. Her mother did not.

The disappointment in his glacial blue eyes was evident, but quickly hidden.

"I'm so glad you took the time to come out today, my dear."

Sabine nailed him with a direct gaze. "James stopped by and insinuated that I should—or else."

Her father frowned. "What did the boy say?"

"He suggested that he could get to either me or Mom at any time." Sabine knew that her father wouldn't let any physical harm befall them at James's hands.

Her father's eyes hardened. "I'll handle that."

"Dad, we want to move on. Both of us. We're ready to be released from your service."

"What do you mean?" he asked, an edge to his question.

"I mean that I'm moving forward with a divorce from Richard. And Mom wants to be free to live her life as she chooses."

"A divorce? Why?" He seemed genuinely puzzled.

"Because I don't intend to live my life in the public eye

any longer. I'm not going to accept that kind of humiliation again, and I can't live with a man who cheats."

"All men cheat." Her father appeared baffled by what she'd said.

Her mother made a disgusted sound but didn't speak.

"No, Dad; you cheated, and Richard cheated because you both believed you were more important than mere mortal men. That you could do so and we would accept it as part of our lives. We didn't and don't. No woman should have to live with her husband seeking out other women in his bed."

"It's normal for powerful men to do this." His Creole accent was more pronounced when he became agitated.

"No, it's not. And we don't have to live with it. We won't."

Suddenly, her mother stood and leaned over the table toward her ex-husband.

"I would rather die than spend one more day as your wife. Oh, and I don't have to because I finally got the divorce decree. I don't love you. You killed anything I felt for you when your sex tape with those whores went public. You humiliated me to everyone I knew."

"You took that too hard, Elizabeth." His tone was meant to soothe. "There was never anyone but you in my heart." He placed his closed palm over his chest.

Her mother smiled, a cold, hard smile. And totally ignored his gesture.

"But the worst was your bringing James into our lives and allowing him to rule our household. You never disciplined him, and he ruined our lives. He's been like a dark shadow over us all the time."

Her father's face changed. "I could have done better with the boy. But he was my son, and I felt I should compensate for his losing his mother."

Sabine chose to ignore his comment, and said, "While you've been here, he's been running amok. We need reassurance that you can keep him out of our lives."

Her mother sat down and glared at her father.

"I can see why you wouldn't want James in your lives. But I don't want to be cut out."

"Dad, we're living quietly now. We'd like to keep it that way. Wherever you go, you'll stir up scandal and negative attention."

"I never meant to hurt either of you."

"When you cheat on your wife repeatedly and do the disgusting things you've done, you lose the right to utter those words, Jean-Claude," Mom said.

Dad shook his head. "I know. I get it. But I can't stand the thought of losing you both, or your sister. Where is Rachel, by the way?"

"Rachel is away on a shoot. I'll come out for your parole hearing and do my best to be a fantastic character witness, but you've got to back me up on the divorce in case Richard gives me a hard time. And keep James away—for good."

"Fine. What about Rachel?" he asked.

"What about her?" Sabine asked.

"I want her to come for my hearing."

"I can't promise that for her."

"Get her here."

"I'll speak with her."

"Can you not see that you've ruined the lives of your entire family?" Mom spoke up again.

"I was trying to do what was right," Dad said, looking directly at Mom.

"By lying, coercing, cheating, intimidating, and God knows what else? You knew the law, and you broke it at every turn. Did you think you were so far above it that none of it applied?" Mom asked.

Dad glared at her mother.

"Okay, we're done here," Sabine said.

Her father rose and turned to go. "Remember what I said. Rachel comes, or you don't get to stay all cozy in your hidey-hole." He pointed at her mother. "You'd better watch how you speak to me. Your disrespect will get you nothing."

He turned on his heel and stalked off.

⇒⟫⟪⟪⟫⟪

"So, that's why I asked you to meet me here. I know you'll give me your honest opinions, whether I want them or not."

He stood in front of the five women who'd raised him, beaten him up, and loved him in equal measure his whole life. *The Council of the Women,* as he silently referred to them. Their reactions to his presentation varied. His mother's eyes were slightly dewy, as expected. Maeve, his eldest sister appeared to be digesting the information, while Emma looked as if she were ready to punch him in the nose. JoJo, the next in age besides his twin, Cammie, had a soft, sad expression in her eyes. Cammie came over and put her hand in his.

"I'll start," Emma said. "First, I don't think you began this journey of debauchery with bad intentions—"

"How poetic," Maeve interjected.

Emma held her hand up as if to silence the crowd. "But—and it's a big ole but, Brother, you've not been especially sensitive where the ladies in town have been concerned."

"How do you mean?" Ben asked.

Emma continued. "It's all about point of view. Yours. You thought that as long as you were polite about your *wham-bam-thank-you-ma'am,* then nobody got hurt."

"And they all were so tickled that Ben Laroux gave them some sweet lovin,' nobody complained," JoJo said.

"Ouch," Ben said.

Cammie nodded. "I agree with them. You're very popular. Everybody wants to see if they can sleep with the rock star. Only, you're not on tour. You're a fixture in town, or just outside of town. So, it's like some competition with the ladies around here. You've got a job and all your teeth, rock star. You're the whole package. And you've never given them any reason to think you weren't available."

Maeve took the torch and kept going. "You've kept them just at arm's length, haven't you? But did you ever tell any one of them, besides the married ones, definitively no? Instead, giving them some lame excuse about timing or putting them off? They all still believed they had a shot with you until they saw you with someone else or you just avoided them until they finally got the message."

Ben's frown deepened. They were laying out a tale here that was feeling eerily familiar. "I didn't want to hurt anyone's feelings."

"In doing so, it sounds like that's what happened." Mom rounded out his guilty verdict.

"So all the ladies have been panting after you all this time in hopes that you'll come to your senses and choose them," Cammie said.

"That's ridiculous," Ben said.

"Maybe that's exactly how he wants it." Emma looked over at her sisters.

"No, of course it isn't." He tried to defend himself against her statement.

"It's far easier to be adored than hated. Avoiding conflict is your specialty—always has been, dear brother. You've been a charmer your whole life," JoJo said.

Ben sat down hard on the sofa. They'd chosen to gather in the comfy family room where they assembled on Saturdays to watch college football—the one with the gigantic TV. It was far less formal than most of the rooms in Evangeline House.

He must be the worst attorney on the planet if he couldn't come up with some sort of self-defense against these accusations. Or, he was dead wrong, and they had it all correct.

"Cheer up, Brother. It's nothing we all haven't known for years, along with everyone else in town. They love you anyway, so there's that," Emma said.

"But how can I make it right? Especially this thing with Hailey?"

The women all looked at one another. "That's another matter. It's a shame she didn't tell you."

"Should I try and speak with her? I feel like I should," Ben said.

"Do you have some kind of wisdom to offer her? Do you want to make her feel better, or are you trying to make yourself feel better?" Maeve asked.

Ben ran a hand through his hair. "I'm not sure. I feel like I owe her something. She was carrying my child."

"And she chose not to tell you about the pregnancy or the miscarriage," Mom said.

"Maybe because she had such a low opinion of me that she thought I wouldn't care," he said.

"Clearly, you didn't care much—about her as a person, or you would've felt some connection while you were dating, even if it was casual. That might have been all she needed to know. If she felt like the only reason you might've shown her any special consideration is because you slipped up and she got pregnant, well, can you blame her for keeping silent? If I was casually dating a man who I knew had no feelings for me, and I got pregnant, I doubt I would tell him. At least not until I knew the pregnancy was viable or until I knew what my plan was," Emma said.

"Do you mean if you were going to *abort*?" Jo Jo's children were her whole world, so that wouldn't ever have been an option for her.

"No. *I* wouldn't do that. But a single woman with no prospects might. And if she miscarried early, then I can see where she might not tell you at all. What would be the point? Can't you see that side of it?"

Ben frowned. "I helped create a life. I deserved to know. It wasn't only hers, even if it wasn't intended."

"Then, you should speak with her. Like you said, you can offer your condolences and let her know that you regret if she felt you didn't respect or honor her feelings as a person," Mom said.

"That sounds like something, at least. I can't stand the idea of doing nothing," Ben said.

⇶⬅⬅

"YOU'D THINK HE was some kind of monarch or something, the way he orders everyone around," Mom muttered.

They were home now. Mom had been quiet on the ride back, but Sabine could tell her thoughts were anything but.

Sabine sighed. "He's used to getting his way." She pulled a couple glasses from the cupboard and filled them with ice and water while her mother pulled out the to-go containers of Italian food they picked up from their favorite pizza and pasta restaurant on the way back into town.

"How long does he get to keep doing that?"

"I don't know. I've decided it's time to have a long talk with Richard about a divorce. Maybe once I figure that out and get my life back, I can figure a way out of this mess with Dad." Sabine no longer loved Richard.

He'd hurt her and used her to advance his political career, but his behavior proved far better than his words what lay in his heart. And Sabine refused to be with a man who wasn't trustworthy. She'd been younger once, and believed his words. But, no longer.

"I thought the two of you were such a great match in the beginning," Mom said.

"In the beginning, so did I." They ate for a few minutes in silence.

Her mother snapped the lid shut on her pasta container suddenly and announced, "I'm not taking it anymore."

"What do you mean?"

"I'm starting my life again. After seeing Jean-Claude today, I realize that I'm over him. Like, I don't love him anymore. He's a sad, pathetic old convict who finally got what he deserved. All the manipulation of people's lives, ours included, caught up with him. I don't have to live like a prisoner, my dear, and I don't plan to anymore."

"Mom, I get that you're angry, and that you're ready to make a fresh start, but how exactly will that change your everyday life?"

"Maybe it won't, at first. It's more in my mind that I've let your father bind my spirit. I've hidden out, and I've worried. I've lived a prisoner's existence. I know I can't do certain things until you've made your break from Richard because of the risk of exposing your privacy and it hurting your business and bringing you unwanted attention."

Sabine's heartbeat accelerated, like it always did when they discussed the possibility of exposure—her greatest fear. No one would trust her with their secrets here again. They would believe she'd deceived them. She had, in so many ways. Her official identity wasn't who they believed. But she was Sabine, and she'd been authentic in her dealings with them. Hopefully, if this all went haywire, she would be able to convince her patients, and the friends she'd made, of this. A small, but insistent voice asked what would Ben think of her?

No, she didn't owe him anything. They weren't an item. But sins of omission had an insidiousness about them. There was something between the two of them. Maybe it was basic physical attraction—but what if there was more? What if she were a divorced woman and free to act on her desires? Sabine had such conventional views on marriage that were so deeply ingrained from her Catholic upbringing. They could take the girl out of the church but not the guilt from the girl. She'd always believed marriage was for life. Divorce was a sin. *Wasn't it?*

Her good sense warred with her rigid moral code. But somehow she'd always been able to suspend her self-inflicted flagellations to provide a well-balanced perspective for her patients, without imposing that rigidity on them. She simply didn't judge them—only herself.

Maybe it wouldn't affect Ben that she was married, or that she was a well-known senator's wife who had changed her name to hide out here in his small town. It wasn't Ben's concern unless she made future overtures toward seeing him socially. Otherwise, they would run into one another on occasion and that would be it.

As Sabine gathered up her leavings from dinner, she pondered what true freedom might be like for her down the road. She'd been so bound up in the emotional complexity of her situation for such a long time, Sabine hadn't allowed herself to glimpse or imagine the future, long-term, once all this was over. Would it ever truly end?

If her mother could do it, so could she. Tomorrow Sabine would contact Richard and discuss their next steps, and hopefully their futures without each other. Richard's political career hinged somewhat on his family-man image. Favorability ratings had dropped since he'd publicly announced they were "taking some time to reevaluate." That had been almost two years ago, right after his reelection. Her absence obviously mattered. A state senator's wife maintained a very busy schedule. Theresa Habersham had dropped off the face of the earth. Richard had dodged questions about her to the point of outright lying. He'd had to imply that she was still distraught over her father's conviction, which had been a huge media circus, and asked for complete privacy. Then there'd been the miscarriage.

Of course, there had been reporters who had sniffed around trying to find her. But, she'd done a pretty significant job of covering her tracks. Her clinical license was registered in Alabama as Sabina O'Connor, which was listed on her birth certificate as part of her full name, making it legal. Her public name had been Theresa Habersham. Her family and Richard had always called her Sabine, as a nickname, but no one else had. Her ridiculously long birth name was Theresa Sabina O'Conner Prudhomme. Her married name was Habersham. For two years, it had worked.

And, so far, the cover-up of Richard's shenanigans with prostitutes while attending meetings in New Orleans had been kept under wraps. Dad had a hand in keeping that quiet, but it could blow up at any time. Sabine wondered if it would matter for more than a full news cycle to his constituents. With all the awful things going on in the world, and the shocking exploits of today's politicians, it was doubtful a prostitution scandal would even register on the scale. No more than having one's hand caught in the cookie jar. Almost expected.

But somehow, being married in politics mattered. It was okay to be a philanderer, so long as one was married. It made one seem grounded and serious to the voters. Go figure.

"Honey, you've been quiet. I realize my announcement might have shocked you. But I'm doing this for both of us. It's still my job to set a good example for you—to show you strength. Don't worry. I would never place you in a vulnerable situation by telling anyone our secret. I just plan to live again instead of hiding inside my own skin in shame."

Sabine exited her own thoughts and replied, "I'm glad. It's time we both got back to our real lives. It might take some time before we're able to be completely honest with everyone in town, but the time will come. Soon. I'm going to call Richard tomorrow. You've inspired me." Sabine and her mother embraced. "It's going to be okay."

"I'm so ready for this," Mom said, fresh tears shining in her lovely eyes.

"Me too."

Chapter Seven

B EN COULDN'T REMEMBER the last time he'd experienced such physical symptoms. He was sweating, but it
was quite cool in here. His hands were shaking slightly—and
even before the biggest trials, his hands *never* shook. And his
gut. He thought he might throw up. Was he ill?

"Hey, bud, you don't look so hot. You okay?" It was his
sister, Cammie.

"I feel like shit."

"It's nerves."

Ben opened his mouth to hotly deny such nonsense, then
closed it. He was nervous. It was such a foreign sensation to
him. His normal, easy confidence had taken off for the hills.

"Don't worry, Brother, I won't tell anyone you've been
taken out by human weakness. You're going to do fine,
okay?"

"Thanks, Cam."

Ben had asked Hailey to meet him at Evangeline House
for privacy's sake. The last thing he wanted was the gossip
mill to crank up to full steam if anyone saw them somewhere

together in public. Mainly, because she was engaged to Jeff, but also because Ben had no idea how this meeting would go. Hailey was a nice girl, and he didn't want to expose her to public drama.

Ben hoped there wouldn't be a scene, because he hated emotional scenes. Didn't everyone? But given his own nerves, he could only imagine that Hailey might be feeling the same. Evangeline House was the best choice for this discussion.

Ben still had Hailey's phone number in his list of contacts, so he'd simply called her. She'd been hesitant to speak with him, at first. Ben could hear Jeff talking in the background, so that might have been the reason. But she agreed to come over. He wondered if she'd mentioned it to Jeff. Ben hoped she had. Meeting with another man's fiancée without his knowledge broke his bro code in a big way, even if it was Jeff's back Ben was going behind.

Ben was seated in the same room where he and Sabine had shared their near-perfect evening. It warmed his insides and settled his nerves a little as he remembered. Just thinking about her calm, reasonable demeanor did that. Maybe he should see her in a professional capacity.

Voices broke into his musings. He stood as Hailey entered the room; she was willowy and blonde, with large brown eyes and a pretty smile.

Cammie's hand rested on the doorknob. "I'll be down the hall if you need anything. There's iced tea, water, and some snacks on the table. No one will bother you." She smiled at Hailey.

Hailey thanked Cammie and approached the table. Ben's stomach turned a flip. Oh, that wasn't good.

But he shoved down the worst of it and managed to greet Hailey. "Thanks for meeting me."

"Sure." They did a quick, awkward embrace, as grown-ups did when thrown together after time had passed.

"Please sit. I'm sure Jeff told you about our run-in at the office the other day."

Hailey shook her head. "No. He didn't mention anything. I know you aren't his favorite person, but he didn't tell me that anything out of the ordinary happened."

"Then this will be more awkward than I'd expected."

She frowned. "I wondered why you asked to see me."

No point in beating around the bush. "Jeff told me you'd miscarried. My baby."

Comprehension dawned in Hailey's eyes. Not shock, but comprehension. "I wondered if he'd be able to restrain himself from telling you eventually." Her expression was sad but resigned.

"Hailey, why didn't *you* tell me?" Ben asked.

"Why would I tell you? We weren't a thing." Her gaze was steady.

"But you were pregnant with my child."

"The only reason you would have cared is because I was pregnant. You didn't care about me." She said this in a sad, but matter-of-fact manner.

"I cared." But Ben realized in that moment that she was right.

"Ben, you have a unique gift of making women feel special but keeping yourself holed away someplace where you can't feel—really feel. I believe you would have done the right thing, whatever the right thing was, if I'd carried the pregnancy to term. But I didn't have any interest in being with someone who wasn't in it at least fifty percent for me."

Ben sighed. "I'm sorry, Hailey." Her revelation had hit him like a sledgehammer between the eyes. "I'm beginning to see a pattern. I honestly believed that I've been treating women well. But it's been recently pointed out that I've hurt people. I hurt you."

"Yes, you hurt me. It hurt to know that the person who I made a life with cared nothing about me. But I was careless too. I knew better than to involve myself with someone so emotionally unavailable, and even though we were both using protection, the pregnancy happened. I would rather have gone it alone than trap you."

"But instead you suffered your loss alone."

"Yes. But, I'm okay. I saw a therapist right after, and she helped me through the worst of it. And quite a bit of time has passed. I still see her sometimes."

Well, shit. He'd bet money on who that was.

"I'm glad you've sought counseling and are in a better place. I hear congratulations are in order for you and Jeff?

You're getting married?"

She grinned then, and a lovely blush stole over her cheeks. "Yes. We are very happy. Please understand; he's not as much of a jerk as he seems. Back when I told him what happened, he wanted to kill you. Or anyone. He's very protective of me."

Ben understood then. Why Jeff singled him out as the butt of jokes in the office, or figured out ways to constantly place him on the defensive. "I can't imagine what he must think of me. I honestly don't blame him."

"Here's a thought, why don't we get together with Jeff and work this out? I mean, long-term, it won't do anybody any good for the two of you to not get along. You're a partner in the law firm where he's trying to make partner. Peace would be best for us all."

"You would be willing to do that? After everything that's happened?" Ben was surprised, to say the least.

"Of course. Ben, I'm relieved that you asked to see me. I wanted to tell you about the baby. But I didn't want to see the look in your eyes when you believed I'd trapped you. You're a good guy. I know that. I think you just need to do some soul-searching where your relationships are concerned. Figure out why you don't let anyone scratch the surface. Everyone in town knows about Lisa. Maybe you need to get some closure there."

Hailey smiled, a sad smile, and patted his hand. She was sad for him as well as her own loss, he could tell. Was everyone sad for him now? Now that they had begun to realize he couldn't connect with other females besides Lisa?

"Do you think everyone knows this about me?" he asked.

Hailey shook her head. "Not everyone. Just a few of us have likely figured it out. But, like I said, everyone knows the mind-job Lisa did on you. I think some women have taken it as their personal challenge to be the one who breaks through and becomes the *one* to make you forget her."

"You're an amazing girl, Hailey. I hope Jeff understands how lucky he is."

She laughed. "Oh, he does. That's why I'm marrying him."

"Well, I appreciate your insights. It's not easy to admit to having a problem. And I'm pretty sure I've got to make some changes."

"Don't worry. I'll keep your secret." She grinned and stood.

"Maybe I'll go to a therapist," Ben said.

"You should try Sabine O'Connor. She's amazing."

He groaned. "Somehow I knew she was the one you were going to recommend."

"Oh? You know her?" Hailey's eyes lit up.

"We worked on a court case together."

"Well, give her a try. She's the best."

And now he knew exactly why Sabine believed him to be such scum of the earth. She'd already heard every detail of this disastrous situation. And then he'd gone out of his way to defend his treatment of women to her.

He gave her high marks for professionalism. A woman with less self-control might have laughed in his face during his man pride speech after their date. She'd even kissed him, knowing what she knew about him. What did that say about her? Either she was desperate, or maybe it spoke to her own self-esteem that she was willing to bottom feed with the likes of Ben Laroux.

He'd gone from strutting around as the town's favorite son to the lowest form of life. And the change had all occurred in his head—and heart—once he'd gotten a large dose of truth.

"You okay?" Cammie broke into his maudlin thoughts.

"No. I don't think so."

"Look. I know this is a big, fat attitude adjustment for you, but you're not a bad person."

Cammie slid into the seat next to him and covered his hand with hers.

"I suck. All this time I believed I was doing them some kind of favor, spreading myself evenly among them. Allowing just enough of myself to keep them wanting more."

Cammie laughed. "Good heavens, Brother; it sounds like you think you've kept the females in town running on sweet Ben love."

Ben allowed himself a slight grin. "There's such a *demand*."

"I think you should focus quality over quantity moving

forward. What about Sabine? She appears to be quality."

Ben snorted.

"What? What happened with Sabine?"

"All the women in town have been telling her their Ben stories and problems. How do you think she views me? Especially after hearing Hailey's saga?"

Cammie grimaced. "Hailey is her patient?"

He nodded, his mouth set in a grim line.

"Oh."

"Now you see my issue with dating Sabine."

"I can see how she might have some predetermined ideas about your character, but I still saw the way she looked at you. And I believe it isn't hopeless."

Ben smiled at his twin. "You always look on the bright side."

"So do you. That's why you're such a fantastic attorney. And if anyone can solve this problem and make a case for Ben, the good guy, it's you."

Ben stood and pulled Cammie to her feet. "Thanks for the pep talk, Sis." He gave her a quick hug. "And thanks for being here today."

"I've got a couple weeks off from filming, so I'm making the most of them."

His gaze focused on her belly, which was still pretty flat. "So, have you felt any kicks yet?"

Cammie's grin was so huge it nearly split her face in two. "Here and there. We'll find out the sex in a few weeks."

Ben couldn't wait. He adored all his nieces and nephews. But he instinctively knew Cammie's child would be special because of their tight bond.

Her face became serious then. "Ben, you've worked this out with Hailey. She isn't holding a grudge, right?" He shook his head. "Then you've got to forgive yourself. We all have personal revelations as we grow and mature. Remember what went on with Grey and me when I moved back?"

Cammie referred to the situation with her husband, Grey, and their very complicated history. They'd fought tooth and nail to be together after a past filled with angst and regret.

"Yes, well, I had to swallow a ton of pride and admit to some things about myself I wasn't proud of, and so did Grey. We learned a lot about ourselves, both good and really awful."

"You've never been awful," he said.

"You don't think so, huh? Well, life and its situations make us say and take some pretty questionable actions. So, you've just learned some uncomfortable things about yourself that you're not proud of. Okay. Move forward differently. Make amends where you feel you should. No one hates you."

Ben's heart lightened just a little at Cammie's words. He had the love and support of his family, at least. But he did have some amends to make.

SABINE MADE THE call once she'd arrived home from work. Mom had gone grocery shopping, or so her note on the fridge said.

"Richard? It's Sabine." Silence.

"Just a moment." His deep voice was clipped. Sabine heard a heavy thud, then a click, like a door shutting and bolt being thrown. A deep inhale, then exhale. "Sabine. I'm glad you finally called. Where are you?"

"Richard, it doesn't matter." She took a deep breath. She hadn't expected to react to his voice with shaking hands and such timidity. "We need to discuss a divorce. Soon."

"No. No divorce. It's bad enough the position you've put me in. I've made ridiculous excuses to the constituents. I need you to come home."

"I am home. I don't live with you anymore. You humiliated me and assured that I could never trust you again. I guess I never could." She had loved Richard. He'd been her first love.

"I love you, Sabine—"

"No. Stop. You can't say that. The moment you consorted with other women, you lost the opportunity to ever say that again. So, just don't, okay? When I left, I wasn't strong enough to fight you and all the politics. I am now. I want a divorce. I want it now, and I want it quietly."

"You sound like you hold all the cards, Sabine. I have a feeling you don't want to be brought back into the circus. But I can't let you go that easily."

"Why, Richard? It's not like you need me. You've done just fine since I left." She assumed he had, at least. Sabine had tried hard not to keep up. The less she knew, the cleaner and more separate she'd felt. Richard's actions had left her coated with an inexplicable nastiness she'd worked hard to physically and emotionally distance herself from.

"How would you know? I wanted children. Someone to carry on my family line. Our children. You've deprived me of that. Your father would have enjoyed that."

"How do my father's wishes enter into this? You can't want to be associated with him since his conviction. That can't help you get reelected."

Richard sighed a heavy sigh. "It's not his public support I need, but his connections that aren't seen by anyone else. Sabine, you of all people know how valuable that is in state politics. Plus, divorce carries such a nasty stigma for a male politician."

"So do hookers," she said, no noticeable emotion in her tone.

"Well, that hasn't gotten out, and hopefully it won't. Your father made certain it didn't, and last I heard, he was against your divorcing me."

"He's on my side now. I have a life to live, and it's not as a politician's wife in Louisiana. I won't be shamed and made a fool of anymore."

"Sweetheart, nobody knows about that."

"*Do not call me sweetheart.* What happened to you, Richard? That's not the man you were when we met." She worked to keep the shrill out of her voice.

"You never were made of the stuff to take it on, were you? It takes a Teflon coating, you know? Letting things slide right off is easier."

Sabine shook her head in disbelief. This was the man she'd loved and married. "No, I'm not coated with Teflon, for sure, which is why I want a clean break—a no-fault divorce."

"Maybe we can arrange a deal. I'll need to think about the details, but it will definitely include your public endorsement. Reelection is right around the corner, you know."

"Public endorsement?"

"You know, something like you getting up on stage and introducing me at the governor's ball, and saying how we're still the best of friends, and you endorse me a hundred percent—yadda, yadda, yadda…"

"Those things get a lot of regional press." Alabama was only two states away, and the governor's ball drew politicians and professionals from several Southern states.

"We can only hope."

Sabine's stomach threatened to retch. Someone might recognize her. If that happened, then all this was for nothing. The life she'd been building here in Alabama would implode. Her patients—She would be exposed as a liar and fraud.

"You still there?" Richard nudged.

"I don't want to make public appearances."

"You abandoned me and our marriage. I tried to be a loving husband and give you time to grieve and heal. But I need you to do this, and if you don't, I'll make sure everyone, where you are, knows exactly who you are and what you've done—and who your father is. So far, I haven't bothered you out of some misguided belief that you'd return to your senses and come home. Clearly, it's time to talk turkey, Sabine. I'll sit down and figure out terms and let you know."

Sabine was shaking from head to toe now. "Why? Why would you do this?"

"Because you're my wife, and your place is with me. I think the law will agree. Oh, and because I love you, of course." The line went dead.

Sabine stood, her phone still dangling from her fingers when Mom found her some time later. "Sabine, honey, are you alright?"

"Huh?" Sabine took a moment to refocus. "No. I—just spoke to Richard. Nothing's fine."

"Sit down."

Sabine sat.

"What did he say?"

Sabine relayed their conversation word for word. She was too stunned to do otherwise.

Mom frowned. "Well, at least we know what we're up

against now. He's shown all his cards."

"What?"

"You didn't blackmail him? You could, you know. And you have the leverage with your father. Without his support, Richard can take a hard fall from grace."

"Yes, but he'll take me down with him."

Sabine thought about her mother's words. It all seemed so skeezy, but Richard had brought them down to this level, so that was where they would begin. Now, she'd have to employ the same kind of character-degrading values needed to survive and emerge the victor from the political sludge. While she'd been in the public arena, Sabine had done her best work for women, children, education, and any cause she could improve by using her influence and position as a state senator's wife.

She wasn't ashamed of the good work she'd done, only what surrounded by political agendas, money, and power did to those who were corrupted by it. Like her father and husband. They had started out as good men with the best intentions.

Were they just weak? Would a better man have avoided such temptation? Or was it an infectious disease where no one elected to office was immune, and eventually everyone succumbed to some degree? She simply knew that whomever she became involved with moving forward wouldn't be in that arena. Period.

BEN CALLED THE office instead of her cell phone. This was business. He needed someone to talk to who understood the situation. Who better than Sabine? She might not respect him or his behavior, but at least she would have all the facts.

He got the office voice mail, which wasn't surprising, since it was after five, so he left a message with the pertinent information. Name, callback number. No, he wasn't considering suicide.

Then, he headed home. As he'd locked up his office, he spotted Jeff, who gave a brisk nod. Jeff must've found out from Hailey about their meeting, because he hadn't been quite as rude lately. Not warm and fuzzy, but not as overtly hostile.

That was one heavy burden lightened, but Ben was still struggling mightily with the guilt of idiocy and past self-delusion. His whistling, everything-right-with-the-world self-confidence was shattered. He wanted it back. No, he wanted something less foolish. It had been an illusion.

As he drove through town, the idea of being alone tonight squeezed at him like a crushing weight. He spotted several cars at the *Buzzer*, the local sports bar. It had been a while since he'd hung out with the guys. Before he thought better of it, Ben pulled his truck beside an older model blue Ford with rusted spots. He recognized the truck as belonging to an old high school buddy, Roland. Lord, he hoped he hadn't slept with or dated any of Roland's exes. Roland might forgive him since Ben had helped him get community service instead of jail time after his second DUI. Of course, seeing Roland's truck parked at the bar didn't bode well.

Ben looked down at his attire and realized he might appear just a little fancy for the venue. He untucked his shirt and pulled off the tie. Not enough. He grabbed the old red Alabama T-shirt out of his gym bag. He pulled on the pair of boots on the floorboard of his truck. Too bad about the dress pants. He'd been in court today.

It would have to do. He locked up his truck and headed inside. The interior was dim, lit along the walls with neon beer signs. The smell of boiled peanuts mixed with various forms of alcohol hit at the same time he felt the crunch of the peanut shells beneath his boots.

"That's quite a getup you've got working there," the bartender observed.

"Yeah. Best I could do straight from work."

"What can I get you?"

"Bud." Ben didn't recognize the guy behind the bar with the long, dark hair tied back into a man bun. "Where's Joe?"

"Joe's got gout. He's taking some time off. So, you've got me. Name's Ace." He tapped his very muscular chest as if daring Ben to defy him.

"Ben. Ben Laroux. Nice to meet you." Ben stuck out his hand, like he always did.

He and Ace shook, but before Ben could even pull back his hand, he was squeezed from behind in a colossal bear hug.

"Ben, my man. What's with the fancy Nancy outfit?" Bubba Joe Hebert finally let Ben go before he passed out from lack of oxygen.

Bubba had played center on Ministry's offensive line back in the day and never let anyone forget it. He and Junior, Ben's brother-in-law, were brothers.

"What's up, Bubba?" Didn't every small town have a Bubba, and a Junior, or three for that matter?

"Dude, haven't seen you in here in a coon's age. How's it hangin'?" Bubba said.

"Yeah, we thought you was too slick and shit to hang with us, big lawyer man," Roland chimed in.

Ben looked over to where Roland, who looked as if he'd already had a few beers, waited for a response. "Well, Roland, I was slick enough to get your ass community service and parole last year when you got that second DUI over in Cheneyville, wasn't I?"

"Uh, yeah. Sorry, dude. I didn't mean no offense. Just giving you the business. We just hardly see you around here anymore."

Ben slapped his two classmates on the back. "I'm reassessing my priorities today, gentlemen. Next round's on me. As long as y'all don't drive yourselves home."

They nodded and grinned a little drunkenly. Which meant Ben would be arranging a ride home for them all.

The third beer slid down smoother than the second. It had been ages since Ben had over-imbibed. Or been even the slightest irresponsible. Oh, wait, he'd take that back. Hailey. And the other women. That had been stupidly irresponsible.

Just as beer number four was cued up and ready to go, he got a whiff of perfume. And heard a female voice, and then her laugh. *Lisa.*

Ben whipped his head around in the direction where he'd heard her. She was two tables away, but there were several people between them. She was laughing at something, her blonde hair shining down her back. Steve stood beside her, his arm draped casually across her shoulders.

Should he go over; say hi? No. He was almost drunk, and certainly not at his best to have any sort of coherent conversation. Then, without warning, Lisa turned and met his gaze. Her eyes lit up, then, she *waved.* She waved as if nothing had ever gone on between them. As if she hadn't stolen his future happiness by cheating on him with his best friend and breaking his heart. She'd *ruined* him for other relationships.

And she'd *waved?* All this time he'd believed he was okay. But seeing them happy together wasn't okay. Or maybe it just was unexpected. He was having a hard time taking in air.

Ben slapped two twenties on the bar and stormed out, knocking over his barstool in the process. "Make sure those two have a ride home." He motioned toward Roland and Bubba.

Ace shot him a look that said, *I'm a bartender, so I've been exposed to a lot of weird shit, so I'll just take the money and handle it.* "Sure man. No problem."

Ben busted out of there, gasping for air, and made his way toward his truck. But he knew he couldn't drive—too many beers.

Pulling out his phone, he fumbled, trying to get to his contacts. "Hello?"

"Hello? Who is this?" Shit, who had he called?

"Well, shit," he muttered, staring at his phone.

"Sorry?" a female voice answered.

"I was trying to call my sister," Ben said.

"Are you okay?" Sabine asked.

"Okay? Uh, I don't know. I guess I'm okay." He was borderline wasted after four beers. What a lightweight. He was slurry, even.

"Ben, where are you?" Sabine sounded worried.

"The bar. The Buzzer. Need to leave."

"I'm on my way home. I'll swing by. Are you outside?"

"Yup. Right by my truck."

"Don't you dare try and drive. I'll be there in two minutes."

"I won't. Scout's honor."

"I've heard that before. Almost there."

"Yup."

⟫⟫⟫✦⟪⟪⟪

SABINE'S HEART THUMPED too fast in her chest. He'd drunk dialed her office number. After hours, her calls were auto-

133

matically forwarded to her cell. The ring was different, so she could identify it. But, why her? He didn't seem like much of a drinker. In fact, from what she'd surmised, he hardly ever drank much more than a beer at a time. Something was off; she could feel it.

As she rounded the corner at the red light, she caught sight of him, sitting on his tailgate. His head was bowed, and he almost looked ridiculous in his suit pants, cowboy boots, and ancient Alabama T-shirt that hugged his muscular torso. Almost.

He'd caught sight of her, and his expression changed from dejected to what appeared to be relieved. Then, just as she rolled down the window to call out to him, a gorgeous blonde woman approached, distracting his attention from Sabine.

Sabine wished she'd never witnessed the play of emotions that crossed his face in that moment. The pain in his eyes made her want to weep—and it made her want to kill this woman who'd obviously hurt him so badly.

It was as if this blonde flipped a switch in Ben, animating him to a deeper level—certainly one Sabine hadn't known existed until now. He'd changed, right there in front of Sabine.

Sabine wanted to watch. Like the voyeur therapist she was, she was fascinated by the drama playing out between these two humans who'd clearly shared a past filled with deep emotions and drama. It was fascinating—and private—

she realized.

So, Sabine pulled the car into a parking space a few slots away, hoping to get some idea what was happening. So, sue her, she still was curious.

Besides, he'd called her, whether he'd meant to or not. So, she had every right to be here and to check on him. But she would wait a few minutes and give the two some privacy. Sabine cut the engine and rolled down her windows. And waited.

She could hear them talking softly, but there was a breeze, so their voices carried. The woman's tone was soothing and sad. This must be Lisa. *The* Lisa Cammie had mentioned. Ben's voice sounded rough, angry, and belligerent. Sabine hadn't ever heard smooth-talking Ben sound so out of control before. Maybe it was the alcohol. Or, maybe it was raw emotion. Indecision warred within her. Something deep inside told her Ben, without the alcohol wouldn't want to lose his cool, or his pride with this woman, or any woman.

So, Sabine made a decision that might cost her dearly. She first put on lipstick and fluffed her hair. And fixed her cleavage. Suddenly, she was glad she'd worn the high heels today.

"Hey, you. I got your message. You ready to go?" Sabine didn't normally flaunt her God-given looks. But she hadn't been born a woman for nothing.

Ben's head snapped up and his eyes connected with Sabine's. She sent him a message in that gaze. *Save your pride, man, and get in the car with me.*

He got the message. His miserable, bleary eyes cleared as if she'd slapped him silly. "Oh, hey there. Lisa, this is Sabine. I don't think you've met."

The blonde woman's eye opened just a fraction wider, and then, to her credit, she smiled at Sabine. A big, wide, friendly grin. "I'm Lisa. I haven't seen Ben in ages, and I hoped we'd have a chance to catch up."

Okay, Sabine hadn't expected this. Jealousy, maybe, or competitive female response of some sort. But overt, honest friendliness. No wonder Ben was over the moon about this girl. She was perfect. Sabine might have a little girl crush developing.

Ben came over to where Sabine stood and placed an arm around her shoulders. Another surprise. She instinctively leaned into his armpit. He smelled like deodorant, bar, and sweat. It was a little warm out this evening.

He managed to smile tightly at Lisa and said, "Maybe later. Sabine and I have plans later this evening. I hadn't planned on more than one beer, but I ran into Roland and Bubba and, well, Sabine was on her way home anyway." He shrugged, then grinned down at Sabine with such familiarity and appreciation, she felt it all the way through her woman parts.

Sabine stuck out a hand to Lisa. "It was so great to finally meet you. Maybe I'll see you again before you leave town."

Lisa laughed. It was full and lovely sound. "That's what I

came out to talk to Ben about. We've come home. We're moving back to Ministry. Steve and I discussed it, and we decided we've been gone from home too long. There's no reason to stay away—especially now that I know Ben's happy. I'm surprised no one told me about you by now."

"We've been keeping a very low profile because of a court case we both testified on. Different sides. We didn't really know each other at the time, but you know how touchy that can be." Sabine gave her a knowing look.

Sabine was nearly holding Ben up now. And he was getting heavy. Clearly Lisa hadn't noticed. "Okay, big guy, let's get you home."

Ben had a somewhat dazed expression, but managed to wave to Lisa as Sabine turned him around and led him to the passenger side of her car.

Once they were inside, she cranked up the A/C and asked for his address. Just as they crossed his cattle guard, he threw up all over her leather interior.

Chapter Eight

〜〜〜

SABINE ROLLED THE windows down and kept driving, trying not to gag. "Couldn't you have warned me? I would have stopped, you know."

Berating a sick person was beneath her and she knew it, but it was her car. She liked her car.

No answer.

They arrived at his front door within thirty seconds, and they both hopped out the second she rolled to a stop. He made it as far as the bushes at the side of the house. She went the other direction, gulping in fresh air.

There wasn't anything sexy about him right now. Nothing. In fact, he might never be sexy again. She might always associate him with this awful smell. She'd done that in the past with nasty things.

After his dry heaving ceased, he sat down on the front steps. Of the porch. Of his gorgeous house. She hadn't really noticed the house as she was sucking in cold air through her nostrils. Now she did. No wonder all the women in town were after him. They wanted his house.

And she didn't blame them. She simply stared, forgetting for a moment about the owner, who'd clearly had a bad day, up 'til this point.

"Wow. It's beautiful," she whispered.

"Thank you, I think." She snapped her head around, and recalled the whole situation then.

He looked pathetic now, shirtless, with his stained suit pants. He'd taken off his boots and tossed them on the porch, but still wore his black dress socks. Then, she unforgivably fought the urge to smile. And lost.

"You're quite a sight right now, you know."

"I'm at one of the lowest points in my life and you're laughing at me? You're a *therapist,* for Chrissake."

"I'm not laughing, exactly. I mean—how can I put this as so not to be insulting?"

"You can't." But then he looked down at himself and shook his head. "This is what I've sunk to." Then he appeared to reconsider. "Okay, give it your best shot. But you only get one."

She grinned. "So, do you remember the first time we met, and then when we went to dinner?" He nodded and cringed. "You asked why I didn't like you." He nodded again.

"Yes, so I was hard on you, and believed you to be a too-handsome playboy who only cared about himself. You tried to defend that persona, but I had my own ideas about you already."

"Clearly," he drawled.

"Well, I'd say that today has pretty much leveled the playing field. I've never seen one human so humbled and humiliated in such a short amount of time. Plus, I have a feeling it started before I came into the picture today."

"Hailey told you about our meeting?"

She nodded. "I can tell you this because she gave me written permission, with parameters, of course. Some things are private. She felt bad for you and wants to help you on your road to self-discovery. She said she referred you to me and hoped you would reach out to me professionally."

Ben began to unbutton his pants.

"What the hell are you doing?"

"Taking off my pants. They have vomit on them."

She turned her back. "You could have given me some warning."

"You've seen me at my worst, so you might as well see me in my boxers," he said.

"Um, no thank you."

"I want to clean out your car, but I don't think I can right now."

"I'd pull out the floor mat, but I have an aversion to that." She pointed toward her car.

"That? You mean throw up?"

She gagged. "Stop it. It's bad enough that I'm going to have to buy a new car."

"A new car?"

"I'll never get the smell out."

"Of course you will. I mean, I will. Just not tonight."

"What are we going to do? Your truck is back at the bar."

"I have people who owe me favors."

"Who owes you favors?" she asked, her eyes narrowed.

Ben narrowed his eyes. Then put his hands on his hips of his boxers—that he wore—without pants over them. With his very muscular legs sticking out beneath them. "I was referring to my family members, and half the town. I'm constantly doing their bidding and at their beck and call, so some of them help me out from time-to-time, though I only ask when I really need a favor."

"Oh." Sabine sat on the porch beside him, but not too close.

He rolled his eyes dramatically. "So, here we are, a couple of burdened souls, me, in my underwear, and you with a carload of my stomach contents. What's our next move, Counselor?"

"Shouldn't I ask you that? How are you feeling, by the way?" He appeared almost normal now.

"I'm just peachy, now. And to answer your question with a question, do we really want to drag anyone else into this?" His tone was droll.

Sabine frowned. "I haven't done anything wrong. Looks like the embarrassment's on you this time," she said sweetly.

He'd been the one who'd had too many beers, and the one who had embarrassed himself.

"That's cold. Aren't you supposed to show infinite kindness and understanding?"

"You're not my patient—yet."

"Yeah, about that—I called your office before I stopped at the bar today—to schedule an official appointment."

And just like that, they'd circled back around to their earlier conversation.

"As a new patient?" Sabine wasn't certain how to respond.

Ben sighed. "I'm a mess, Sabine. Everything I believed about myself and my life has all changed." He snapped his fingers. "Like that." He was dead serious.

Her heart tweaked for him in that moment. "Hailey said you might call. But shouldn't you find a therapist who is less *involved*?"

Ben shook his head. "Are we involved?" He still looked pitiful, but also a little hopeful. "You're the only one who can really help me. Think about it; you've got all the inside scoop. You know the other side of the story. Hailey even gave you permission to share what you thought would help me get to the bottom of my issues."

Sabine frowned. "What issues are you referring to?"

"My issues with women."

"You told me you thought you'd been fair and straight in your dealings with women in your history." Sabine tried not to focus on his bare legs.

"That's the problem; I'm rethinking my position."

So was Sabine, sadly. What might be the best position for him to take her on the porch? "I see. If I agreed to be your therapist, we would have to set up serious, um, ground rules." Maybe the ground would be better.

Fortunately, they had complete privacy out here. She fought the urge like mad to scoot closer to her potential client and find out what lay beneath those blue plaid boxers. Her good sense and professionalism warred with her very long-ignored womanly needs.

"Are you having sexy thoughts about me?" Ben asked, breaking into her sexy thoughts. Because his sexy had returned.

"Huh? Of course—not." Her eyes were unfocused.

"You are. You want to sit on my lap again," he accused.

"That—wouldn't be wise." But God, it would feel so good.

"Stop it! I'm asking for help, here, and you want to climb the tower of Ben."

"Okay, this isn't headed anywhere good," Sabine said.

"Make you a deal." He appeared deadly serious.

"I'm listening."

"You stay here tonight—" He held up a hand to stop her shocked protest. "Listen. I'm suggesting I sleep off my beers, make a call to my buddy to have your car cleaned, and we discuss plans for my therapy. And I'll make eggs in the morning. If you still look at me like that after I've sobered up, then, I'll have no choice but to kiss you again."

She couldn't really see a flaw in his plan. Certainly, there were many, but right now, she was seriously charmed by a stinky, post-vomitous guy with a great house. "Um. I'm not sure that's wise."

"Why?"

"Because I'm a little distracted by you sitting there in your underwear."

His eyes changed, the atmosphere between them became charged. "I knew it."

"Go take a shower and brush your teeth."

Both laughed at that. Sabine had no idea where this might lead, but either way, she was certain it was a bad idea. *Bad.*

⟫⟫⟫⟨⟨⟨

BEN HAD SHOWN her the way to one of his extra bedrooms with an adjoining bath, which was surprisingly equipped with shampoo and other items an overnight guest might require, even a new toothbrush still in a cellophane wrapper. Sabine preferred to believe he hosted his nieces and nephews on occasion instead of random female overnight guests.

Surprised that she was even considering this impromptu sleepover, Sabine pushed down her doubts and followed her instincts, which told her she wasn't a stupid woman, and Ben wasn't a bad guy. He wasn't Richard. Of that she was certain. Tomorrow would tell the tale.

It had been an unnatural amount of time since she'd

been with her husband, and there'd been no one since. For all the sensationalism regarding Ben, Sabine felt secure that he wasn't some kind of depraved rapist.

In fact, weirdly, she believed she knew him well enough at this point. Enough to trust him to relieve her sexual tension. It sounded strangely clinical when she thought about it that way, but her body was near-feverish with the anticipation of considering a possible sexual relationship with him. Just knowing he had the capacity for self-realization and a desire to change put her fears to rest regarding his past with women.

She walked into his kitchen the morning after a surprisingly restful night's sleep, barefooted, and sporting the loose pair of boxers and extra-large T-shirt he'd loaned her. He'd been the perfect gentleman and kissed her on the cheek before heading to bed last night.

Sabine wasn't prepared for the wave of desire that hit her on seeing him standing at the stove, clearly cooking breakfast for her. His dark hair was wet from the shower, and he was barefoot as well.

"Good morning." Sabine's stomach fluttered when he turned around and grinned.

"Hey there. How did you sleep?" he asked.

"Surprisingly well, thanks."

"Hungry? I've got bacon, eggs, and biscuits."

Was he for real? No wonder the women in town all wanted him. He cooked too. All prissy judgment flew out the window. Might as well lump her with the rest of them and be done. He was flipping perfect.

They sat at Ben's kitchen table, sharing scrambled eggs. As Sabine took a sip of her orange juice, she sighed.

"Everything okay?" he asked, politely.

"Peachy."

"So, you and me. Maybe we should discuss all this stuff. Seems I need to work on myself, and you need to—what *do* you need, Sabine? You're not especially talkative about feelings and such, being a professional feelings person, and all." His eyes were questioning, and his tone sincere.

His sincerity rattled her. It was the perfect time to come clean. He should know about Richard.

Instead she heard herself say, "You looked like you were about to take off on foot when your blonde friend showed up yesterday."

"Okay, so no feelings." Then he said, "Fine, we'll talk about me, since I'm in such need of professional counseling. She showed up out of nowhere inside the bar, and I wasn't prepared to see her, or Steve."

"How do you feel about them moving back to Ministry?" Sabine asked.

"I'm not sure. Lisa's been gone a long time, and as much of a shock as it was, I really don't know how I feel about either of them. I didn't want to punch Steve in the face like I did initially, so I guess time and space makes a difference. They have two kids together. Time to behave like a grown-up about it, I guess. I guess seeing them at the bar didn't hurt so much as it was a shock to my system."

"She seems nice." That was all Sabine could honestly say, based on her exposure to Lisa.

"Yeah. I guess she's nice. I've spent years angry with her and Steve for betraying my trust, so nice hasn't exactly been how I've perceived either of them."

"Are you still in love with her?" Sabine asked; she had to. Better to get his gut reaction.

Ben appeared confused by her question. "With Lisa?"

"Yes. With Lisa. Your expression was—intense—when you looked at her."

He shook his head. "No. I don't think so. I mean, I can't say I didn't feel a gut punch at seeing her again, but it didn't feel like love, more like, stunned."

Sabine had to admit relief.

"As your therapist, I'm trying to understand where you are, emotionally, with seeing her on a regular basis again." She took a bite of the fluffy eggs. "No time like the present. Maybe our therapy could be a little less structured than normal sessions. I mean, this is nice." Sabine didn't exactly mean over breakfast in his house, but maybe a casual setting.

He appeared thoughtful. "I have an idea."

"Oh? Let's have it."

"Since Lisa believes we're dating, why don't we let her— believe it—I mean?"

"Why do you want her to think that?" Sabine's pulse

leapt at the idea of dating Ben, even as a ruse.

To be his one and only. Clearly, she'd been bitten by the Ben bug.

"If we were 'dating' I'd be protected from all the hubbub. If you and I came out as a couple in town, then I wouldn't have to address the ensuing mass curiosity about how I *feel* about Lisa moving back. And I wouldn't have to deal with Lisa and Steve coming at me with awkward overtures. If they think I'm otherwise occupied in life, then we can all move on without the bother of getting in each other's' way."

"But I saw your face when she told you she was moving back. You really were affected."

"I was pretty inebriated and completely blindsided. Almost like I saw someone back from the dead."

"Hmm. It's a decent idea, but what about this?" She motioned her hand between the two of them.

"You mean the chemistry between us. The one you won't discuss?"

"Uh, yes, that. Don't you think it could get in the way of the *pretend* dating and therapy?"

"Only if we let it. It's definitely odd, but maybe it could work for us. We could have our therapy sessions during dates. You know, when we go out to dinner and such. That way, people will see us together, talking, and no one will think anything is odd about it, and it will solve my dating issues."

Sabine thought for a moment. "I guess it wouldn't take time out of my schedule, and I do have to eat. And you wouldn't have to fend off other women while working on your issues that way. You could pay me in meals."

He smiled at that. "And sex? It's settled, then. We're dating." He stuck out a hand for her to shake as if they'd struck a bargain.

She shook it, but when she did, he pulled her toward him and kissed her. She ended up straddling his lap once again—this time on the kitchen chair.

"Ooh. This is never going to work." She sighed into his mouth.

"I think it's already working perfectly."

And suddenly he pulled out a condom with a question in his eyes. Were they taped to the bottom of the kitchen table? All she could do was nod and bite her tongue from begging.

Ben kissed her without holding anything back. God, she'd waited two years for this. Or, maybe a lifetime.

He lifted her into his arms as if she weighed nothing and carried her to his huge master bedroom, and dumped her in a puddle on the bed. She laughed out loud. She'd never laughed like this with Richard.

Ben slid next to her on the bed.

He reached over and pulled out the clip from her thick, dark hair, allowing it to fall free around her shoulders.

"Ah—okay." Before Sabine realized what was happening, they'd backed up toward the big carved mahogany headboard and Ben had pulled back the heavy, gray duvet, exposing crisp, white sheets.

She inhaled his clean, soap and man smell as he leaned down and nuzzled her neck, then he moved his sensuous lips to her jaw, and, oh, her lips. Sabine sighed as he found her mouth in the most erotic kiss she'd ever experienced. Her clothes weren't off yet. *Damn.*

Ben laughed deep in his throat. "Okay, so you don't want to go slow the first time. But I insist on your being completely naked."

Her nostrils flared. "Oh—yes. Completely."

Somehow, he had the boxers and T-shirt off in seconds. She hadn't bothered putting on a bra this morning. The man had mad skills; she'd give him that.

"I don't want or need foreplay, okay? I just want you inside me. Now. *Please,*" Sabine begged.

Ben appeared uncertain. "Never heard that one before, but your wish is my command."

Sabine nearly screamed her first orgasm before he'd gotten fully ensconced.

⟫⟪

BEN HAD UNDERSTOOD that Sabine was different from the moment they'd met. He never even considered a ridiculous two-date rule with her, and it wasn't because she'd treated him like a total scumbag. She'd made the ground shake for him. And now, he understood. In this moment, he knew.

Lisa hadn't been his soul mate; she'd been the precursor. Sabine was the one he was meant to be with. On some level, he'd known it months ago, and since he hadn't stopped thinking about her since they'd met, it made sense now, utterly perfect sense.

As she stared up at him, her gaze slightly unfocused, he grinned. "Feel better?" Of course, he wouldn't show all his cards now.

She would think him insane. They'd made love three times without words, taking very short breaks for him to renew his stamina.

"That was—um—thank you." She smiled hugely, and her beauty nearly overwhelmed him.

Had she just thanked him for sex? He wanted to tell her that he loved her, and that she completed him like no other woman ever had.

But he said instead, "No, thank *you*. That was amazing." He leaned down and kissed her forehead.

"I totally get it now."

"Get what?"

"Why those women are in therapy."

He frowned. "So, I'm now a piece of meat—to you?"

She laughed. "No. I just now understand what it's like to be on their side of the fence and wanting more."

"You want more?" That sounded promising.

"Only if you're up for it." It was a challenge.

Ben never backed away from a challenge. "I've created a

monster."

⊱⟫⟪⊰

HE'D CALLED SOMEONE, she wasn't sure who, to take her car early this morning for cleaning. Since it was Saturday, she didn't have appointments booked. For awhile, she'd scheduled a few on Saturday mornings, but since those patients were now much-improved, Sabine decided to take the entire weekends off, and only see emergencies on Saturdays.

Sabine had taken a shower and was wearing an old T-shirt of Ben's with a pair of his sweats. They were huge, but she was comfortable, and while she waited for Ben to check on his animals in the barn and muck a few stalls, Sabine thumbed through a *Garden and Gun* magazine and watched some local news.

She couldn't bear to break their tenuous trust today though, even while everything inside her screamed that she tell him about her father's upcoming parole hearing and the fact that she was a married woman. It was too soon.

"Hey, you."

She nearly jumped straight up from her sitting position on the couch. She hadn't seen or heard him come in because she'd been so lost in her thoughts. "You startled me."

He was standing in front of her, wearing a ripped, old T-shirt, filthy jeans, and he was drenched in sweat.

"I'm just gonna hit the shower." He wiggled his eyebrows. "You're welcome to join."

Boy-o-boy was she tempted. "I just got out, but thanks for the offer."

"I'll just be a minute."

As she watched his spectacular jean-clad rear retreat into the bedroom, she sent up a prayer for wisdom and courage. And self-restraint, because she was gonna need that the most.

Sabine grabbed her nearly-dry clothes out of the dryer and slipped them on while he showered. Best to be fully-dressed when he got out. Her guilt was headed into over-drive, so she'd best be suited up with as much armor available to her as possible.

Not that her skirt and blouse provided much protection from Ben Laroux's prowess, but at least she felt a little more like her old self. The one that wasn't naked in his bed and begging him to do her again and again.

He entered the room and thankfully had clothes on. His hair was still slightly damp, but at least they were back on a somewhat level playing field.

"Hank just dropped off your car. Says it's good as new."

"Who's Hank?"

"He owns the detail shop in town. He was a year or two behind me in high school."

Sabine nodded. "Let me know how much I owe you."

Ben laughed. "Are you kidding? I'm way on the owing side of this one."

She smiled. "Okay. I'm not going to argue with that."

"Why don't we head into town and I can pick up my

truck? I'll buy you lunch, and we can start my therapy/dating while we're at it."

The quick stab of guilt came out of nowhere, but she said, "Sure. Sounds fine."

⋙⋘

SABINE'S CAR SMELLED like Ben had never christened it, thankfully. So, she wouldn't have to budget for a new one. His truck was still parked in the same spot where he'd left it the day before. It had several small pieces of paper slid under the windshield wipers. Two pink and one pale yellow.

Sabine raised her brows. "Probably concerned about why my truck was still parked here."

"I'm sure they were." She laughed.

He hopped out and grabbed the notes, read each, and stuffed them in his pocket.

Leaning down into her passenger window, he said, "Should we head over to the barbecue place?"

She nodded. "Sure. Anything important?" She inclined her head toward his pocket.

He blushed. "Uh. Just a couple offers."

"I'll bet." She rolled up the window, causing him to pull back quickly.

"What the—" he yelped.

She smiled and put the car in reverse.

He followed in his truck to the restaurant where they'd shared their first meal together. Sabine shook her head at the changes since then. The changes in their relationship, and the ones within herself toward Ben.

They ate, they laughed, and they talked. But Sabine didn't divulge anything he didn't already know about her. It was fun, relaxed, and they drew some curious looks from the other diners. It was lunchtime on Saturday, so the place was nearly full. Ben waved at, smiled, or shook hands with numerous folks as they passed the table coming or going.

"Do you ever get any peace?" Sabine asked.

"Huh?" His expression showed real confusion.

"You can't even eat a meal without being interrupted every minute or two on a busy day."

He seemed to digest this a moment. "I really hadn't thought about it. It doesn't bother me, if that's what you mean."

She understood it and had lived that life. It had driven her crazy that wherever they'd gone, Richard was constantly interrupted from his meal and forced to discuss local and state issues. So, she guessed she was overly sensitive to the intrusion. Of course, he'd adored the attention. They'd been so young to be in such a position in politics. His junior senator position made him an up and coming star.

"You okay?" Her silence had obviously been noted.

How could she tell him she'd been a politician's wife, that her father had been a politician, and that she'd jump in a lake and never come up before she'd live that life again? "I'm fine. Just getting full from these ribs and potato salad."

That was true enough. She loved barbecue, but didn't indulge very often. Her treadmill would get a good workout tonight.

"This has been fun. I know it's meant to be work, but I enjoy your company. This morning was amazing, but obviously you know that."

"So, about the notes. Let's see them." Sabine gestured an empty spot on the table.

"You really want to?"

"I think I need to know what kind of interactions you have with women regularly if I'm going to help you mature in your relationships."

He pulled out the crumpled scraps of paper from his pocket.

Sabine smoothed them out. One was from a girl named Candi, who suggested Ben give her a call and they could hook up sometime. She'd dotted the "I" in her name with a heart.

"Tell me about Candi with a heart," Sabine suggested.

"She's a tech at the drive-through pharmacy. And we went out maybe three times."

"Sex?"

"On the third date only."

"Why didn't you go out again after that?"

"She told me she loved me." He winced.

"How old is sweet Candi?"

"I have no idea. Maybe twenty-five?"

"How many times did she try and contact you after your third date?"

He outwardly cringed. "Ten or fifteen, maybe. I called back, but told her it wasn't her, but me, and that I wasn't looking to get serious."

"The second you slept with her, she opened her heart to you. That third date, she believed you wanted to continue seeing her. That's why she slept with you. But you were done with her. Women make love; they don't just have sex." As soon as she said the words, Sabine nearly slapped her hand over her own mouth. Here she was, less than twenty-four-hours out of his bed. "Except me. I was the exception. I was physically desperate."

His eyebrows went up. "I'm confused. Everything you say about other women doesn't apply to you?"

"Let's go with that assumption for now, okay? You know I needed release—not love."

He studied her. "How do I know you won't need to seek therapy from our night together?"

She laughed out loud. "Oh, get over yourself. It was fantastic, but I'm emotionally intact, don't worry."

"Well, let me know if you need to talk about it, okay?" He grinned.

"Stop. Just stop."

He held up his hands. "Fine. I get what you're saying about Candi and the others. We were on different wavelengths and saw things differently. I didn't mean to hurt anyone, as I've said before. I'll call Candi and apologize for misusing her and for the miscommunication. In fact, I made a list."

"A list. Of women?"

He nodded, his expression grim. "I needed to really think about each person I've been with or dated and how it went. I now realize there were quite a few *miscommunications* and timing snafus. We wanted different things."

"I'd say so." But a list and a plan was a good strategy for him to follow. It would help ease his conscience to make amends, would help those who were hanging on to hopefully find closure.

"I didn't want to have a real relationship or commit. I just hadn't found anyone before or since Lisa who I really connected with."

Sabine was silent for a moment.

"Until you."

"Me?"

"Yes. You."

Chapter Nine

❧

SABINE RETURNED HOME in a tizzy. Her response to Ben's admission had been interrupted by his mother and new stepdad, Howard, stopping by their table. Sabine was never so thrilled to see anyone in her life. She'd had no response to give Ben. Thankfully, there hadn't been a need, since their private conversation couldn't be finished.

She'd excused herself then, after pulling out her phone as if she'd gotten an urgent message from a patient, leaving Ben staring at her as she'd never seen him. With complete vulnerability. It was too much. She needed time to think about what he'd said. Think about what she hadn't told him and how she might break it all to him. Soon.

Were they headed down a relationship path? Together? She was married. To a Louisiana state senator who didn't want to let her go—without conditions that might be her ruin. Her father was in the federal prison camp in Alabama. Ben had no idea who she really was. No one did.

She was a first-class fraud, and it might hurt Ben's professional reputation if anyone found out. It would hurt Ben.

He'd just been appointed to the governor's *ethics* board, for heaven's sakes. She had an awful feeling this was all going to matter to him. A lot. Until now, Sabine hadn't felt such an urgency to confess her secrets. They'd become close quickly.

As she let herself into the house, she noticed it was unusually dark and quiet. "Mom?"

There was some shuffling, and muffled sounds coming from her mother's bedroom. "Oh, God. *Mom.*" Sabine burst into her mother's bedroom fearing the worst.

It took her a moment to process what was happening. Her mother was in the bed—and so was Norman Harrison. And they were naked. *Oh, God.*

"Sabine. Are you alright?" Her mother sounded positively cheerful, but pulled up the covers. And Norman, while covered from the waist down, appeared a little less comfortable, still smiled and waved.

"I-thought—I heard—" Sabine stuttered.

"It's alright, dear. Why don't you make some coffee while we get dressed?"

"I'll just go make coffee."

Sabine moved in a daze toward the kitchen, unable to process the scene that had just met her eyeballs. Good Lord, she and her mother had both gotten laid within twenty-four hours. She was waiting for the lightning bolt.

"Are you okay?" Her mother approached, wearing her robe and slippers.

"What were you thinking, Mom?" Sabine went on the

offensive.

"You really don't want to know, but it was lovely," Mom said with a grin.

"Ew. I don't mean literally. I mean that finding you in bed with a strange man was disconcerting to say the least."

Her mother pulled off a dramatic eye roll. "Are you kidding? First, young lady, you didn't come home last night either, which tells me you took care of some pretty sexy business with Ben Laroux, or you foolishly missed a prime opportunity. Second, do you think I'm a nun? Or that I haven't missed sex like any other red-blooded woman? I've been seeing Norman, so he's not some *strange man,* as you put it. He's a lovely, kind, and considerate person, who knocks my socks off. And third; I told you I planned to move forward with my life, so this is what that looks like. Get used to it. I love you dearly, but don't be such a stick in the mud."

As Mom finished her tirade, Norman, now fully clothed, approached and placed an arm around her mother's shoulders and kissed her temple. "Sabine, I know it's a shock to catch your mother in bed with an old man, but I promise my intentions are honorable toward her."

Sabine softened watching the two of them together, obviously happy. "I apologize to you both. I have no right to judge anyone else."

"I knew it! You and Ben were together." Her mother grinned from ear-to-ear.

"I'm not discussing what happened with Ben. I'm going to my room to catch up on my backlog of paperwork," Sabine said, then exited with as much dignity as possible.

She fired up her computer, ready to do a little more research on Ben's appointment by the governor. If it was public knowledge, then she might not feel as guilty for reading the outside of his mail.

She didn't want him to think she'd slept with him or agreed to date him because he might somehow help her pull strings with her father's case. While she understood that her father's case was federal, he was incarcerated in Alabama, and Ben was clearly in the governor's good graces. It just didn't feel right, the way she'd kept such secrets from him, after he'd been placed in this new highly political position. It gave her a stomach ache and reminded her of her old life in politics.

⤞⤝

BEN RAN A hand through his hair. His frustration at the interruption of his and Sabine's conversation was eating at him. He was dying to know what her response might have been. Did she view him differently now? She'd slept with him, so surely if she still believed he was the lowest form of life, that wouldn't have happened. They'd connected at a deeper level than just sex, he was certain of it. Of course, her point to him regarding the women he'd slept with was that they'd believed it had been a deeper connection than just sex as well. Point taken.

But, really, it *had* been deeper with her. For him, anyway. This turnabout being fair play and all was beyond disconcerting.

He was home now and he sensed Sabine all around. Her scent lingered in his house. Ben fought the urge to call her up and invite her to come back over. His sanctuary suddenly seemed empty without her here. It hadn't ever lacked anything before. She'd ruined him.

He needed a distraction. Looking over, he noticed the stack of mail. As usual, it was piled up because he'd been avoiding it. So, he grabbed the pile and began the boring process of attending to the things that required action. Fortunately, he'd already thrown away the ads and junk mail, so all that remained were the bills and correspondence. Some things, he took care of online, but other items continued to arrive, monthly, to his home address, without fail.

Small towns trailed the rest of the world when it came to technology. He doubted the local hardware store would ever catch up to online billing. In fact, they still carried monthly paper accounts, instead of taking payment when items were purchased for its regular customers. They just "put it on the bill." Granted, most of his outdoor supplies were ordered by phone and delivered when Ben wasn't at home, but it was an old-school way of doing business. He guessed it was a comfortable way, but it created a ton of bookkeeping and paperwork for poor Jan.

The letter from the governor's office jumped out at him. Ben knew it was coming, but hadn't been especially excited about attending his first task force meeting. Of course, this letter informed him of the upcoming date and alerted him that he would be receiving a packet within the week, via certified mail, with the cases the board were to make inquiries into. He did look forward to being part of the solution to help clean up corruption and waste in the state, but he dreaded carving out time from his already busy work schedule. His hope was that this additional commitment didn't end up causing him to be less available to his family when they called upon him. Because as much as he complained and gave them crap about it, it was the best part of his week.

Tutoring Lucy in math and babysitting Dirk and Susie for JoJo grounded him like nothing else. Those hours meant something to them all and, in a few years, Uncle Ben wouldn't be cherished and needed in quite the same ways. It made him sad. He couldn't imagine how his sisters dealt with the kids growing up and becoming less dependent on them as parents. In fact, he was getting a little choked up about it himself.

Ben's deepest held secret was in desperately wanting children of his own to love, parent, and nurture. He just couldn't think of anything he longed for more. Well, he guessed they needed a mother, preferably one with silvery blue eyes and midnight black hair. Their children would be stunning.

Ben had watched as others were experiencing satisfying lives and relationships while he'd sat, emotionally stunted. But suddenly, the sensations of genuine emotion were returning, thanks to Sabine. Yes, he had some real soul-searching to do, but now that he'd begun to understand his inability to connect with women, and how his actions had impacted others, it was like rebooting his inanimate self and reattaching the wires. They sparked and sputtered, and he wasn't moving smoothly yet with the new upgrade, but he sensed the potential.

He tossed aside the governor's letter with a renewed sense of determination to prioritize the people in his life over the things and career. Gathering things had never been his goal. Doing good for the people he loved and the people who needed it was way more important. Ben liked his house and property and had worked hard to earn and maintain it, so he was proud of it. Beyond that, the stuff didn't matter so much.

Sabine mattered. And she was beginning to matter more and more. She was the real deal, as he'd commented before. Honest and trustworthy. That mattered.

⤜⟫⟪⤛

"THANKS SO MUCH for your help, Doctor O'Connor. I'll do my best to try and stop correcting my family and neighbors' grammar. I guess I can see why it might be annoying. But it irritates me to the moon when they don't even *try* to use the proper words and pronunciation."

Sabine smiled at Mrs. Boone. "You can't change others and their behaviors, Mrs. Boone—only how you respond to them."

The tiny, seventy-plus year old woman patted her on her shoulder and shuffled out. Her children referred her to counseling after throwing up their hands over *her* behavior. Her bossy, know-it-all manner had become so irksome they'd begun to avoid her. Sabine thought that while the woman was overbearing, she was also lonely and attention-seeking. So, it seemed they were dealing with a chicken/egg situation.

Sabine rolled her shoulders, trying to ease some of the day's tension and remembered the mail she'd picked up earlier.

Sabine spotted the large envelope on the corner of her desk, where she'd haphazardly placed it, along with the other items that had been slipped through the slot. Her hand shook when she read the return address. Sabine tore open the offending correspondence. *If you want your divorce so badly, plan to attend. You'll need to arrive a day early to go over wardrobe with the staff and our public plan of action. We will discuss details of the divorce settlement at that time as well. I've notified my attorneys, and they are currently drafting an agreement. I don't expect you'll require any further representation. In fact, I highly discourage it. Send your travel details and arrival information to my assistant. Her contact info is listed below.*

Included in the envelope was an invitation to the Louisiana state governor's ball—in two weeks. She had two weeks to figure out how to navigate her future.

She wondered how Richard had gotten her work address, but worrying about that would be a waste of time. He, like her father, paid people to find things out. Plus, he had a copy of her birth certificate in the safe at their home in New Orleans. Her perfect and beautiful home in the Garden District. She'd had a full-time staff there and never had to do her own laundry. How her life had changed. And, oh, how she preferred her current quaint lifestyle.

Sabine closed her eyes and sighed, sending up a silent prayer for wisdom and guidance. She'd been in such a rush to find out what Richard wanted, she'd ignored the other pieces of mail. For some reason, she was compelled to complete the task.

As she looked down on her desk at the rest of the pile, the logo jumped out at her. "OFFICES OF THE UNITED STATES ATTORNEYS." The parole hearing. Sabine's stomach dropped, and she scooted over to the sofa in her office and sat. This wouldn't be welcome news, no matter what the letter revealed, simply because it would require something of her, and she was about tapped out.

Maybe she should wait to open it until she got home and uncorked a bottle of red. Yes, that was a better way to deal with this today. With that mildly comforting thought, she locked up her office and headed home. Picking up her cell, she voice-called her mother's number to make certain to avoid a repeat of catching her and Howard in the act again.

"Hello?"

"Hey, Mom, I'm on the way. Do you have plans for dinner?"

"Norman and I are planning to join Cammie and Grey out at the farmhouse. There's leftover red beans and rice when you get hungry. Oh, and there's a bag of salad greens as well."

"Sounds great. Have fun. I'm pretty beat, so I'm planning to do some paperwork and turn in early tonight."

"You do sound tired, honey. Be careful driving and I'll see you soon."

Her mother's concerned voice soothed her, as it nearly always had. It didn't really upset Sabine that Mom was sleeping with Norman. Now that the shock of it had worn off, Sabine saw the real benefit in Mom finding comfort and hope for a future beyond the pain-filled past with her father and his betrayals. She'd said she was moving on with her life, and sure enough, she had begun the process with a literal bang. And, from what Sabine could tell, that bang was agreeing with Mom.

When Sabine arrived home, Norman's truck was already in the drive, so telling Mom about the upsetting mail she'd received wasn't an option this evening.

Gathering the offending papers, Sabine entered the house through the interior garage door. Mom and Norman were just inside the kitchen and jumped back when she opened the door.

To hide her own embarrassment, Sabine joked, "I would tell you two crazy kids to get a room, but—"

"Honey. I'm sorry. It's like we're teenagers again." Her mother's face was flushed.

Sabine waved off her apology. "Don't mind me. Y'all go on and do your thing."

"We were just on our way out. Can we bring you home a plate of Cammie's fine cooking?" Norman asked.

"As tempting as that sounds, I'm going to make a salad and call it a night; but thanks for thinking of me," Sabine said.

"Well, you have a nice evening. I won't keep your mother out too late."

"Honey, I'll just be a few miles down the road if you need me."

"Sure. I'm fine. Enjoy."

Her mother frowned slightly as she scrutinized Sabine's phony smile. "Something's up with you. Let's have it."

"Have what?" Sabine gave it one final valiant effort to shake her mother.

"You tell me, Daughter. There's no fooling your mom. You look like somebody kicked your puppy."

"*Mom!*"

"Well, you do. Out with it or I'm sending Norman home and you'll have to live with the guilt of ruining my evening."

Sabine frowned at her mother, much as she might've when she was a decade or two younger. "Fine."

"Norman, could you excuse us a moment?" Mom asked.

"Of course. I'll just be in the other room." He nodded toward the family room. "I think there's a football game or something on."

Sabine gave him a weak smile. "Thanks. I don't want to ruin your evening."

"Think nothing of it. I have a family, and they come first."

Once Norman had cleared the room, Sabine sighed heavily and said, "I got two letters today. One was from Richard and the other from the US Attorney's office."

"Nothing like a double-whammy. Well, what did they say?"

"I only got through the one from Richard. I haven't worked up the courage to open the other one yet."

"Bring them in here and let's do it together. Wine?"

"Sadly, I had the same thought. I hardly drink, but this feels like something that requires liquid fortitude."

Her mother made a "bring it on" motion for Sabine to open the mail, then yelled toward the living room, "Norman, we need wine, if you'll do the honors. And please tell your family we'll be a little late. If you want to go on without me, I understand. Otherwise, please pop the cork on the good red and give us girls a half hour to deal with this little hiccup."

Norman entered. "It would be my pleasure."

Sabine shot her mother a *does he know* look.

Norman placed two glasses in front of them, uncorked the fragrant pinot noir, and exited the room.

"He guessed from my behavior there was an issue with us hiding from someone or something. Plus, I had to tell him about my past. I couldn't very well sleep with a man without being truthful about who I was." Guilt for doing exactly that sucker-punched Sabine in the gut.

"I guess you were right to explain. It must be such a relief to confess the secret to someone else." Sabine cast her eyes down in shame. "I haven't told Ben any of it yet."

"Don't you think he's trustworthy?"

"Maybe he is, but the honesty ship might have already sailed on my part. I first thought he was such a scumbag because of all the things I'd heard about him. So, I didn't even consider moving forward with any kind of relationship."

"You didn't value him enough to tell him the truth."

"No. Not at first. But now—well, now I do, but he thinks of me as such a trustworthy 'real deal' kind of person. I mean, I'm *married* and have a whole other identity beyond who he believes me to be. Like, even another name. How honest and trustworthy does that strike you? Everything he knows me to be is a big, fat lie."

Mom took a big gulp of wine. "I see your quandary,

dear."

Sabine snorted a little. "Yes. Quandary. That's a pretty fitting description for it."

"So, break out this mess and let's have a look." She motioned to the papers Sabine had placed on the bar where they sat.

Sabine shoved the letter and invitation in front of Mom.

As she read it, her mother's frown grew deeper. "You've got to confide in Ben. He's an attorney. He could represent you. If not represent you, he could certainly advise you."

"Absolutely not. Even if he were still willing to speak to me after I confessed my secrets, I can't imagine he would consider helping me out of my mess."

"I do believe you're underestimating your young man."

"He's not *my* young man, Mom."

"Hmmph." Her mother snorted.

"Plus, I have no intention of dragging him into this disaster."

"I believe you should reconsider that position. You might not have a choice; have you considered that?"

No, she hadn't, actually. "I'll cross that bridge if it gets that nasty. One way or another, I'll get a divorce. I don't want to have to threaten Richard with exposure to the public or ask Dad to not support him, but if he gets ugly, it might come to that."

"Honey, so far Richard has only been unpleasant. But take it from someone who's seen the ugly underbelly of the way these guys operate; you don't want to threaten one if you don't have to. We have no idea how far Richard will go to protect his reputation or his candidacy. You're MIA from the public, and have been for going on two years. Let's not allow him the motivation to make that a permanent reality. I don't want to scare you, but I also don't want you to feel secure around these people. They change. Politics changes them. Richard isn't the man you fell in love with or the man you married. I guarantee he's grown a politician's conscience—none at all."

"I—hadn't really thought it through." Sabine was shaken by her mother's words.

It was true. She didn't know her own husband anymore.

"Ben would know how to handle this. You heard about how he handled that situation for Sadie Beaumont, right? That Tad Beaumont was a real shitty piece of work, and rumor has it that Ben figured out how to neutralize him and his real threats against Sadie and their daughter."

Sabine silently nodded. She knew the secrets there, far more than her mother even would imagine. Ben had handled that very tricky and threatening situation. It was one of the few instances she'd been around him early on and seen the altruistic side of him. It had confused her.

But could he forgive Sabine for her lies and omissions? She guessed there was one way to find out. "Okay, I'll speak with Ben."

Her mother covered her hand with her own. "Good girl.

It's a wise decision. I'd feel so much better knowing you had him in your corner during this battle."

Sabine smiled at her mom.

"Now, let's open the other one. First, more wine." She topped off both their glasses.

The letter revealed date and time of her father's parole hearing and instructions on the family's role in the proceedings. They would have the opportunity to speak on his behalf for approximately five minutes, total. "They're only giving us a week to prepare?" Mom asked.

"It likely won't take more than a half hour to prepare something to read to the board," Sabine said, her tone sourer than she'd expected.

Writing a persuasive letter didn't sound especially difficult to Sabine. She would have to stretch the truth to the barest threads, of course, but pleading for the release of her father on the grounds that the family loved and needed him, and that he wasn't a danger to anyone shouldn't technically be a hard thing to do. Ethically, it would be a doozy.

"Do you think we can get Rachel to go with us?" Mom asked.

"All we can do is ask. Once this is out of the way, and the board decides one way or another, we can move forward. As much as we don't want to deal with Dad as a free-roaming citizen again, at least we won't be sitting around on hold waiting."

"Once your divorce is final, you can go about explaining

to each patient why you changed your name and kept a low profile. I'm sure most are women, and they'll understand how intimidated and embarrassed you've been by all this. I know you can salvage your reputation even if someone spills the beans before you're ready to tell everyone."

Sabine cringed at that thought. "I can only hope, but I really pray it doesn't come to that."

"Would you prefer that I stay home with you this evening?"

"What? Of course not. I would feel awful if I caused you to cancel your plans."

"If you're sure, I'll take that fine man out there out for the rest of the evening."

Sabine smiled her gratitude. "Thanks so much, Mom. I feel such relief at sharing this burden with you."

"Of course you do, sweetheart. That's why I squeezed it out of you."

Her mother winked and waved as she marched toward the living room in search of her man.

The house felt hollow and empty once Mom and Norman left. Sabine paced around; she was edgy and anxious, and unable to relax, all due to the corner she'd lied herself into with Ben. Now, she would ask him for forgiveness, *and* possibly his help. She didn't have the right to expect either.

Chapter Ten

B EN'S PHONE WAS blowing up. Texts, voice mails, and social media were filled with messages questioning whether he and Sabine were an item. He figured enough people had seen them together more than twice that the alarm had been sounded. It was time to confirm the farce so that he could live more peacefully. If it was widely known that he had a steady girlfriend, then he could focus on healing past hurts and moving forward toward a real relationship with Sabine.

She just didn't know it yet. He'd seen the panic in her eyes when he'd dangled the possibility over dinner before they'd been interrupted the other night. They hadn't spoken since, but it was time for some more "therapy."

As he drank his coffee, Ben read through the morning paper. He'd gotten an early start, so he'd stopped by the diner and ordered breakfast. Matthew, his soon-to-be brother-in-law, was there, clearly annoying Thelma, the waitress who'd worked there since he was a kid. Matthew produced and directed his sister, Cammie's cooking show.

He made a point to stop by the diner every morning for breakfast, and to aggravate Thelma.

Ben watched their antics with a grin. "Oh, and Thelma, could you make sure the omelet only has egg whites? You know how I detest the yellows."

"Yeah, Mr. Stick-Up-the-Ass. I've got your egg whites." Thelma sneered at him, then smirked when she turned around.

"You really shouldn't make enemies of the locals," Ben said to Matthew from across the aisle.

"I know I shouldn't, but it's the best part of my day," Matthew replied.

"Emma would have your hide."

"She has my hide daily." Matthew grinned.

"Y'all are gross." But Ben was especially thankful for Matthew's role in bringing his sister, Emma, back to life. Figuratively, of course. She'd been stuck in a far worse rut than Ben for years—not allowing herself to become involved with a man because of a past misstep, not to mention her ex-boyfriend's role in keeping men away from her without her knowledge. Matthew had been the one to bring change and help her find love again.

"Just wait until you get gobsmacked, my brother. You'll be just as gross and won't care who knows."

"Well, I'll forgive you since Emma is happy."

"I hear you've gotten cozy with our town therapist," Matthew said.

"Gossiping, Matthew?"

"Just checking in at the source."

"Well, it's true that Sabine and I have been seeing one another. You can make of it what you want." He nodded toward Matthew.

Ben rose and left a twenty on the table, blew a kiss to Thelma, who rewarded him with a wide three-toothed smile, and then he headed out to his truck.

As he drove toward the office, his focus moved away from his current social media activity and toward his clients. He had a couple cases that would require extensive research. Fortunately, there were interns and legal assistants to help with that, but Ben had to direct them to the precise information required to make his points in the upcoming trials, should the opposition decide not to settle.

Trials required mountains of paperwork and extensive research of items that might or might not be used, depending on which direction the case went. Ben was always prepared.

As he entered the office, his excessively efficient assistant, Chase, met him at the front door with coffee. "Did you hear the news?"

Ben raised his brows in question. "What news?"

Chase made an irritated noise. "Of course they didn't give you a heads-up. Could we step into your office for a minute? You'll want to buzz right in and not make eye contact with anyone. I'll do my best to clear the way."

He trusted Chase to look out for his best interests. And

nothing was worse than being the uninformed, so he followed Chase with his cell phone to his ear and eyes cast toward the floor. He heard George call his name, but simply held up a hand as if he couldn't be interrupted at the moment. When he and Chase shut the door to his office, Ben turned the lock. "So, what's up?" he asked.

"You're not going to like it, and I hate that they left you in the dark until now," Chase said.

"Out with it."

"Steve and Lisa Stark are joining the firm."

"What? How did this happen without my knowledge?" Ben shook his head to clear it.

The news stunned him.

"Senior partner decisions. Clearly they went above your head. His daddy and Mr. Babin have been golfing buddies since college." Chase shrugged dramatically.

His contract stated that the two senior partners could hire associates without his assent. So, they'd gone behind his back knowing he might take issue with the new hires. Sneaky and underhanded, but not beyond their rights.

Ben ran a hand through his hair. "Well, damn."

"I can't believe they would do this," Chase said, obviously defensive on Ben's behalf.

"They do what they want and ask forgiveness later. It's business."

"Are you okay? I don't mean to overstep, but *everyone* knows the insult those two dealt you when they got together."

Ben shrugged. "I'm fine. I knew they were back in town. I suppose they have to work someplace. It's bound to be a bit awkward around here for awhile, but I can't hold a grudge forever. Plus, it's not like I still have a thing for Lisa anymore. I'm seeing Sabine O'Connor now, so there shouldn't be too much talk."

Chase grinned hugely. "I'm so glad you've found someone who's your equal. She's *fantastic*. I watched her give testimony during trial, and was so impressed. Good for you, Boss. Well, I guess we should let them break the news to you." Chase unlocked the door.

"I do appreciate you looking out for my best interests, Chase."

"Well, I know you'd do the same for me. And we staffers keep our eyes and ears open, you know." Chase opened his eyes wide as if to accentuate his point.

There was a brisk knock on the door just before Mr. Babin opened it, not waiting for a reply. "Good, you're off the phone. I need a minute, son."

"I'll just be outside if y'all need anything," Chase excused himself.

"Thanks, Chase," Ben said.

"That boy's a little light in the loafers, don't you think?" Mr. Babin said.

"He's gay, if that's what you mean. And he's the most efficient assistant I've ever worked with." It wouldn't do to punctuate to the senior law partner how ill-advised his obvious prejudice was toward Chase's sexual preference. That might have to be a hard lesson Mr. Babin learned on his own someday.

"Anyway, I need to tell you that George and I are bringing in two seasoned attorneys to the firm."

"I've heard."

Mr. Babin's relief was obvious, judging by the heavy sigh and loosening of his shoulders. "Well, son, that's good. We were a little worried about your reaction to the hires."

"I realize it's allowable to exclude me from some things, but this was offensive. If you believed I'd have a real problem with Lisa and Steve, why would you jeopardize office relationships by going behind my back? Why not have an adult conversation with me before it was a done deal?" Ben asked.

Mr. Babin's face became ruddy and he coughed, clearly he hadn't expected Ben to question his ethics or his character. Likely, he believed Ben would throw a mild temper tantrum similar to something Jeff might have done. That, he could have dealt with like a superior. This seemed to throw him off.

"Well, I guess we didn't go about this in quite the right way, now did we? You are, after all, a partner here. I apologize for the disrespect, Ben. Your work here has been exemplary and an asset to the firm. I'm truly sorry if we offended you."

"You did. But it's your right to hire whomever you choose. I will make the best of it, but I believe I've been here long enough and put enough on the plus column in the books that we should remove the codicils in the contract so that we're equal partners in all aspects. I don't like surprises or things going on behind my back that affect me directly."

The man nodded gravely. "I'll speak with George, and I'm sure he'll agree that it's past time." Mr. Babin stood and shook Ben's hand. "Please call me Stan."

That was a first.

"Steve and Lisa's offices will be at the other end of the suites, so you shouldn't run into them more than necessary. But they will be moving their things in today, just so you know."

"I'll be on my best behavior."

"You're a good man, Ben."

"Thanks, Stan." The older man nodded and shut the door behind him.

Well, this was not how he'd planned for his day to begin. Clearly, life was about to change significantly around here. Before he had a chance to ponder that thought any further, another knock sounded.

"Come in."

"Ben?"

Her voice had haunted him for years. Now, while it only gave a slight twinge, it still impacted him, he had to admit. Since the evening at the bar, Ben had been anticipating the moment they'd actually have to interact again.

"Hi, Lisa."

She was lovely, of course, and so familiar. Her straight blonde hair and near-translucent pale skin remained the same. Her figure was still thin, though slightly curvier since bearing Steve two children. A boy and a girl, if he wasn't mistaken.

"I guess you've heard, huh?" Her smile was tentative, as is she wasn't certain of his reception.

"I did. Congratulations to you both, and welcome to the firm. You came to work at the best place in town." He stood and came around the desk, hand outstretched, ready to shake hers.

Lisa took it. She smiled fully now. "I know this has to suck for you. I mean, we're back in town and now working at your firm. Years have passed since we—uh—hurt you. Neither of us took what we did to you lightly, Ben. We moved away to try and make things a little less painful for you." Lisa did appear pained.

"Besides being run out of town?" He shook his head and chuckled just a bit. "I'm sorry. I couldn't resist a jab. Yes, I was hurt and angry with both of you for a long time. But you have a family, and you should be near your families while you raise your kids. I'm okay; don't worry."

"Thanks, Ben. Facing you was what we were dreading most. I hope we can figure out a way to work together without things being awkward." She looked around. "Nice office."

"Please let me know if you need anything. Chase, my assistant, is brilliant, and can do or find anything you're looking for before you even realize you want it." He realized he meant every word, and that was a relief.

Someone tapped on the semi-opened door, then pushed it opened. Steve. Sure, why not? "Ben. It's so great to see you."

"Steve. It's been a long time. I was telling Lisa that I hope you'll both come to me if you need anything while you're making the adjustment."

Steve shook Ben's hand and then unexpectedly pulled him in for a man-hug. "I've missed you, man. It's been too long. I hope we can go out and have a beer soon."

"Uh, sure." Ben really hadn't expected such a punch in the gut at Steve's sudden show of emotion.

"I would really love for us to get together with you and Sabine—isn't that her name? She is lovely," Lisa said.

"Yes. Sabine is great, and I'm a very lucky man. I'll check with her and get back to you on a time. She's a clinical therapist and stays pretty booked up."

"Wow, that's an impressive line of work. It takes a special person to deal with such raw emotions and honesty every day."

"As opposed to a good dose of dishonesty that we get hit with by our clients and on pretty much a daily basis," Steve said.

They all gave a little laugh at the sad truth of that.

"Well, we'd better get back to our move-in. Great to see you again, buddy. I hope we can all bury the past and look forward to good times ahead," Steve said, then waved and left the office.

Lisa smiled at him again and said, "I really do hope we can move forward as friends. It will be nice to have that again. We've both missed you."

Ben understood her feelings. He missed them both too. "Me too, Lisa."

A warm emotion settled inside his chest. Could that be peace? This unresolved issue between himself, and Lisa and Steve all these years had burdened his soul. Now, he felt lighter and calmer.

He wanted to share this with Sabine. Knowing she'd likely be with a patient, he texted her. *Hey there. Just found out that Lisa and Steve joined my firm. They just left my office. Believe it or not, all is well. Would love to see you ASAP.*

He had no way of knowing when she would get free to respond, but he continued checking his phone throughout the day. Ben completed a difficult deposition in the conference room with a construction site manager and his personal attorney, who advised against his answering nearly every one of Ben's questions, on the grounds they might incriminate the company who employed him. Ben represented the prospective homeowner who was injured during a final walk-through of their new home when a poorly installed wrought iron light fixture fell on her head, causing massive trauma, both physical and emotional. Both wanted to settle out of court, but it wasn't looking good.

Management had placed the man in a crappy position to defend such terrible safety practices, based on what Ben had learned so far, from some of his coworkers.

No doubt the liability was squarely on the company, but since the company had let their insurance lapse, some of the owners had been named personally in the suit. It wasn't sitting well with corporate.

Ben stopped by the offices where he'd been told Steve and Lisa were working out of to see how things were going, but the lights were off. Their desks were set up and they looked to be about halfway moved in, based on the boxes scattered about and the lack of pictures hung on the walls. Ben stepped inside to survey things and caught sight of a family photo on what he assumed was Steve's desk. The four of them were laughing together on the beach, dressed in white linen and denim. They were tanned, and obviously happy. Ben wanted that. Not with Lisa, but he wanted what they had together. A family.

Ben left the office with a strong desire to see Sabine. He didn't want to examine why that was, exactly, but she was utmost on his mind. He'd not heard back from her since the earlier text he'd sent, so he decided to swing by her office and offer to take her to dinner. Or not. He really needed to see her. She might not be on a "really need to see him" basis, but he was there with her.

When he arrived, he noticed her car still in the tiny parking area beside her office. Ben pulled off to the side, just out of sight from the front door, rolled down his window, and cut the engine. He wouldn't want to be accused of stalking, but he did want to see when she came out the door. There was one other car, a large black sedan. Must be her last patient. He had paperwork to do, as always, endless paperwork. Ben kept an eye peeled as he worked through the transcripts of the brief he was currently editing.

After about five minutes, a sudden movement caught his eye. From where he sat, he doubted Sabine would even notice him. So, when the dark-haired, extremely tall, and somewhat brawny guy backed out the door ahead of Sabine, clearly shouting at her, while she poked him in the chest, Ben didn't hesitate. By the time Ben cleared the front of his pick-up, the asshole climbed in the black sedan and squealed tires out of the parking lot, flipping Ben off as his back bumper scraped the curb.

"Are you alright? Who the hell was that?" Ben's emotions were all over the place.

Sabine seemed angry, more than scared. "Come inside." She motioned him to enter her office.

He did, noticing the comfortable atmosphere. But right now, he wanted to know if she was in danger. "Please tell me what's going on."

"Sit." She pointed to the sofa.

She sat across from him on a matching chair. She appeared conflicted. "I need to tell you something—something I should have shared before we slept together. Please understand that I've been trying to find a good time to have this conversation."

A confession. Well, shit.

"I'm married. And, I'm not who you think I am."

"Married?" She might as well have hit him in the head with a two-by-four. "Was that your meathead husband who just spun out of here?"

"No. That was my brother."

"Nice guy." Ben's head was about to pop off. "You're married, as in, I have a loving husband and I'm sneaking around behind his back, married, or I'm getting a divorced married?" Ben wanted to know.

"It's more complicated than that." She stood and paced. "My husband is a Louisiana state senator, and I changed my name to move here with my mother and get away from him."

Ben frowned. "I'm assuming there's more."

"My father is Jean-Claude Prudhomme." She stared at him, as if to let that sink in a moment.

It did. Images of a media circus and nationally televised trial, comparable in media coverage only to what he could remember as a kid of the O. J. Simpson or Menendez brothers' trials. But it had been a couple years ago, and Prudhomme had been convicted as a pariah of the worst kind for the consequences of his actions in law circles. Sabine was Theresa Prudhomme Habersham, which also meant she was married to Senator Richard Habersham.

"Holy shit, Sabine. How have you kept that a secret?" He was stunned.

"It hasn't been easy. And I've contacted Richard about a divorce. I've just heard back from him. And my father's parole hearing is soon. So, yes, I've lied, and I've kept secrets. I'm a total fraud."

"I believed you were the real deal," Ben whispered, mostly to himself.

Sabine turned to face him, but her eyes were downcast. "I should have told you. I kept looking for the right time."

"I came over here because I felt an overwhelming urge to see you—be with you. The you I thought you were. Now, I'm not sure who you are."

"Ben—" She reached a hand toward him, but he held his up in defense of her plea.

He stood and walked out the door. He had to think.

Chapter Eleven

BEN DROVE TO his mother's house, almost without thinking. He didn't call first, though now that she was married, maybe he should have.

When he knocked on the door, Howard opened it, took one look at him, and called out to Maureen Laroux, "Honey, Ben's here and he looks like somebody kicked his puppy.

"Son, did somebody kick your puppy? 'Cause I know people who can take care of people, if you know what I mean." He winked, then ushered him inside.

"Howard, one of these days, we're going to hold your feet to the fire and get the truth of what you did all those years for the government," Ben said, as he followed Howard to the kitchen.

"Well, there's the problem with that whole tell ya/kill ya thing, and your mother would have my hide if I harmed a hair on one of her kiddos, if you know what I mean, son."

"Honey, is everything alright?" Mom floated into the kitchen, or it seemed so, anyway. She nearly floated everywhere these days since she'd married Howard last year.

"I'm okay. I just felt like stopping by," Ben said.

"Why, Ben Laroux, you're a terrible liar. Should I call your sisters? What is it, darlin'?"

"Oh, God, no. Don't sound the alarm."

"Then you'd best come clean, son. Or, you know she will," Howard suggested. "I'll be happy to step outside and let you and your mother have some privacy."

Ben sighed. "No, it's alright, Howard. You're the only male ally I have in this godforsaken place. Maybe you can help me understand what the hell is going on."

"Oh, dear. What's happened? I heard Lisa was back in town. I really thought you were over her," Mom said.

"Lisa? This isn't about Lisa. It's Sabine, Mom. But she's not really Sabine. She's got a different name, and she lied about her father being dead. I just came from her office, where she confessed all her secrets."

"Sabine's not Sabine? Well, that's surprising. So, she lied to you, and apparently lots of other people in our family and this town. That—could be a real problem for all of us who trust her. Hmmm." His mother went over to the kitchen sink and filled up the teakettle.

Ben stared at her as if she'd lost her mind. "Mom?"

"I'm thinking. We need tea." She calmly lit the burner and pulled out several teabags and moved to the refrigerator and retrieved a lemon. Ben stared at her.

"It's her thinking process when she's trying to figure something out." Howard motioned with his hand toward

Mom's doings.

Ben nodded. "I remember. She used to bake when we got in trouble while she decided what to do with us. We knew how bad it was going to be by how high the baked goods were stacked."

"I'm going to need a shot of good Kentucky bourbon in mine, dear," Howard said.

Mom nodded, but it was obvious her thoughts were on the problem at hand. "Yes, of course. So, Sabine, whom our family members have entrusted their deepest emotional turmoil, tenderest of heart issues, and most difficult problems to solve, has revealed that she's not who she seems?"

Ben nodded, but was now thinking about some of the family issues that Sabine played such an integral part in helping solve. She'd been a godsend to his new niece, Samantha, whose deceased mother had been mentally unstable and borderline abusive, and Sabine had helped Grey and his sister, Cammie move forward beyond their very deep and seemingly impossible past issues to find a happy future together.

"So, Sabine has proven with her deeds that she is a person of substance and good intentions, yes?"

"I thought so," Ben agreed.

"Maybe our Sabine has carried around so much baggage of her own that she hasn't been fortunate enough to have someone like herself to help her solve the burden." Mom was still solving out loud.

"Your mother has a pretty solid point there, son." Howard poured a substantial shot of whiskey into the dainty teacup Mom slid his way. He offered the bottle to Ben, who shook his head. The last thing he needed was a fuzzy mind and a hangover.

"I left out the worst part—she's married, Mom."

Her mother's face fell. "Oh, honey. I'm so sorry." She came over and sat next to him, taking his hands in hers. "I've seen the two of you together, and I can tell you that whatever the state of her marriage, it can't be especially viable. She's been here going on two years without a husband. Technically, she might be married, but she doesn't have a marriage. No one can be apart that long and keep things on track." Howard coughed, perhaps reminding her how long they were apart before finding one another again.

"But she didn't tell me. Granted, we haven't been close for very long, but it feels so wrong. I thought she was such an honest person," Ben said. "And we've been—uh, close."

His mother patted his hand. "Honey, people do things in desperation sometimes—often because they believe there isn't another solution."

Howard came over then. "Benjamin, I was involved in some seriously secret shit for more years than I can say—because it was secret, you understand—and there are lots of reasons folks keep important information to themselves. Often, it's a matter of not trusting others with their secrets because secrets can be dangerous in the wrong hands. Now,

I'm not sayin' Sabine has some deep, dark something going on, but if this family feels she's worth giving the benefit of the doubt then I'd be of a mind to extend that opportunity to her."

"So, I should hear her out instead of shutting her down like a whiny ass that got his feelings hurt?" Ben asked, realizing his mother and stepfather were right.

Sabine might be in trouble. Surely his pride could move aside long enough to give her a chance to explain herself. Especially since he'd felt such a bone-deep connection from the moment they'd met. Didn't that deserve a chance at more discovery? Surely his *forever* intuition meter couldn't be that flaky. Because if it was, he would require far more therapy than at first he'd believed.

"So you'll give her a chance to explain?" Mom asked.

"I will. I really care about her, and you know how long it's been since that's happened."

She leaned over and kissed his cheek. "I know. I'm your mother, and I keep my eye on these things. And what I don't see, your sisters keep me informed of."

Ben stood. Coming here was absolutely the right decision. "Thank you both for listening and for your good advice. I know it's the right thing to do."

Howard thumped him on the back with his huge hand that resembled a bear's paw. "Son, I never had a family of my own until now, and I'm doing my dead-level best to catch up on all this fathering."

Ben laughed because he understood how genuine Howard's words and his heart truly were. He loved their mother and wanted only her and their happiness. "Thanks, Howard. I'd call you Dad, but it might be a couple decades too late."

Howard laughed, a big, booming sound. "It's never too late, son."

"Night, Mom. Love you." He hugged his mother.

"I love you, Ben."

⋙⋘

SABINE BARELY SLEPT. Her mother had called to let her know she would be out late, so there hadn't been an opportunity to spill her upset when she'd gotten home.

So, she'd gone to bed and cried herself to sleep—something she hadn't done in a very long time. This morning her eyes were beefy and swollen. She tried a cold rag and green teabags.

"Dear, what are you doing?" her mother asked from behind.

Sabine nearly shrieked. "Mom, don't sneak up on me like that." Sabine wore her robe, slippers, and had a towel wrapped around her wet hair. She stood, by the kitchen sink steeping teabags for medicinal purposes.

"Yes, but what are you *doing*?"

"My eyes are all red and swollen. I'm going to put teabags on them."

"I've got some cream for that. I'll go get it. In the meantime, you can come up with your best explanation as to why your eyes are red and swollen."

"I'd rather not. I don't want to be late for work." But her mother had disappeared into her bedroom.

She continued with the teabag cure. "Ow." Who knew green tea burned?

"I told you not to use that. Your eyes are too irritated. Here, try this."

"Thanks."

"Out with it."

"Fine. James stopped by the office yesterday and we argued."

"Why is he here?"

"More of Dad's messengering, I guess. But I think he's gone rogue. Anyway, I showed him the door, and Ben saw it. I told Ben I was married and who I really am."

"Well, no wonder you're all smushy this morning. I guess our hero didn't take it very well?"

"No. He just seemed—so disappointed. Told me he believed I was the 'real deal.'"

"Honey, Ben is the real deal, and he will get over his wounded pride. Anyone who knows you at all would believe you've kept things from them for a good reason. Give him a little time. I guarantee he'll come around and want to know the whole story."

Sabine wouldn't count on that after seeing the look in Ben's eyes just before he drove off, but her mother's words did give her some hope. "Thanks, Mom. I hope so."

Sabine brought the eye cream to her bathroom and carefully applied it to her poor eyes. Her mother's words did bring some comfort. As did her eye cream.

As she finished getting dressed, she kept checking her phone, though there wasn't any real reason to believe she would hear from Ben.

By the end of the day, she was back to feeling a little emotionally ragged again. When she stepped out of her office to lock the door, she sensed someone behind her. Heart pounding, she turned, pepper spray at the ready. Just before she released the trigger, Sabine realized it was Ben.

"Oh, my gosh, I nearly doused you with police-grade pepper spray. Don't sneak up on me like that." She noticed his expression was grim, and not at all his normal, teasing, smiling one.

"Sorry. I didn't mean to scare you. I came because I want to know what's going on with you. Clearly, you've got a whole history you've kept from us all. If you want to clear the air and explain yourself, I'm willing to give you that opportunity."

"I'm not sure you want to know." Sabine sighed. "Obviously, I'm not who you think I am. I mean, I am, but there's a lot about me I haven't told you. And I don't know if you'll ever want to speak to me again once you know the whole story."

Ben's expression was somewhat as she expected; hurt,

angry, but mostly he appeared curious, which she hadn't anticipated.

"How will I know if you don't tell me?"

Sabine's heart beat heavily in her chest. She tried to control the tiny bloom of hope taking root there. He hadn't outright banished her from his life for her lies. Surely that was promising.

"Could we go someplace quiet? It's a long, sad tale."

"How about I pick up some food, you go home and change out of your work clothes, and meet me at my house? That way, we won't be interrupted and you can leave whenever you want. This sounds like it might turn into a long evening." Ben's expression was still dark and serious, but he hadn't kicked her to the curb.

Sabine tried a smile, but it fell flat on her lips. "Sounds like a good plan. I'll bring along a few things to show you from home to better explain the situation. And Ben—" Their gazes connected. "I'm really sorry about this. I've been planning to tell you everything, but the timing hasn't worked out before now."

"I'm willing to hear you out. But I can't say I'm not hurt and extremely disappointed by all this." He shook his head.

"And I appreciate it," Sabine said. She'd been such an idiot to not let him know sooner who she was. Of course, her real feelings and trust in him was just recently confirmed as a viable thing. Before, Sabine's opinion had been so colored by her patients' experiences and gossip about him that her angst and confusion about who the real Ben Laroux was had clouded her judgment. He'd proven to her over and over during and since how truly honorable he was. Trustworthy and solid. She'd be a fool to let a man of his loyalty to family and friends get away. Plus, he was about as hot as they came.

Now, how to break it to him that she was everything he believed she wasn't? And more?

They parted ways and headed to their respective vehicles.

BEN PICKED UP the ribs from their favorite barbecue place, doing his dead-level best to dodge a few folks who tried to engage him in conversation. But, damn it, they just wouldn't leave him be. "Ben, my man, I hear you're seeing the hot therapist. Dude, she's awesome. Shawna swears by her. Says Sabine keeps her 'focused' on what's important. I swear Shawna was planning on leavin' me before therapy. I even went a few times. I guess it's not a good idea to go to the bar every night after work."

Ben pasted on his listening face he used in court when he was impatient with a witness. "Wow, that's fantastic, John. I know Shawna's a great girl. You'd better treat her right and hang on to her." Ben slapped John on the back and headed out the door.

Any dumbass, especially a mid-level intellect like John, who was lucky enough to marry a girl as smart and pretty as Shawna Gates ought to know hanging out in bars every night was a really bad idea.

Which brought him back to Sabine. She gave great advice to others. Good, sound, *honest*, and helpful advice. It just confused him even more. How could a person be such a walking, talking dichotomy? Unless there was a really good reason. He was hanging on to that. It had better be a good one. Normal people didn't lie about their husbands, their identities, and whether or not their fathers were dead.

Sabine seemed very connected to her mother, and from what he could tell, their relationship appeared similar to that of his sisters with his own mom. They laughed and talked comfortably, touched, and hugged. Ben was intuitive about noticing small details as people interacted, and he'd not noticed anything strange between Elizabeth and Sabine. Except, maybe, they shared some pretty knowing looks between them. If they carried secrets, that made sense. Ben had just assumed it was a mother/daughter silent understanding thing.

The smell of the substantial orders of ribs, smoked sausage, potato salad, and baked beans were causing his brain's focus to switch unwittingly to his stomach as it growled in protest and refused to be ignored.

When he pulled into his driveway, he saw that Sabine had already arrived. She hadn't taken much time at home before coming here straightaway. The expression on her face when Sabine had confessed her secrets would stay with Ben a long time, maybe forever. She'd been so ashamed. Her fear of his reaction hurt him.

He parked and carried the bags up to where she waited on the front porch.

She hardly met his eyes. "Thanks for suggesting we come here. I really do want to have the chance to explain myself," she said, and then raised her gaze to his. It conveyed a lot because, despite all he didn't know about her, Ben believed he knew her heart.

"Well, I'm starved, and from what I know about you, you likely are too. And neither of us will be at our best on an empty stomach." He put his key into the lock and opened the front door, and motioned for her to precede him.

⯈⯈⯈❈⯇⯇⯇

"SO, YOU'RE MARRIED? Tell me about that." Ben hit her with the question as soon as they'd sat down at his kitchen table and dug into the ribs. The same table where they'd shared scrambled eggs and laughed together after giving his king-sized bed a workout Sabine would never forget.

She took a long draw from the bottle of water in front of her. Might as well start there. "Technically, yes. We've been apart since I've been here in Ministry. Richard and I met when we were both very young. He was a progeny of my father. This is going to be a long, complicated story."

"I've got time," Ben said.

He'd demolished a slab of ribs already and was now working on the links of smoked sausage and potato salad.

Clearly, talking and eating wasn't a problem for him.

"Obviously, my father is Jean-Claude Prudhomme, former district attorney of New Orleans. Right now, he's in the federal prison camp not far from here."

"I'm familiar with his case and the facility. So, you and your mom are living in Alabama to be near him?"

"Well, that's only the beginning. We're mainly here to get away from all the craziness my father left behind in Louisiana. Here seemed near enough to keep an eye on what was happening with Dad, knowing we would need to go to the prison from time to time. We could never have any peace unless we did."

Ben stopped eating then. He wiped his mouth and pushed his plate to the side. "Why did you leave your husband?"

"He was caught with a prostitute—well, two prostitutes, at the same time."

"So, instead of behaving like the dutiful political wife and standing by your man, you skipped town."

"No one knows about the prostitutes. The scandal never broke publicly. My father managed to clean up Richard's mess before it got out."

"So, Daddy, with all his faults took care of his little girl."

Sabine rolled her eyes. "I kind of wish Richard had been shamed in front of the world. It would have given me a perfect excuse to leave him, because then, nobody would've blamed me for walking away from my marriage."

He nodded. "So, what has he told his constituents?"

"That I've taken some time to recover from my father's trial and public humiliation, and that I'm reevaluating political life."

"So, you've had a nervous breakdown, according to your dear husband."

"Something like that."

"And you've allowed it to stand?"

"At first, I just wanted to run away from the anger and humiliation. Then, I was just so happy to be as far away from him as possible. I'd recently had a miscarriage and was extremely fragile from that."

Ben's eyes changed then. "I'm so sorry, Sabine. How horrible for you to endure losing a baby and then have your sleazebag husband behave that way." His disgust was evident for Richard's behavior.

Sabine smiled a little sadly. "I'm very glad those days are behind me. Richard had changed. Politics changed him, even from the very beginning. The power and popularity of public life became his lifeblood. He drew breath from it. The man I loved and married shriveled and was replaced by an egocentric caricature of his former self."

"I've seen it happen to some of the attorneys who've gotten into politics, unfortunately, as well as professional athletes. It's as if the rules of ethics and decency no longer apply to them."

"Exactly. I believe that's what happened to my father

too. He became so powerful within the legal system that he believed he could control it."

Ben nodded. "Sounds like he did for a long time."

"Unfortunately, all the convictions during his tenure were overturned. Some of them will never be retried, causing dangerous criminals to be set free, which is the opposite of his original intention."

"But he thought he was above the law and manipulated those convictions," Ben said.

"Yep. If he'd let justice work, they'd most likely have been put in prison anyway," Sabine agreed.

"But some of those convictions gained without due process likely put citizens away who were innocent of the charges," Ben said.

"My dad figured they were guilty of something and had slipped through the system already, and should be locked up, which is why he went to such lengths to circumvent the steps. Makes no sense to those of us who work hard to make sure we do things the right way."

"But he'd seen too much by then. Too many violent criminals get off on technicalities and too many victims. I see more than I'd like to as an attorney, even though I don't prosecute. But we must follow the laws and rules as written or put forth legislation to change them. It's all we can do to make change."

"It was vigilante justice, which never bears fruit. He didn't trust the system to do its work."

"Sabine, I see why you wanted to get away from your husband, but it's been two years. Why haven't you divorced him?" Ben asked.

Sabine hoped she could make him understand. "Richard doesn't believe in divorce. Well, in our case he doesn't. He also doesn't think he'll be reelected without a wife. So, he's refused to grant me one until now. And he's threatened to expose my lies here. He knows me well enough to understand that lying low and licking my wounds was tantamount to my healing."

"Let me get this straight; he cheated with prostitutes, which is a deal-breaker in any marriage, yet he doesn't believe in divorce?"

"I know. Maybe it's not that he doesn't believe in it, but that he is a hundred percent against it in his own case. But, I didn't push it while I worked through some of my own emotional crap and, for a while, he left me alone. But I've recently demanded a divorce. Problem is, he's blackmailing me into appearing with him at the Louisiana governor's ball coming up in ten days or he'll blow my cover and rain down the media circus on my quiet life.

"He agreed to the divorce with some pretty stiff contingencies, but wants to talk turkey on the details and have me by his side to demonstrate to the world that I'm still a hundred percent in support of his candidacy. I'm not sure I believe he'll really grant me a divorce once I get there. It may be a ruse to get me to return."

"Ten days, huh? Are you going alone to Louisiana?"

"Yes. I'm leaving Mom here, but since she's now got Norman as support, I feel much better about it."

"How do you feel about facing Richard on his turf?" Ben asked, concern etched on his face.

"I feel like I'd better pull up my britches and engage my super girl powers of bulletproof skin and the ability to fly above the fray."

"How about I go along as your attorney to negotiate your terms for divorce and whatever else you need?"

Sabine's heart nearly melted right onto the floor. "Oh— what a kind offer. I don't know what to say. I'm not sure how Richard would respond to it. He's strongly discouraged my gaining representation, as he feels I don't require it."

"Do you care what he thinks about my being there? If you still have feelings for him, I won't consider it."

"No—no, it isn't that. I just don't want to anger him."

"Are you afraid of him?" Ben's tone became fierce.

Sabine shrugged. "He has a lousy temper, but it's more of a cold, rigid thing, not a physical one. So, I'm not really afraid he would become abusive, but he's pretty manipulative and underhanded—and he knows a lot of unsavory people. I just wouldn't want to compromise the offer of divorce. I want to get in, do what needs to be done, and get out of there with a divorce agreement in hand."

"I want to go with you, Sabine. I don't like the idea of your going into the lion's den alone. Plus, I've negotiated with some rotten characters in my day. I'm somewhat skilled in satisfactory outcomes."

Sabine stared at him with a new understanding. "That really would be an asset for this trip."

"Then it's settled. I need to know the dates and details as soon as possible, so I can clear my schedule for a couple days."

Sabine reached over and picked up her purse. It was a large tote, and she'd managed to shove all the mail she'd received from both Richard regarding the governor's ball and his demands, along with the feds' packet and info about her father's parole hearing. Now, she had to share that info.

She passed the first envelope across the table to Ben. He picked it up and spread the contents out. *Exhibit A.* Sabine couldn't help but thinking he was approaching this with his lawyer brain, which was okay with her, considering he hadn't shown her the door and was offering his assistance. Of course, she had no idea how his feelings might have changed for her since he'd discovered her nasty past yesterday. He hadn't yet said anything personal, or resembling conciliatory. He'd appeared somewhat sympathetic, angered over Richard's behavior, and frustrated at her current situation.

"Okay. I've got something coming up with the governor's task force, but I should be free by then. No court on those dates, so we're good there. I can move around a couple things. Alright. When you hear back from his assistant regarding whatever arrangements they've made, let me know, and you'll counter that with your own conditions and accommodations for your stay in New Orleans. He doesn't have to know where you're staying or that I'm with you necessarily."

Sabine had only seen him in his lawyer mode the one time in court, but his demeanor had been far different and less rigid because he'd been dealing with a victim's family who'd lost their loved one. This Ben was stern and unyielding, with no room for flexibility whatsoever. He was intimidating, but undeniably sexy as well. Well, damn. She hadn't meant to go there.

She noticed he'd stopped speaking. "It's happening again, isn't it?"

She shook her head to clear away the confusion. "What?"

"You're having sexy thoughts about me in the middle of serious business."

"No. I'm not. I mean, I shouldn't be. Sorry. You've been so understanding about all this. I didn't expect it. I figured you'd never speak to me again. I wouldn't have blamed you a bit, you know?" She attempted a smile.

Then, her mouth trembled. *No, she was not going to cry.* Then, against her very determined will, the first tear streaked down her cheek.

⧽⧽⧽⧽⧽⧽⧽

BEN LAROUX WAS defenseless to a woman's tears. They were his kryptonite. Combined with the fact that he had fallen ass

over teakettle in the real kind of forever love with Sabine
O'Connor, or whatever the hell her name was, seeing that
single tear track down her face nearly did him in.

Real emotion was not necessarily the norm in his daily
life, so he recognized it when it hit him between the eyes.
His sisters had cried a lot throughout his lifetime—a lot. But
he could always distinguish between the phony drama and
the real pain. And he hated the real stuff. It made him
helpless. That was how he felt now, with Sabine both
admitting her desire for him and her vulnerability to his
kindness and support when she believed she deserved
neither. Her father and soon-to-be ex had emotionally
abused and put her and her mother through years of hell.

"There's dishonesty, and then there's self-preservation,
Sabine. I hated finding out this way, but you were up against
a wall, and I get it. I'm disappointed that you didn't trust
me, though I can't say what I would've done in your situation. Trust is earned. I'm not sure we've known each other
long enough to cement that kind of bond. So, what I'm
saying is, I'm not going to hold it against you, but I want
you to trust me now. To help you get free of your past and
move forward."

By now, Sabine was openly crying, her eyes red and lovely skin splotchy. She was heartbreakingly beautiful to him.
He reached for a tissue box on the counter and handed it to
her.

"It's just so wrong that I didn't trust you and you're willing to help me, and that you actually *forgive* me. Trust is such a huge thing, and I feel like I blew it big time."

"I'm a fact-finder, Sabine. You deal every day in people's emotions, but I want the whole truth. Now that I have it, I can let go of my hurt feelings. I believe you. And I'm so freaking crazy about you that I'm thrilled you're not with someone else. It means you're available." He pulled her into his arms, hoping to soothe.

She clung to him, and calmed almost immediately. "You're such a good man, Ben Laroux. I'm so sorry I didn't see it at first."

"Well, how could you have noticed with all the women telling tales in your office? Of course, you believed me to be a world-class sleaze. I guess I kind of have been in some ways."

"But I see the real man under the sleaze now, and I'm so glad." She took full advantage of the tissues by drying her eyes and blowing her nose.

>>>«««

"YOU *ARE* AVAILABLE aren't you? I mean, when all this is over?" he asked.

A thrill shot through Sabine's heart, and let's face it, other places as well. "I'm planning on being very available. In fact, I'm somewhat available, at the moment." She raised her brows suggestively.

"I knew it. Sexy thoughts. Thank God." Ben didn't hesitate, lest he lose his opportunity, Sabine figured.

It had been almost two weeks since when they'd first made love, and she'd fantasized about it a hundred times since.

"I've been hoping you'd invite me over for more at home *therapy*," she said, as he kissed her jaw.

He growled. "I didn't want to come across as too forward or aggressive, or maybe too needy." They were standing near the kitchen counter now.

"Needy?" She laughed, but then she moaned as he did a thing with his tongue behind her ear that melted her knees out from under her.

Good thing he had a hold on her and scooped her up, which was convenient, because it allowed him to carry her directly to his bed. The same bed that was the scene of *all* the things they did to one another the last time she'd been a visitor here.

As he laid her gently on the comforter, he said, "I've been in such a needy state for you, I didn't want you to think I was pining for you—I was, by the way. Because every time I look at you, you reduce me to a horny fourteen-year-old boy who's just gotten to second base for the first time."

He'd somehow managed to remove her lightweight cotton sweater and was working on her bra closure. "You are a mighty talented fourteen-year-old, young Ben."

"Ah, to have had such skills at a tender age."

She giggled at his wicked humor. "Carry on."

But he pulled back for a moment. "I've missed you; I've missed touching you and kissing you. I love the way you smell and the texture of your hair. I hope you understand how emotional this is for me with you. I lose focus at work because I can't stop thinking about you or seeing your face in my mind's eye."

"O-oh, Ben. I've been so wrapped up in my own guilt and worry that I couldn't allow myself to think about what this moment might be like."

"Well, what's it like?" They were now lying face-to-face with their entire bodies touching all the way to their toes.

She sighed, long and deep. "It's wonderful." She smiled and gently kissed him on the lips. "I *am* available, Ben."

"Let's just see how available." His laugh vibrated deep in his chest.

And Sabine relished his meaning. Right now, she was his. While the law said otherwise, nothing could change where she was and whom she was with. And nothing could change what was in her heart.

Somehow, he'd managed to get them both completely naked now and magically he'd produced a condom. She'd have to give it to him, there were certain things she was glad he'd had plenty of practice with.

He kissed her with a passion that left her gasping for breath as his hands ran down her body, making her moan and plead for release.

She could hardly keep a single thought in her head, but

found her power in his moans as she touched him gently at first. Then, as he fell back and allowed her more access, she became bolder. His body was pure masculine perfection.

"Ahh. You're killing me." Sabine heard her opportunity in his surrender. She pushed him on his back and climbed aboard.

Chapter Twelve

"HEY, BEN?" BEN was working on some trial notes, but was interrupted by a quick knock, followed by his door being opened.

"Steve." He hadn't changed much over the past few years. How many had it been? Five? Six? Maybe he'd put on a few pounds and had a more mature look about him.

"I'm glad I caught you in your office. I've been meaning to stop by and say hello."

Ben was torn. This was the guy who'd been his very best friend. His brother he'd never had. And Steve had betrayed him in a way no brother would ever dare. He'd stolen the woman Ben loved. Only, she wanted to be stolen. In a million years, Ben couldn't have imagined speaking to Steve again, much less their becoming friendly again. But he was faced with this impossibility. It was a test.

"Yeah. I figured we'd bump in to one another sooner or later. How are you settling in?" Wasn't that the exact same question he'd asked Lisa?

"It's going alright. We've bought a house not far from

your mom's place. It was always my favorite part of town—Lisa's too." Evangeline House was situated in the older section of Ministry where the trees were huge and ancient and the houses were all historically significant. And expensive. It was where Steve's dad lived as well. It was a beautiful area.

"I'd heard the Alexandria place was going on the market," Ben said.

"We were very lucky. We got a tip they were planning to list it. Mrs. A was going into the nursing home and the kids weren't able to keep it up and pay the taxes and insurance to keep it in the family."

"Congratulations. It's a great house to raise a family."

"Listen, man, I know we've got a helluva past between us—" Steve began.

Ben snorted, he couldn't help it. It was such an understatement. He guessed he couldn't be as big of a man as he'd believed he might.

Steve held up his hands in surrender. "No, I'm not going to pretend it's just something that happened between us. It's something I did. We did. It was wrong. I take responsibility for allowing myself to fall for Lisa. Not that I could have helped my feelings, because I was crazy about her when the two of you went on your first date. I did try to deny my feelings, and I never let on to her how I felt."

"You mean until she reciprocated your feelings?"

"Yes. Neither of us wanted to hurt you. She loved you.

Hell, I loved you. You were my best friend. I've never had a friend like you since, and likely won't again. But you deserved better from both of us. I just wanted you to hear it from me."

Ben was humbled by Steve's words, because he believed them. "It sucked so badly because I lost you both at the same time. I didn't have a best friend to turn to when I lost the love of my life. So, it was the double-whammy that did a number on my life for a long time. It changed me."

Sharing like this with another guy wasn't easy for him. He'd gotten used to being bullied about his feelings by his sisters, but this was awkward.

"I get it, man. I just don't know how I can ever fix it. Sorry, not giving up the wife."

They both laughed.

"I'm over Lisa, just so you know. I'm pretty crazy about Sabine, so no worries there."

"Well, that's a relief because you're still the best-looking son-of-a-bitch I've ever seen. Not sure what kind of deal you made with the devil, but finding a woman will never be a problem for you."

"The trick is finding the right one," Ben said.

"Are y'all talking about me?" Lisa slipped inside the office at that moment.

"I've always said you've got the best radar around."

She grinned. "So, Ben, when are we all going out together?" Lisa asked.

"I'll check with Sabine, but she and I are going out of town for a few days, so it will likely have to be after that."

"Oh. That'll be nice. I hope it's a romantic trip," Lisa said.

"Not exactly. She's got an ex we need to dispose of." He nearly smacked himself on the head. What had possessed him to spill that information?

"Oh? Like an ex-husband? How do you plan to dispose of him? This sounds fascinating." Lisa's eyebrows shot up.

"Do you need any help?" Steve asked.

Then, an idea occurred to Ben. Three legal minds were far better than one. If he could only get Sabine on board with the possibly brilliant plan that was beginning to form in his mind. "You know, I might just take you both up on that and we can call all this even."

"Sounds like there's a twist to ridding her of the ex," Steve said.

"He's her current husband, and soon-to-be ex-husband, just as soon as we can get down there and negotiate terms. But he's an attorney and a Louisiana state senator, and not exactly a straight arrow. Sabine doesn't want to piss him off, and he is only giving her a divorce if she does a song and dance in public to show support for his upcoming candidacy. I don't like the smell of it."

"Louisiana, did you say? Not good. Their laws are sticky with Napoleonic Code and all. He can get her for abandonment if she's been gone over six months," Steve said. He was a crack divorce attorney and was up to date on all the latest loopholes.

"Do you know Napoleonic Code?" Ben asked.

"I did a comparative analysis between it and pretty much the rest of the country. I was fascinated by the fact that so many of those archaic laws are still on the books. It's like a tiny foreign country two states away, legally speaking. The divorce laws are different than here because it's a fault state, where we're a no-fault state. They look at blame and morality before granting divorce and setting forth terms and judgment. Historically, the deep Catholic influence still remains."

"So, the fact that he cheated with minor prostitutes wouldn't sit well with the judge?" Ben asked.

"Oh, poor Sabine. What an asshole. How can I help?" Lisa's outrage was clearly genuine.

"First, as you both know, everything we've discussed is completely confidential. Sabine hasn't confided in anyone else. No one here knows her true identity besides her mother. I'm sharing with the two of you because I believe if we approach this as a team, we can better any unknowns that could pop up. From what Sabine has told me about this snake, I get the feeling Richard Habersham has no intention of letting Sabine go without a fight."

"Since we're just getting our feet wet here, we're not booked up with clients and cases yet. Plus, we owe you big-time. Why don't you let us go to Louisiana and help you get your girl freed up for you?" Steve suggested.

"I'm not sure Sabine would be on board with that. She's intensely private. And having her personal dirty laundry aired out and shared is already likely going to be a real problem for her. Hopefully, I can lay out the merits for having the two of you assisting us so that she won't see my sharing as such a breach of her trust—I mean, I shouldn't have told you, but the benefits are so beyond hurt feelings. I just hope she'll come to see that."

Lisa shook her head at him. "I'm glad you told us, but you shouldn't have shared without checking with her. I won't blame her for being royally pissed. You're used to solving problems in the best, most efficient way you see fit. You came up with a way to help her, so you moved forward because you knew we won't tell anyone because of office privilege. She won't see it that way."

Ben wasn't sure what he should do. "Well, shit."

"Dude, I think we should go to Louisiana on the sly. I can feed you information on the laws and tell you how to counter whatever is happening. We can do research behind the scenes and be your backup. Sabine doesn't have to know we're there."

Steve's knowledge of Napoleonic Code and Louisiana law would be invaluable when dealing with a team of opposing counsel.

Ben didn't want to be at such a huge disadvantage. "I'll think about it. I'm sure they're going to hit Sabine with a list of terms as soon as she arrives, so we'll have to counter on the fly," Ben said.

"You're leaving out Sabine's wishes as you're discussing her life here," Lisa reminded them.

"Just anticipating what we might be up against, honey. By the way, are you in?" Steve asked her.

"Are you kidding? Of course I'm in. Sabine's going to need a woman's perspective in play during this fiasco. I'm certainly not leaving it up to the two of you." Lisa was a family attorney, and handled divorces. Most often, she represented women who'd been emotionally or physically abused, or bullied at the hands of domineering husbands. Ben knew her legal history, as she'd been written up in some of the legal magazines for cases she'd represented. Plus, whether he'd wanted to hear it, word got around.

"I know Sabine will appreciate you having her back from the female perspective. The two of you handle more divorces than I do, I've got to admit."

"So, when do we leave?" Steve asked.

"Day after tomorrow. Can you swing it with the kids?" Ben asked.

He'd never met their children, but he'd bet money they were adorable, considering both Lisa and Steve were both aesthetically gifted, and brainiacs to boot.

"Are you kidding? Both our parents fuss and argue about whose turn it is to take the kids. They beg us to go on trips so they can have them to themselves overnight. It's a blessing and a curse," Lisa said.

"Well, that's certainly going to be helpful in this situation," Ben said.

"The question is, which set of grandparents gets to watch them? Or, will they split their time equally between the two?" Lisa asked.

"I'm betting money on the second scenario." Steve laughed. "Can you imagine our breaking it to one or the other that they weren't the chosen pair?"

Lisa rolled her eyes. "Not in a million years."

The yearning in Ben's chest was becoming familiar. Witnessing Lisa and Steve banter over their children with such affection shined the light on what was missing in his life. Of course, rushing something like that was foolish, but he still wished for it like greener grass on the other side of the fence.

"So, you and Sabine discuss having kids?" Steve gave words to Ben's thoughts.

"Not yet. Right now, we're focusing on getting her free to move on with her life."

"Kids make everything worth the struggles." Lisa mooned her agreement with Steve.

She pulled out her cell phone and clicked on a photo of two tow-headed little ones who almost looked like twins, they appeared so close in age.

"Wow. Great-looking kiddos. How old?" Ben asked.

"Jonathan is two, and Emma is three and a half," Lisa said.

"I can't wait to meet them." He meant it.

"You always had a soft spot for little ones. How's your nephew and niece? Dirk and Lucy, wasn't it?" Steve asked.

"Dirk's almost fifteen, and starting to date. JoJo thinks all the girls these days are far too aggressive, but Dirk seems fine with it. Lucy's great. She's almost eleven now. Pre-teen hell, according to Maeve, but pre-algebra is our thing. I tutor her pretty regularly, so she and I are tight." Ben knew his pride in his family was obvious. "JoJo has little Suzie, who's four, and Cammie married Grey Harrison last year, who has a daughter, Samantha, about the same age as Lucy. Oh, and Cammie's pregnant."

"Wow. Lots of changes in the Laroux family. I heard about your mom getting married as well," Lisa said.

Ben nodded. "Howard has been a real godsend for Mom; I have to say. He was certainly a surprise. I'm sure you heard that he's Maeve's biological father." With all the gossip in town, it would be strange if they hadn't.

"The gossip mill is alive and well here in Ministry. No way that could have flown under the radar around here," Steve said. "I'm thinking that was a blow to the family."

"Nobody ever thinks their mother capable of such a secretive past. But we did wonder where Maeve's dark blue eyes came from. Howard has the exact shade," Ben said.

Ben's cell phone rang then, breaking up the discussion. He noticed that it was Sabine's number on the caller ID. "Excuse me a moment."

He stepped toward the corner of the room. "Hey there. What's up?"

"Just wanted to check in with you. I got a call from Richard's assistant letting me know the accommodations for my stay. I guess he's planning to pay for it."

"Turn it down. Tell her you will make your own arrangements and let them know when you arrive. The less you do on their terms, the better. No need giving them more information than is absolutely necessary. That way, he can't get the upper hand right away."

"O-okay. What should I say if she asks where I'm staying? Should I tell her you'll be coming with me?"

"No, don't mention me at all. Best to make Richard and his counsel believe you'll be in a vulnerable position alone. But I don't want them to place you in a hotel where they can keep tabs on you twenty-four-seven. He will try to bully you into doing what he wants, so be prepared to simply say no. Or, you could say you're staying with a friend and it's none of his business what your plans are."

"I'm fine with saying any of those things to him. I don't have a problem standing up to him. My concern was his seeing you as a rival. If he believes I want a divorce because I've found someone else, he'll never agree to one."

"Why don't we get together this evening and go over a game plan? In the meantime, send me the names of your favorite hotels. I can have my assistant, Chase, make reservations through the firm. Now that I'm your attorney, it can be written off as a business expense."

"Okay. I've canceled my patients for three days to be sure I'm covered, time-wise," Sabine said. "Why don't you come over to my house for dinner? Mom is making étouffée tonight. You got a problem with crawfish?"

"No problem at all." He disconnected the call and turned around. He'd nearly forgotten Steve and Lisa were still in his office.

"Sounds like everything is going to plan. You can fill us in tomorrow on the details.

It would be risky, but Ben agreed that it would be best they stayed nearby. "Okay. I'll keep you posted."

The couple left his office and Ben sighed. Now, he truly was having serious reservations over having deceived Sabine by omission. Her safety was utmost on his mind, and he couldn't think of a better way to ensure it than having silent backup with collective knowledge of the law.

The only change in the plan he might suggest is that he and Sabine go to his place tonight and repeat their last meeting's activities. It wouldn't be especially polite to suggest a change in venue at this point, so he would suffer from wanting her in silence.

⋙⋘

RACHEL'S NUMBER APPEARED on Sabine's caller ID on her drive home. Finally, her sister was returning her call. "Hey, Rach. Everything okay?"

"I was going to ask you the same question. You sounded a little frantic on the last message. It's not like you."

"There's a lot going on over here. Dad's parole hearing is coming up in a couple weeks and he wants you there."

"No effing way, thank you very much."

"I figured you'd say that. But it's more involved than that. He's insisting his entire family's attendance will carry more weight in swaying the parole board to let him loose. And he backhandedly intimated he would be less inclined to cause trouble for Mom if we got you on board."

"He basically threatened to make things more difficult for Mom if I didn't show?"

"Basically. And it would make the difference in Mom's life moving forward, without his interference or his being a huge pain in the butt for who knows how long."

"He's not a father, he's a sperm donor," Rachel hissed.

"I know you feel that way now. But, right now, the sperm donor is in the driver's seat."

"Unless none of us show up."

"We couldn't do that, Rachel. For all his faults, you know he loves us, don't you?" Jean-Claude Prudhomme had been a loving father to his girls when they were young. They knew he cared for them, but he'd become so obsessed with his own world as they'd grown up. When he'd brought James into the household, it was as if a line had been drawn, and Dad and James were on one side of it, with Rachel, Sabine, and Mom on the other.

"I have a hard time remembering that person," Rachel said.

When the scandal had broken several years ago involving Dad and the disgusting antics with other women, it had been the break of decency and all pretense between them pretending they were a viable family unit. She and Rachel were grown by then, and Mom was done suffering her husband's indiscretions in silence. But Dad refused to allow Mom her freedom. His ego and pride were so overblown by then that he refused to admit the mess he'd made of their lives. He couldn't accept fault or blame. Still, Sabine wouldn't say he was a bad person, just extremely misguided, and so catered to by those in his circle that he'd lost touch with decent values most average humans maintained in their lives. He'd achieved some sort of demigod status and was insulated from the real world.

While a district attorney's position might not sound like it, it really was a hugely powerful position in a city like New Orleans. He'd been as much a figurehead as an attorney. Being an elected official in such an extravagant place full of vice and corruption had gone straight to his head, and been fed by the staffers and social climbers—like James's mother. There was a nasty underbelly strongly associated with that world. One that Sabine was thrilled to never revisit, would never revisit.

"Hey, are you still there?" Rachel's voice brought Sabine out of her musings.

"Oh, sorry. Just thinking about Dad's descent into the dark side. You know, he wasn't always like this."

"I can hardly remember the father he was before James came into our lives and ruined everything. The sad thing is that we tried to make that work. Dad just let him rule the household. He was horrible."

"Yeah. It's a personality disorder he was born with. We couldn't have fixed him even if we'd tried harder or done everything right. His drug-addicted mother ruined him before she gave birth to him. His brain was fried and mis-wired from all the partying when she was pregnant. He doesn't have a conscience or empathy. That's why we must be cautious around him, Rachel. Don't make James too angry if you can help it. He is capable of real violence. I'm guilty of reacting poorly to him too, but we should keep in mind that if he snaps, it could be irrevocable."

"God, you scare me when you go all therapist on me. I'm glad you understand why our family is so incredibly screwed up, but it's pretty damned depressing, I have to tell you."

Sabine laughed. She was home now, sitting outside in her car. Ben would arrive in a half-hour or so.

"Oh, by the way, I'm sleeping with Ben Laroux."

A shriek. "Ben La-who? And you're sleeping with him? Get out!"

"He's a local attorney. And he's quite frankly the best-looking human being I've ever laid eyes on. Gorgeous."

"Why didn't you just lead with that? It would have been

a much more fun conversation. Thank God, Sabine. I thought you would revert back to virgin status or go sequester yourself in a damned nunnery if you didn't get laid soon."

"What about you? How's your love life?" Sabine asked.

"My love life or my sex life?" Her sister's voice took on a teasing quality.

"I retract my question. Not sure I want to know that." Sabine changed the subject.

"So, Mom's sleeping with Norman Harrison." Best just to put it right out there.

"*What? Gross!* I did *not* need to hear that. What else are you going to tell me?"

"I'm going to New Orleans to meet with Richard and his attorneys to negotiate my divorce." So much had gone down since the last time they'd spoken. Sabine hadn't realized just how much until now.

"Do you want me to have a damn heart attack? What's the catch? I know he's not letting you off that easily."

"You're right. I have to go to the governor's ball with him and show my support for his candidacy." The very thought of dressing up and taking Richard's arm made her stomach hurt.

"Sounds like sleazy, snot ball, Richard," Rachel said.

Rachel had never been sold on Richard as a brother-in-law. Sabine wondered now if anything had ever happened to cause that besides the things she knew about.

"I'm coming home. Tomorrow. I've just wrapped up a shoot here. When are you going to New Orleans?"

"You're finally coming home? Tomorrow? We're leaving day-after-tomorrow."

"Well, I'll get to see you for a little while, and then I'll stay with Mom while you're gone."

"I'm so glad, Rachel. How long will you be in town?" Sabine asked, thrilled that her little sister was finally coming for a visit, but sorry they wouldn't have much time together.

There was a pause. "Not sure. I've got a break in my schedule. We can talk when I get there. Well, gotta go. See you tomorrow afternoon."

The line went dead. Something was up with her sister. When it rained, it poured as always. Mom would be so happy to see Rachel, so Sabine wouldn't share her concerns. It would all come out eventually.

When she entered the kitchen, her mother kissed her on the cheek. "Hello, dear. How was work?"

"People. Problems," Sabine answered, and shrugged.

"Well, I know you did your best to help them solve every one," her mother said. "When can we expect that handsome hunk you've been seeing?"

"About twenty minutes, I'd guess." She sniffed appreciatively and her stomach growled. "Smells divine."

"Well, you'd better go back and freshen up, then. I've got things well in hand here. I hope that young man likes to eat," Mom said, gesturing to the very large pot of étouffée bubbling on the stove.

Sabine smiled. "He does; don't worry."

As much as she looked forward to diving into her mother's Cajun feast, part of Sabine wished she'd suggested a rendezvous at Ben's place, for obvious reasons. Just thinking of him made her restless. She hoped she'd be able to concentrate on his words instead of watching his mouth and remembering what he'd done with it the last time they were together.

Splashing cold water on her heated cheeks to cool them, she tried to reset her naughty thoughts about Ben. Better get it together. This was serious business they had to discuss. And she was a serious person, or had been until Ben Laroux entered her life and turned everything upside down. Not that it wasn't upside down before. Maybe he just righted it and she didn't recognize how things were supposed to be. That was a nice thought.

Sabine changed into soft, faded jeans and a cream, light-weight jersey knit tunic. She'd come to realize how well-built she was for this Southern, cozy life here in small-town Alabama. No more planning her wardrobe every week with her assistant, keeping the constituency in mind, or waking every morning, a rigid moment-by-moment schedule set forth by the staffers. Now, she had patients to see. But Sabine was doing what she loved. She poured her heart and soul into helping the citizens of Ministry work through their problems and heal their hurts. Sure, there were some she wanted to kick to the curb, but she did her best for them as well.

A knock on the door and her mother's voice broke up her thoughts. She quickly brushed her teeth—because nobody deserved to greet her face-to-face at the end of the day before she'd had a serious visit with her toothbrush. Especially since she intended to get *way* into Ben's personal space at some point this evening. Even if it was just for a goodnight kiss.

Sabine entered the kitchen, where Mom was fussing over Ben. She'd put him at the small breakfast table that was set for four. Four? Oh, maybe Norman would join them. Mom knew the score as far as the subjects they'd planned to discuss this evening. And Norman was up-to-date on pretty much all the family secrets, so she figured having him here wasn't a problem. Norman had proven to be smart, trustworthy, and completely loyal to her mother, thus far. Who was Sabine to question her mother's decision to confide in him? After all, she'd shared their dirty laundry with Ben. Not that she wanted any of this to go any further. With every person who knew a secret, it increased the possibility of someone letting something slip. And if Sabine had learned anything, it was that secrets had a way of getting out.

"Hi there," Sabine said to Ben as she entered the room.

At seeing her, he transferred his gaze to her from her mother. The change in his expression was immediate and intense. He raked her body with his eyes, and caught her stare. Her body's response weakened her knees.

"Hey there, yourself." The tone of his voice sounded completely innocent and welcoming.

She knew better.

"I hope you don't mind that I've asked Norman to join us," Mom said.

Ben's lustful look vanished immediately, replaced by a questioning one. "Is he aware of all the facts?" Ben asked.

"Yes. I trust him completely," Mom answered.

Sabine added her agreement to that. "Norman is in the loop. The only other person who knows everything is my sister, Rachel. I mention Rachel because I just got off the phone with her on the way home. She'll be here tomorrow and will be with Mom while we're gone to New Orleans," Sabine said, then checked her mother's reaction.

Tears filled Mom's eyes. "Oh, how I've missed your sister. Did she say what time she planned to arrive?"

"Sometime tomorrow afternoon. I'm not sure how long she's planning to stay."

"Our home is her home, as she well knows. She can move in permanently, as far as I'm concerned." Mom stood and walked over to the built-in bookcases beside the fireplace and pulled down a framed photograph. She stared at it for a moment, then brought it over and handed it to Ben. "This is the three of us a few years ago."

Ben took the frame and studied the photo. "Rachel's tall, but I can see a strong resemblance between your girls," he said to Mom as he handed back the frame.

Mom laughed at the understatement. "I'll say. Besides the height, they almost look like twins. Their eye color is slightly different, and Rachel is three years younger, but it's almost shocking to most people who see them together the first time, or when someone sees one and doesn't know the other. It can be confusing too."

The sound of a door opening and closing grabbed everyone's attention. Norman entered the room, smiling. "Hello, all. Sorry I'm late to the party."

"Nonsense. You're just in time. I've gotten some fantastic news. My daughter, Rachel, is coming home tomorrow."

"Well, now, that's a reason to celebrate. It'll be nice to finally meet her. I hope you've told her about me—us," Norman said to Mom.

"I've told her some. I'm guessing Sabine has filled her sister in more than I have." Mom looked over at Sabine, expectantly.

"I might have mentioned the two of you were getting pretty tight. Rachel is open-minded. Don't worry, Norman, she's not going to read you the riot act. She's as thrilled for Mom's happiness as I am. We're just glad she's moving on with her life. It's been a tough few years for all of us with Dad's behavior, and then his public media circus and trial."

"In an effort to not speak of your father, I'm going to suggest we load our plates with this food I've spent the day preparing," Mom said.

"No need to suggest it twice," Ben said. He stood with his bowl in hand. "Show me the way."

❧

THE DINNER TALK remained light and they stayed away from any heavy subjects. Ben told some funny family stories from his childhood. As the only boy with four sisters, and the youngest to boot, he sounded like a holy terror. Not like Sabine's brother, James, of course, but a precocious child, to be certain.

Mom shared a few somewhat embarrassing memories about Sabine's childhood, and pointed out what opposite personalities she and Rachel were. "You'd swear they were from different planets if they didn't look so much alike."

Of course, Ben pressed her on what those contrasts were. "I was a nerd, according to my mom," Sabine supplied.

"Not possible," Ben said, grinning.

"Not a nerd, honey. You were quiet and liked to read. And you loved your cats."

"You just stated verbatim the definition of a nerd. Of course, as a therapist, I must state that there's nothing wrong with a slightly introverted young woman with social mistrust issues and a love for rescuing animals."

"Of course there wasn't anything wrong with you. I mean, look at you." Mom gestured toward Sabine with her hand.

"Nothing wrong at all." Ben continued to grin.

"What?" She threw her napkin at him.

"I love hearing your history," Ben said. He even had a dopey look on his face.

"Stop it, Mom. Don't say another word. Ben's eating this up." Sabine held up a hand. "Enough."

"Aw, honey, don't be embarrassed. You were adorable."

Sabine picked up her plate and brought it over to the sink. "I think we should change the subject, if y'all don't mind," Sabine suggested.

"We do have some pretty serious things to discuss," Ben said.

"I'd love to hear your plans, if you don't mind my sitting in," Mom said.

"No, of course not. I don't have any secrets from you. In fact, you know Richard, and you might think of something that I haven't. Dealing with him is going to be challenging," Sabine said.

Mom nodded. "Ben's going on this trip isn't going to help his mood, for sure."

Ben piped up. "I'm not planning on getting in the mix unless I have to. I'm going to stay behind the scenes and make sure all goes as it should. As long as the attorneys are straight and fair in their dealings with Sabine, I'll lie low. But I'll make sure I've got eyes on her the entire time and that we stay in contact."

"And what if Richard tries to pull a fast one?" Norman asked.

"Then I'll make sure he understands that we'll not tolerate his intimidation or bullying Sabine."

"I'm afraid he's going to bring the circus to town here and try to ruin my life in Ministry if I don't fall in line with his demands. He understands how important it is to me to maintain my personal and professional reputation."

"And I wouldn't put it past him to use it to his advantage to manipulate Sabine, either," Mom said. "But you know that his campaign and his reelection mean everything to him, so keep in mind that might be his Achilles' heel. Without his political career, he has nothing of value, in his mind."

"The question is, how badly does he want his way? And what lines are he willing to cross to get it?" Norman chimed in. "I hate to see y'all push this fella beyond what his good nature might allow. Once a person goes too far, they stop worrying about the consequences, and the means no longer have to justify the ends. So, don't push him too far."

"What about your dad?" Ben asked.

"What about him?" Sabine's response sounded defensive, even to her own ears.

"I mean, what is the relationship between your husband and your father?" Ben asked.

"My father has helped Richard keep his dirty laundry from the public to spare me shame. At least that's what Dad said. I'm not sure what their actual relationship is. I know Richard has a healthy respect for my father. He's never wanted to cross him politically, but that was before Dad was put in prison."

"So, it's complicated. Richard might not want to rock that boat with your dad," Ben surmised.

"I can't see Richard doing anything to thumb his nose at Dad intentionally, so long as it was in line with his own purposes. But with Dad in prison, Richard might be more likely to go his own way, even if it hurts me, because he'd be less worried about political reprisal for sure."

"When is the date of your dad's parole hearing?" Ben had pulled out his electronic calendar, obviously intending to enter the dates.

"Next Thursday, April twenty-sixth," Sabine said.

"Okay. That gives us tomorrow, which is Thursday, and Friday to prepare for Saturday's governor's ball, and make headway with the divorce talks."

"Are you planning to be at the ball?" Sabine asked Ben.

He smiled. "Not in a way that I'll be noticed by anyone."

"Are you planning some James Bond covert stuff?" Sabine was curious what he planned now.

"Let's just say I'm going to cover your back so you don't have to face the evening on your own."

"I have an idea." Norman raised his hand as if in science class.

They all turned in his direction. "What if you set up a line of communication during the ball, or maybe the whole time?"

"You mean, like an earpiece? Listening devices?" Sabine

asked.

"Great idea. That way, if I lose sight of you or can't be in the same area, then we'll still be able to communicate."

"Won't someone be able to tell?" Sabine asked.

Norman smiled. "I know someone who has all the tools. The best tools in the spy business."

Again, they all looked his way, waiting. "Howard," he said, in a way that said they should have already guessed the obvious.

Ben slapped his hand on the table. "Of course. Why didn't I think of it?"

Sabine had seen and heard small bits of info when she'd been around the Laroux family that Howard had been involved his entire adult life with some super-covert government operations. In other words, he'd been a high-level operative—a spy. "Ben, I'll let you discuss this with Howard. I know we can trust him."

"Of course we can. And my mother too. I hope you don't mind, but she and I already had a—conversation. She was pretty adamant I give you a chance to explain yourself."

Sabine's heart fell. "I hope she doesn't think any less of me." It was a little embarrassing, having this conversation in front of her mother and Norman.

"Are you kidding? She thinks you hung the moon, which is why she set me straight very quickly."

"You weren't going to give me a chance to explain. She had to talk you into it." That hurt a little bit, Sabine had to admit.

Ben's mouth was grim. "Mom only reminded me how compassionate you'd proven yourself with our family's very delicate issues. And she left it to me to conclude that I should at least give you the opportunity to tell your side of the story."

"It's alright, really. If I were on the other side of this, I'm not sure how I would have reacted," she admitted.

"I wish I hadn't needed the reminder. But I couldn't have stayed away; you should know that."

Mom stood from the table to break the awkward silence that followed Ben's heavy words. "Why don't you two go in the other room and finish hammering out your travel plans while Norman and I clean up this mess? Y'all let us know if there's anything else we can do to help. I want to get things looking nice for Rachel's arrival tomorrow," Mom said.

Sabine gave her mother a quick hug. "Thanks for cooking tonight, and don't worry, Rachel doesn't want anything special. She only wants to be with her family."

"Will she go to the prison with us next week?" Mom asked.

Sabine shrugged. "That's completely up to her. Rachel's response to Dad's actions is not the same as mine. The two of them had a different relationship."

"She was his baby girl until he brought James into the family." Mom sighed and nodded. "I don't think she'll ever forgive him for that."

"Maybe not, but when we spoke earlier today, I let her know what was at stake if she chose not to participate in the parole hearing."

"She's a good girl, and she loves her family. I hate to use guilt to persuade her, but for all of us to be truly free of your dad's thumb, it's necessary."

"We'll never be truly free of him; you know that, don't you? Once he's out of prison, he'll figure out a way to insinuate himself into our lives to create a new normal," Sabine said.

"Let's just hope he's able to handle my new normal," Mom said, and glanced over at Norman lovingly.

"Mom, it might take Dad a little time to get used to your being with someone else. I know you're legally divorced, but the two of you were together since high school. You're his family too, even if y'all aren't married anymore. Just be prepared for an adjustment period on his part. It's going to hurt him that you've moved on and found someone else. So, be prepared to show him a little compassion," Sabine said.

"Like the compassion he showed me when he was screwing half the women in New Orleans?" The bitterness in her mother's voice told Sabine that Dad still had the power to hurt Mom, which meant she still cared about him, even if she wanted her freedom and a future with someone new.

"He won't equate that, you know. His behavior over the years has put him in the current situation where he finds himself now. He's lost everything and has had plenty of time to reflect. But Dad only has us now, and you're part of us. So, while you don't want to be married to him, don't abandon him completely while he's transitioning from prison to a life without his wife, family, or career. None of us are proud of his actions or of what he's done to our family. We're all very angry and distrustful of him. It's like we don't know him at all."

"I'll say. But I don't want to be near him. In fact, I honestly don't want to have any contact at all with him. And Sabine, I shouldn't have to. I've gotten my divorce settlement from his attorneys, so why should I continue to be held captive by his needs?" Mom asked.

She had a great point.

"Because it's what we do for family. And we'll all be far better off if we, including you, are not hostile to Dad while he adjusts to life after prison. No, he doesn't deserve it from you, especially. He put us all through hell, but hopefully, if he's in a good place soon, then we can all get on with our lives."

"I don't like it, but I'll be as civil as possible. Only because I'm in a happy place, myself."

"Don't worry that I'll have a problem with it, honey. I've waited a long time to find you, so I'm willing to wait until you settle your business so we can be together," Norman said.

"You see now why I want so badly to be free of the nasty past with your father? Because this guy's here now, and I don't want to make him wait another minute."

"Well, hopefully once the parole hearing is over and they release Dad, things will settle quietly and quickly."

"We can hope. Now, we can do these dishes and let the two of you get to it. C'mon, Norman." She threw him a dish rag.

Sabine turned toward Ben. "Do you want to go into the family room and finish planning our trip?"

He motioned for her to precede him. "Lead the way."

Chapter Thirteen

TWO MORE DAYS. Richard was nearly counting the hours until Sabine was home. She'd been gone far too long. He'd *allowed* her to stay away because it was what she wanted, and because it had given her time to get over the miscarriage and his little misstep in their marriage. Now, she was coming home to divorce him, or so she believed. There would be no divorce. This was her home. Now that her father would be getting out of prison, nothing would keep her from taking her rightful place at his side. He felt confident she would realize it once she returned.

She'd sent back a message refusing to stay where he'd planned for her to. That was curious. The Sabine he'd known hadn't naysayed his suggestions, as a rule. Why would she change the plan? Perhaps she was trying to show him that he could no longer tell her what to do. He gave a small chuckle. Good for her. He liked the small show of spine. Sabine had always been somewhat opinionated, but she'd been a dutiful and obedient wife. Until she'd found out about those blasted girls.

The hookers had simply begun as a distraction, a mere folly, while Sabine moped about losing the pregnancy. She'd been so whiney about it that Richard had been forced to find something to entertain himself. Sabine had kept him straight; she'd been his conscience whenever he'd begin to drift from the straight and narrow, and she likely hadn't even known it.

It was why he needed her back. She'd been gone too long, and he feared the future of his career without her beside him. His staffers had done their best to advise, cajole, and threaten to quit if he didn't get his shit together and put things back on track. He learned that he liked sex. With barely legal girls. A few might not have been completely legal, but he hadn't known it at the time. That was his story and he was sticking to it. It had nothing to do with Sabine. He loved Sabine. With her near, he didn't do the things that would get him into trouble. So far, Richard had managed to keep his activities out of the press and under the radar.

The vices were closing in. He'd begun to drink more and, not being an idiot, he realized none of this would go on unnoticed or unreported forever. He needed Sabine. And he refused to take no for an answer.

Sabine was lovely and so classy and elegant. She was his walking credential for reelection. He'd discovered she'd been treating half of that podunk Alabama townsfolk for their mental disturbances and family issues. Hell, most of them likely had issues alright. Uncle-daddy issues. Bunch of inbred hicks.

It angered Richard that Sabine spent her days listening to people blather on about their problems. *He* had problems, and she was his cure. And he meant to see that she never stepped foot back in that ridiculous pissant town once she got back to civilization.

Now that she'd made her plans to come home, he could move forward with his. He'd picked out a lovely red gown that would do wonders for her curvaceous figure and complement her dark good looks. He hoped she hadn't gained any weight. Her mother had been living there with her, and likely cooking every night, so he hoped her size was still the same.

Sabine's dad, Jean-Claude had been in touch recently. He'd not-too-subtly warned Richard to treat his little girl like a princess while she was in town. Little did the convict realize that Richard was no longer his boy, and he wouldn't take orders from his father-in-law now, or in the future. Jean-Claude hadn't ever been in favor of their divorcing in the past, but somehow Sabine had changed his mind recently. Richard no longer worried about Jean-Claude's wishes now that the former district attorney had been taken down so publicly and permanently. He'd lost his license to practice law and all his power.

That made Richard a free man, politically, because Jean-Claude no longer held the puppet strings that orchestrated the control Richard had respected as part of the hierarchy of the structure of politics within the state. Sure, Jean-Claude still had cronies who would slap him on the back and pay lip service to his friendship, but he wasn't a mover or shaker any longer, just a sad, dried-up old loser, who'd ended up in prison. Of course, in Louisiana, those old guys could end up governor, if history was to be repeated.

Maybe Richard could walk both sides of the line and no one would be the wiser. At least for a while, until it was impossible to hide his true intentions. It was feasible that Sabine would be willing to fall in line with his suggestions and plans without a fuss. After all, they'd been crazy about each other once. They'd planned a life together. If he could remind her of that, it just might work. If not, he'd need to find another way to persuade her.

He hadn't come this far to let her bring him down because she wanted to change her mind. Plus, he'd missed her. Having a wife was a comfy, cozy thing in his case.

➤➤➤《《《

BEN HAD LEFT Sabine's house with a hard-on and a smile. The best and worst of things. She'd not invited him to spend the night, but he'd not expected her to. He'd slyly suggested she accompany him home, but she'd thought better of it since her mother was flitting around the house tidying up and getting ready for her sister Rachel's visit the next day.

He'd wanted to be with Sabine so badly, especially after the goodnight kiss she'd laid on him outside in the moonlight just before he'd climbed inside his truck. More like a full-body frontal press that left Ben nearly panting for more. It was a new sensation for him. Longing might be a more apt description, knowing she was so close, and accessible, should he push a bit harder. But the thrill was in the waiting, and how precious being with her was to him. Because it would only be better the next time.

He drove all the way home with the same goofy expression on his face. And the boner.

Until his cell phone rang. "Hello?"

"How did it go with Sabine?" It was his mother. He'd meant to call her and fill her in.

"Oh, hey, Mom. We're good. She's got a pretty complicated situation on her hands, but you were right, as usual. I should've taken a breath and asked why she didn't tell me the truth up front. I'm heading to New Orleans in a couple days to help her negotiate a divorce agreement with her husband's attorneys. It could get tricky, since she doesn't want to let on that I'm going to be there. Sabine believes he'll be more likely to cooperate if she's alone. He's a pretty slick politician, a state senator, with connections."

"Honey, should you talk to Howard about this? I mean, I know you've had to deal with some pretty ugly characters in your line of work, but how do you know this guy's not *dangerous?*" Mom asked.

"Based on what Sabine says, he's unpleasant, but not dangerous. But it might help to have some earpieces to communicate through, since we don't want to let on that she has me there as back up unless things get ugly."

"I'll put Howard on speaker."

"Okay."

"Son, I don't like the idea of you both walking into a situation out of town with a slick politician without knowing more about this character. Do you mind if I do some background work on him?"

"As long as you keep it completely legal, Howard. He's also an attorney, so I don't want to draw fire by blurring the lines and end up hurting Sabine."

He heard Howard's deep rumble of laughter. "Don't you know by now that my security clearance allows me to check out most anything and anyone without legal concerns? Of course, I only use my powers for good and only in situations where they would stand up to a certain level of scrutiny, should it come to that. Doing a background check through my information channels on a questionable politician and getting his history is just a quicker way than if you did it through yours."

Ben did have sources available who gathered information as well. "True. I'd like to avoid asking favors in this case from my sources, so if you'd check out Richard Habersham, Louisiana state senator, I would appreciate it.

"I told Mom we could use earpieces and mics to communicate without anyone noticing, if you have access to the equipment. Habersham will think Sabine is there on her own, so I want to maintain contact at all times."

"If you can stop by tomorrow, I'll outfit you."

"Thanks, Howard; I'll give you a call when I'm on the way."

➤➤➤❮❮❮

SABINE'S LAST PATIENT of the day had left a message that she wasn't going to be able to make her appointment, which caused Sabine to breathe a massive sigh of relief. Not because she didn't want to see Mrs. Weed; it would simply make it easier to get home earlier to spend a little extra time with Rachel and Mom together before rushing off to New Orleans with Ben tomorrow.

Poor Mrs. Weed had had a recent come to Jesus with herself—her words—and she'd recognized her deep-seated bitterness and disappointment within her life had permeated her relationships with others. Sadly, it had left her lonely, and with few friends. Of course, a few run-ins with towns-folk had also helped serve as a catalyst toward making this important step toward self-improvement.

Today, it seemed that Mrs. Weed had scheduled a last-minute engagement with a new friend from the garden club. It had been a suggestion of Sabine's that she try participating socially instead of sniping at people regarding their short-comings or repeating nasty gossip in the aisles of the grocery store. It seemed the woman had taken her advice. Likely, Sabine would hear the result of the outing at their next appointment.

As soon as she was able, Sabine gathered her things and locked her office. She was excited to see her sister. It had been nearly a year since Rachel had come home. Last time, she'd only stayed overnight, and then she'd been off to her next commission. Freelancing was a perfect profession for Rachel, especially at this time in her life. She had nothing tying her down—no husband or children. But Sabine also knew that Rachel struggled with commitment, even if that commitment was staying in one place for more than a few weeks. She was like a beautiful bird that loved to fly from place to place, but never took the time to build a nest.

Mom had left a voice mail earlier to let her know Rachel had arrived safe and sound. Ben had sent her a quick text confirming their hotel reservation that Chase had made for the two of them. She dialed his number as soon as she got on the road.

"Hey there." He'd answered on the first ring.

His deep and familiar voice caused an unexpected warming in her chest.

"Hi. I was on my way home from work and wanted to check in with you about tomorrow."

"I'm headed over to Mom's to get some equipment from Howard. Seems he has pretty much all the latest super spy equipment we could ever need."

She smiled. "Someday maybe we'll find out his former job description."

"On his death bed, if we're lucky," Ben laughed.

"Ha. Or not. He might take it to the grave."

"Well, lucky for us, he's there to help. Hopefully, everything will go smoothly and we won't need anything besides listening equipment, and Richard won't even know I'm there with you."

"Hopefully he won't. He was a jealous type, even though he cheated. He's also the kind of man whose ego wouldn't allow the thought that I would ever have found someone else besides him, or that there would be another man I'd prefer. I want to get the divorce well underway before he discovers that."

"What do you think his reaction might be if he finds out you've been with someone else?"

She shuddered slightly. "I'm not sure. I hardly recognized him anymore when we spoke. He was a stranger, and I've been gone a long time. He was cold, but still behaved as if he owned me and could tell me what to do. In fact, I was surprised he was okay with my changing the hotel reservation. I didn't tell him where I was staying. Of course, I didn't know at the time, because Chase hadn't yet made the reservation."

"We're staying listed under my name instead of yours so he can't find you. Just in case," Ben said.

"Good plan. If he thinks I'm alone, I wouldn't put it past him to have me followed or watched." Sabine was now remembering how her life had been in the political arena, and how much she'd hated it.

"We'll make sure that's not possible. Even if we have to lose the tail or switch cars. I know it sounds like a movie, but I really don't trust Richard, and I don't want anyone watching you—us."

"I agree. And I remember how it was living in a highly political family and being married to a politician. High stakes, always, and underlying threats. We had security and drivers. He'll want to offer me that to keep tabs on me."

"That's it. How about we introduce me as your driver? I can't believe I hadn't thought about it before. That way, I can be nearby all the time. You can insist. And I'll have to do your bidding."

"You'll need to get a black suit and a hat. Perhaps a pair of driving gloves?" Sabine giggled at the thought of Ben working as her driver/security personnel.

"I'll be your bodyguard." His tone suggested that and so much more.

"I like the sound of that."

"Then it's settled. I'll figure out a chauffeur's uniform, and instead of renting a car with a driver for you, I'll work on 'borrowing' a black town car from a rental company. Maybe Howard can help with that too. I just pulled into their driveway, so I'll let you know how it all works out."

Sabine was sitting, parked in the garage, still talking on the phone. "I'm home too. I'd better go on inside and greet the prodigal daughter before they come out here looking for me."

Sabine pressed "end" on her phone, still smiling. Having Ben accompany her to New Orleans was probably the best-case scenario she could have imagined. She'd hit the man jackpot with him, to be certain. Too bad it had taken her a while to wade through the stories of her patients to realize it. She'd developed an opinion of him based on her perception, not because she knew him personally. Lesson learned.

Sabine heard them before she opened the door. They were laughing together, and it was wonderful to her ears. Mom's was a light musical sound, so airy and bright, and Rachel's laugh, like her voice, was a little husky and sultry. Sabine stood a moment and soaked it in. For about a second, because Rachel opened the door before she'd had the chance.

"Hey, you. I thought I heard the garage door." Rachel snatched her up in a big bear hug.

"Put me down, you Amazon; I can't breathe." Sabine laughed.

Rachel was nearly six feet tall, and looked like a super-model, even in sweats on an ugly day.

"Oh, stop whining; I've missed you, you little peanut." Nobody would ever have called Sabine a peanut. She was a full-sized, full-grown woman. But the oversized one there made everyone and everything seem smaller than they were.

Sabine had made it inside the house now and shut the garage door. "Something smells wonderful."

"I'm making your sister's favorite, jambalaya and pecan

pie," Mom replied. "I didn't expect you for another hour or so."

"My last patient of the day canceled, so I was able to get here a little earlier than I'd planned."

"Well, go change out of those awful clothes and shoes and get comfy so we can catch up on all the craziness and *sex* going on here in Alabama." Rachel's eyes twinkled as she turned Sabine by the shoulders and gave her a tiny shove toward the hallway from the kitchen.

"What's wrong with my work clothes? I have to look professional or people won't take me seriously." Sabine frowned back at her sister.

"You look like an old woman. An uncomfortable, grouchy one. Go."

Sabine took the ribbing in good humor, understanding that Rachel, with her art degree and free spirit would wither and die if she had to put on a pair of sensible shoes and a suit, and keep office hours day after day, week after week. Though Sabine had to admit, her suits were awesome, and her shoes, well, they weren't too sensible.

So, she changed into far more comfy lounging clothing and flip-flops, her oversized sweatshirt covering her rear end. Its green Tulane wave logo splashed across the gray front. The yoga pants hadn't been anywhere near a yoga studio lately, but it was time to get back to her workouts.

Sabine sighed appreciatively over her braless status. Rachel was so right. This was way better. Just the three of them to laugh, eat, and catch up. Heaven.

Though she wanted Rachel to meet Ben at some point before they left for New Orleans in the morning. She might have to wake up her late-sleeping sister if it came to that.

"Now, don't you feel better?" Rachel asked Sabine when she returned to the kitchen.

"Yes. You were right. I'm so used to dressing like that I don't always change the minute I get home. But I'm always so relieved when I do."

Rachel wore black leggings and a flowing, deep crimson T-shirt with a huge question mark graphic across the front. Mixed hammered silver and corded leather jewelry adorned her long, neck and wrists. She wore some sort of flat espadrilles that appeared they'd been purchased from the foreign village of origin a hundred years ago. Somehow, she managed to appear hippy-chic and elegant at the same time.

"Will you look at my girls? I almost wish your father could see the two of you together. Almost. It's such a shame he turned out to be such a rip-snorting disappointment, isn't it?" Mom's comment and question was a difficult one to address.

Rachel and Sabine shared a glance.

"Dad has disappointed us all, Mom. But he ruined your marriage and life together, so I know how frustrated you must be when we're here together as a family and he's not with us, and he's the only one to blame," Sabine agreed.

"Yep, Daddy turned out to be a real ass face, didn't he?"

Rachel added.

"Yes, indeed he did," Mom agreed.

"Alright, you two, no time like the present to hash this out. Dad's parole hearing is next Thursday. Dad has requested/insisted that we all be present and put on a happy family face. I know we all think he's a huge turd, but he's going to get out of prison eventually. He can make our lives pretty miserable if we don't do what he wants; y'all know that, right?"

Sabine didn't like the looks on their faces, so she didn't wait for a response and kept talking. "I think we should go to the prison, appeal to the parole board on his behalf, and leave the chips to fall where they might. We will have done our part and he can't say we didn't. If he gets paroled, he'll be grateful and, hopefully, will do as we ask and not cause a ruckus in our lives moving forward."

"What if it doesn't work?" Rachel asked, her expression skeptical.

"If he doesn't get paroled this go-round, then it won't be because we didn't give it our best shot. That way, he won't hold a grudge. It's the last thing we all need. Mom and I are both trying to make big, obvious steps to move on. He's going to see that and, hopefully, not try and cause a problem."

"Sabine is probably right. We should suck it up and go over and support him in trying to gain his release. He's going to be free eventually. Might as well get it over with. I don't want to live my life wondering when that's going to be," Mom said.

"I just can't even look at him yet," Rachel said. "I'm still so disgusted by his behavior with those other women and how he treated Mom that he makes my skin crawl. Not to mention what he put our family through during his freak-show circus trial."

"That's why we've been hiding out here. It's also why we should support him. To keep him and James from telling the press where we are. It's going to hurt Sabine if the community finds out who she really is. They'll feel betrayed because she's held their confidence for two years. There are so many here who are vulnerable because they've entrusted their deepest secrets and fears to her alone."

Rachel sighed, a long, put-upon sigh. "Fine. I'll do it. But I won't promise to pretend like I forgive him, because I don't. I may never. He was our daddy. I trusted him with my whole heart. I idolized and worshipped him. I believed he did good work and put bad people in prison. I thought he was honest and true to our family—to our mother. He ripped my world apart. Sabine, you were a little older. But I was still starry-eyed about him. I believed in him and I fought the things they said about him. I *defended* him when the accusations came out." A single tear tracked down Rachel's cheek.

"Oh, honey." Mom gathered her up tight. "He did this to us all. You were the most vulnerable because you'd been so kept from the fray."

"I trusted him," Rachel said. "But I'll never trust him again—or forgive what he did to our family."

"You were his favorite. I have a feeling your being there is going to impact him the most. So, whatever you do, don't let him see this anger. I know it's going to be hard, but it will set him off. His ego is still his greatest Achilles' heel, and in many ways he still believes he should be vindicated," Sabine said. She understood, intellectually at least, that Rachel was her father's favorite. It had always stung, but it had been easier to distance herself when it had all hit the fan. Rachel hadn't been so lucky. She'd been devastated.

"Our solidarity will be our strength. It won't be easy, but when it's over, we can come home, here to Ministry, and we'll still have each other for support," Mom said.

The girls nodded. "Okay. I'll do it. So, while you're both here, I guess I should tell you that I'm going to be around for a little while, if that's okay."

"Of course that's okay; in fact, it's better than okay. But you don't sound especially thrilled about it. Is everything alright?" Mom asked.

"Okay is a relative term, I guess. I've been living in an apartment with my friend, Cheryl, just outside of Baton Rouge, keeping a low profile, kind of like the two of you. But every time I run into someone I know, either from college or from home, I have to answer a ton of questions about Daddy and our family. It's like reliving the whole nightmare all over, every time." Baton Rouge was close enough to New Orleans that it made sense Rachel might run into people she knew. Plus, many of her friends from home had attended LSU, and after graduation had stayed in the Baton Rouge area.

"Well, we're all about moving on with our lives over here. So, join the party. Were you seeing anyone in Louisiana?" Sabine asked.

"Nah. I've got some personal commitment issues that are tough to work around right now. Like, I can't commit to more than a single date with one person."

"Wow, sounds like you and Ben would have gotten along great." Sabine laughed.

"Until he found your sister. Now, he's a changed man— can't seem to get enough," Mom said.

"*Mom.*" Sabine scolded their mother for her bold words regarding her relationship. "Do you think you have room to talk? I actually caught you in bed with Norman. A daughter can't unsee that, you know."

"Both of you are creeping me out right now." Rachel covered her ears. "Can you imagine what pictures your words have placed in my mind right now? I'm going to have nightmares."

The three laughed together. "So, Mom, we haven't discussed your new man yet. Tell me about Norman." Then she held up both hands as if to ward off evil. "I mean, tell me about him as a person, not anything about him sexually or how he looks naked. Just getting that straight before you begin."

"Don't be silly, honey. Of course I wouldn't share any of our personal details. Though he does have a cute little dimple, right on his—"

"*Mom.*" Both girls chorused.

"Okay, fine. I was only kidding. He's the kindest, most sensible and loving man I've ever known. He's been a widower for seven years now. His wife died of cancer, poor dear. He's got one son, who is Ben's twin sister's husband."

"Nothing like a small town, huh?" Rachel said. "Norman sounds terrific. Does Dad know you're dating?"

Mom's face fell. "No. He doesn't. And I don't want him to until his parole is settled and he's released from prison. I want to move on with my life with as little drama as possible from your father."

"Well, I'm not going to tell him if that's what you're worried about. I'm glad you've found someone who makes you happy and floats your boat in bed."

Mom giggled. "Oh, he does."

"But I still don't want to hear about that." Rachel made a face.

"Fine, but you should find someone who makes you feel like I do with Norman. Then you'd want to share all your juicy details too."

"Like I said, I can't find someone I like or trust enough to hold the door for me, much less spend time with. I'll just blame Dad for that and move on."

"For sure we've got reason for serious 'daddy issues,'" Sabine said, only half-joking.

But it wasn't a joke. She figured she'd put up with Richard's poor treatment of her far too long due to her own unresolved issues stemming from their father's bizarre parenting that left a hole Richard filled at the right time and place. She'd met him when they were in high school. He was ridiculously good-looking, with such confidence and a bright future. They'd shared his bright future. Both had pursued advanced degrees at Tulane, she in psychology and counseling, he in law.

But his *saving* of her had been what she'd most been attracted to. Even in high school and college, Sabine held resentment toward her father because of James's shenanigans and Dad's lack of willingness to put his foot down. Richard had stepped in as her supporter and protector.

To say that Richard had always been untrustworthy or bad wasn't true. He'd lost his way somewhere on their life's journey together. She couldn't and didn't hate him, but he'd changed so much that Sabine simply didn't recognize him as the man she loved and would certainly never trust him again after he'd so carelessly and blatantly abused her loyalty and their vows to one another. It was a broken thing that couldn't be fixed. Just like her parents' marriage.

The snapping of fingers in front of her face brought her back to the present. Sabine's head snapped up, and her eyes refocused.

"Hello? Earth to Sabine. Looked like you were in a trance," Rachel said.

Sabine shook her head. "Just thinking about Richard and how much he's changed since we met."

"Maybe he's changed and maybe you're just seeing him in a clearer light. He was who you wanted him to be for a long, long time, in my opinion," Rachel said.

Of course, Rachel hadn't ever hidden her opinion of Richard.

"Why didn't you like Richard early on, Rach?" Sabine finally found the courage to ask the question.

Rachel shrugged. "He creeped me out, even as a teen."

Something stirred up Sabine's spidey senses about the way Rachel didn't meet her eyes. "Did he ever touch you or hit on you inappropriately when we were young?"

Rachel shrugged again, clearly not wanting to have this conversation. "Look, Sabine, nothing happened. There's no sense in dragging all this up now."

Sabine heard Mom's swift intake of breath. "Did Richard *do* something, Rachel? Something you didn't tell your sister or me about?"

"Look, it was no big deal. Guys are shits. Richard was more of a shit than normal. He made a play for me when I was in high school. Maybe it was eighth grade. I don't remember. But I kicked him in the 'nads and threatened to tell you if he ever tried it again. He never did, so I pretended it never happened."

Sabine was shaking. She covered her face with her hands. How could she have misjudged Richard so completely? Clearly his perversions had begun well before and gone far beyond her catching him during their marriage.

"Honey, you know this isn't your fault. Richard's wrongs don't lie on your shoulders." Her mother moved close and laid a hand on her shoulder.

"But she's my sister—my baby sister. He tried to abuse her and I didn't protect her from him. Was I ignoring a problem that was right in front of my face all along? Were there signs? How many other young girls did he prey upon who were innocent? I mean, they're all innocent, aren't they? They're children, for heaven's sake."

"You told me he cheated with prostitutes. Were they underage?" Rachel asked.

"I'm—not sure. I have a video as insurance in case he refused to give me a divorce, but I've never looked at it. I was told the girls were young, but no one mentioned they were below the age of consent. I was so upset that he'd done such a terrible thing that I stuffed it away and didn't consider the other possibilities, like his being a true predator to young girls."

"He can't be allowed to walk free from this. I imagine there are plenty other girls out there who Richard has made advances toward. If you have a video, it would prove whether the girls were young, certainly it would give us some idea *how* young," Rachel said.

"I don't think I have the stomach to watch it," Sabine said.

"I do. And I'll bet your lawyer boyfriend does," Rachel said.

"Richard will still expose me as a liar and bring the media circus to town if I threaten him with this. In fact, it will be even worse if what he's done is found out. It will seem as if I've condoned it."

"How about this? You go tomorrow with Ben and do your best to get the divorce. Act like you don't know anything about his being a pervert and try to get your papers signed."

"But how can I stand up and endorse him at a public fundraiser knowing what I do about him?"

"You can't if we find out he's been with underage girls. But you can go and try to get his signature on divorce papers before this blows up. And you can call it part of your plan to bring him down. Get the divorce first," Rachel said. "Otherwise, if it all hits the fan, it may be impossible to avoid being blamed for turning a blind eye if you're still his wife. And then, it may take forever to get the process completed if he's tied up in court should this all come out in the meantime. I guarantee it will come out eventually. Best to be as legally and physically far away from Richard as possible when it all happens."

"Shouldn't you tell Ben about this, honey? He should

know what the two of you are getting in to. The stakes have risen significantly, haven't they? And Richard's staff must know about some of the things he has done, and if the prostitutes were underage. Does Richard know you have a recording of his—activities?" Mom asked.

The light went on in Sabine's foggy brain. "Yes. I believe that's what has kept him away while I've been gone all this time. That makes more sense, now that I realize those girls might likely be below legal age of consent. It makes what he did a felony, instead of just a huge political hit and a fault in divorce." She thought for a moment. "Yes. I'll let Ben know as soon as we're sure." Sabine winced, still certain she didn't have the stomach to watch the video.

"Might you be walking into a trap?" Mom asked, clearly concerned.

"I didn't think so, but now I'm getting a little paranoid," Sabine said.

"Just don't go anywhere without Ben," Rachel said.

"The only place I'll be without him is while I'm actually speaking with Richard and his attorneys about the divorce, and when I'm inside the governor's ball. But he'll be right outside waiting. And we're going to be wired with listening devices that Howard is providing. Ben's posing as my driver while I'm in New Orleans."

Mom laughed. "What a fantastic idea. It gives him a legitimate reason to be at your beck and call constantly the entire time."

"Who's Howard?" Rachel asked.

"He's Ben's new stepfather. Retired spy of some sort, but he doesn't tell anyone specifically what sort of work he did for the government. Very highly classified stuff, we're led to understand," Sabine said.

"Sounds suspenseful. Can't wait to meet him, and I'm thrilled he's on your team," Rachel said. "So, when do I get to meet the new men in your lives?" She looked back and forth between Sabine and Mom.

"Well, you'll be around for a while, so I can't imagine you won't see Norman within the next day or so. And Ben is picking up Sabine in the morning. But you'll need to get up early, or you'll miss them," Mom said.

"I'll be up; don't worry. I'm not planning to let Sabine leave with this guy without my stamp of approval. Especially knowing what we do now about Richard. Of course, I've known all along, but I thought it might have been just a fluke. By the way, Sabine, do you have the video here of Richard doing the bad things?" Rachel asked.

Sabine frowned. She wasn't entirely certain she was ready for this. Not that she still loved Richard, but it was all so sudden and unexpected. But she supposed it was necessary.

She stood. "I'll get it. It's on a memory stick, so we'll need a computer to play it."

"And we'll need to make a few copies, just in case," Rachel said. "Do you have any other sticks or discs lying around that we can use? Or we can just upload it onto the cloud."

"I'll bring my computer. I've got plenty of storage," Sabine said as she headed toward her bedroom where the device and her laptop were stored.

"I've got a USB stick too that I haven't used. I was going to store some recipes on it," Sabine heard Mom say.

Chapter Fourteen

HOWARD LED BEN upstairs to the small study he'd remember his father using when he'd been a child. Beside the fireplace, Howard pulled out a book and pressed a button. A panel literally slid open. Ben blinked. "What the—"

"We're family son; I'm showing you this in case anything ever happens to me. You'll know it's here. The contents of this room aren't to be shown to anyone. I'll leave a contact in the event of my demise."

"The contents of the room—oh." Ben had stepped inside behind Howard as he'd been speaking. The *contents* were right out of a James Bond movie. Everything was carefully displayed. Guns of every size and caliber, and devices that Ben didn't recognize.

"These items are mine, but some are still considered on the low level of classification. Upon my discretion, I can reveal the contents to you. I trust you. But I ask that you not show these items to others as it might cause mild worry to those who don't understand."

Ben again wondered at Howard's life of espionage and who knew what else. "I hope you're writing your memoirs."

"Might do it one day, son. Might do it. Would have to be a PG version with lots of information left out, and certainly anonymous. Wouldn't want to put the family in danger, you know."

Ben chuckled. He honestly loved his new stepdad. "So, what have you got for us?"

"Wires. And earpieces. You can never have too much information. I've put out my feelers for the senator's activities, so I should get something back tomorrow or the next day."

"Do you really think there's more here than meets the eye?" Ben asked.

Howard gave him a deadpan look. "There's always more with politicians, son. Never met one I could trust, or who didn't have a cold, dirty underbelly."

"Okay. So, tell me how to use this stuff. Oh, and one more thing, Howard…"

"What's that, son?"

"I'll need two more sets of wires and earpieces if you have them."

"Sure thing." He reached into the cabinet and grabbed more supplies. "You got backup for the trip?"

Ben nodded. "Sabine doesn't know about them though."

"Boy after my own heart. She won't hear it from me."

Howard went into professional spy versus spy mode and

showed him all the ins and outs of the equipment they would have for their trip.

When Ben was downstairs ready to leave, Mom came out to see him off. "Hi, honey. Do you want anything to eat before you leave?"

"No, thanks, Mom. I need to get home and do some packing for the trip. I've got some last-minute paperwork on one of my cases to finish up too. It's tough to carve out being gone for a couple days."

"I know how busy you always are, so I can only imagine."

Ben turned to Howard. "Thanks for everything, Howard. I appreciate your help."

Howard nodded. "I'll be in touch as soon as I get that information from my source."

"Be careful, okay?" Mom said.

He hugged his mother. "I promise. We'll be back before you know it."

"Oh, and Ben—take care of our girl."

Ben smiled at his mother's reference to Sabine. "You can count on it."

As he drove away from Evangeline House, he called Steve and Lisa. They were all set as well. He planned to stop by and share the equipment with them so they would all be on the same page.

"OH, HI, YOU must be Rachel. I'm here to pick up Sabine." Rachel answered the door the next morning on purpose when Ben arrived.

She'd been looking for him to drive up while Sabine was gathering her things to leave.

"Well, hello there, Ben. I've heard a lot about you. Yes, I'm Sabine's sister, Rachel. Great to meet you." Rachel stuck out her hand for Ben to shake.

He seemed genuinely glad to meet her but his eyes showed no gleam of interest in her as a woman. Rachel breathed a sigh of relief. Ben had passed the test. If Ben had shown even the slightest attraction to her, she'd have likely punched him in the nose at this point, so great was her disgust and distaste with men, in general.

"Sabine, Ben's here," she called.

After watching that god-awful video of Richard with those obviously underage prostitutes last night, Rachel wondered if she could ever truly trust a man again. Richard was so much viler than even she'd believed him to be. And he'd been elected to represent a large portion of Louisiana's citizens' interests in the state senate in all means of issues, from education to laws protecting innocent children from being exploited. It made her sick.

Rachel would personally take Richard down if all else failed. She could certainly come forward and prevent his reelection with her story. Because it was worse than she'd told her mother and sister. How could she have known he was more than just a drunk asshole when that had happened? And she'd been really young back then and believed no one would really take her seriously. Now she knew better.

"So, will you be here when we get home?" Ben asked.

"Seems so. I'm planning to hang with my family for a while. I hear we've got a parole hearing to attend next week."

Ben nodded. "Hopefully this trip will go well first."

"Yeah. Richard's a real piece of work. Sabine'll have to fill you in on what we figured out last night."

Ben raised his eyebrows in question just as Sabine entered the room.

—⟫⟪—

"Good morning." Sabine rolled in a carry-on sized suitcase and a large duffel bag slung over her shoulder.

As usual, she blew him away with her beauty and sex appeal. Her sister, Rachel was pretty, and there was a strong family resemblance, but Sabine outshone Rachel in Ben's eyes.

He took the luggage from her, and asked, "Anything else?"

"Just my purse and laptop case," Sabine said.

"Rachel tells me y'all found out some new info on Richard last night?" he asked.

Sabine suddenly looked ill. "You told him?" She didn't sound happy with her sister.

"I didn't tell him what it was. I figured you would fill

him in on the way." Rachel shrugged, her body language slightly defensive.

Ben knew body language. Something serious was happening here.

"Okay. We'll get on the road and discuss it. Rachel, it was great to meet you. We'll be in close contact while we're away. Try not to worry," Ben said.

"Where's Mom?" Sabine asked, looking around.

"I'm here." Elizabeth came in, sleepy-eyed, in her navy robe and slippers. "Sorry, darling; I overslept."

"No problem. I just wanted to say goodbye before we left," Sabine said.

"Please be careful, and keep us posted as often as possible. I won't sleep a wink if I don't know what's happening."

"Of course we'll keep you updated. Love you, Mom. We'll be fine," Sabine reassured her mother.

Elizabeth looked over at Ben. "These two are my whole life, so you've got half my life right there, you understand."

"I understand."

"Thank you for going with her on this trip. I don't trust Richard, especially now, the bastard."

"He doesn't know about it yet," Sabine said.

Elizabeth frowned, but didn't say anything else, though it appeared she wanted to.

"Do you have your cell phone charger?" Ben asked.

"Got it." Sabine nodded.

"Okay, then I think we're all set."

Sabine hugged her mom and sister and said another round of goodbyes before they finally settled the luggage into his truck and climbed inside.

"Did you think we wouldn't ever get to leave?" Sabine asked once they were finally driving away.

"I figured we'd make it out of there eventually." He understood how it was with family. "Do you recall how many sisters I have? So, times your situation by four, plus a mom. I can't get anything accomplished unless I plan two hours ahead of time when they're around."

She laughed. "Oh, yeah. I wasn't thinking about that. At least you're used to it."

"So, are you going to tell me what this new, earth-shattering information regarding Richard is, or am I going to have to call your mom and sister to get it?"

Sabine looked away for a second. Clearly this wasn't something she looked forward to sharing with him. "Remember the prostitutes I found out about?"

Ben nodded.

"They were underage. Richard is a predator of young girls."

Ben wasn't surprised. He'd seen it so much in his line of work. So often, sex workers were young women who'd gotten manipulated into the business as young, desperate girls, or worse, forced into it. "I would like to say that I'm shocked. But I'm not, Sabine."

"I just didn't give it much thought. Maybe I didn't want

to think of it beyond his cheating on me. The whole idea that he would buy into that world when he is supposed to be making and supporting legislation to protect women and children. It's so disgusting."

"I get the feeling there's more to this."

"There's a video to support our claims. My dad sent it to me as insurance in case I ever needed it. I've had it in my possession but haven't ever watched it. That's how we found out the girls were—young. Also, Rachel admitted that Richard accosted her when she was in high school."

There were tears in Sabine's eyes now.

"You couldn't have known or prevented that, Sabine. You understand that, don't you?"

"She's my little sister and she never breathed a word. I should have known what sort of man my own husband was."

"That's the thing about predators. They are insidious. They play upon emotions and weaknesses. So often a predator can fly under the radar for *years* without anyone being the wiser. They seem to understand how to buy and manipulate silence from others. Getting what they desire is their only game. In your line of work, you see the victims and deal with the consequences of the predators' actions. I see the predators firsthand and, sometimes, I'm asked to defend them. I don't take those cases. But I've seen them and, in the past, I've prosecuted them. They are scary, conscienceless people."

"What should we do about Richard, now that we know?"

"Well, other than get your divorce, we should bring him down."

"How can we do that without bringing me down too? I mean, when high profile wives stay with men who do these things, they get blamed for turning a blind eye and nobody believes they didn't know.'"

"We might need help with this. Would you be willing to allow me to add a few members to the team?" Of course, he already had, and the guilt was killing him.

"No. Not now. We can do this without bringing anyone else into it. We already have the proof we need to start the process once we get home. I just want to get him to sign off on divorce papers, and I know going there and doing what he's asked will be the only way he'll agree to it."

"Okay. Hopefully, we'll get in and out, and all will go as planned. At least no one knows where we're staying. The car will be waiting at the B&B."

"Where are we staying?"

"A little bed and breakfast uptown on Napoleon owned by a sweet couple named Mr. and Mrs. Bergeron."

"Is that the one right down the street from Pascal's Manale?" Sabine had lived her entire life in New Orleans, so it made perfect sense she would know the city like the back of her hand.

"Yes. I've heard of the restaurant. Famous for its barbecued shrimp, right?" Ben had been told many times by friends and colleagues that he should check out Pascal's

Manale next time he was in New Orleans. "Maybe we can slip over there for dinner this evening. I'll wear my uniform in case someone sees us. They'll think you're sharing dinner with your driver."

"An unusual situation to be sure. But not completely unbelievable if one is alone in town. Especially if one's driver is as handsome as you."

"The bed and breakfast was recommended to me by an attorney friend who lives in North Louisiana."

"Oh, and who might that be? It could be we are acquainted. Not likely, but possible."

"Tanner Carmichael. He's from Cypress Bayou, I believe, or somewhere thereabout. We met at a legal conference a few years ago and have kept in touch. He's a good guy. Says the Bergerons are the souls of discretion and personal friends of his family."

"Hmm. I don't recognize that name, but unless we've crossed paths in New Orleans, it's likely I wouldn't. Weirdly, Louisiana is somewhat like a big small town in some ways. Lots of connections. Everybody seems to know somebody that somebody else does."

Ministry was close to a six-hour drive to New Orleans, so it was a fairly easy weekend destination for those Alabamans wanting a change of scenery. So, over the years, it was logical that business and personal connections had been made.

Ben thought they'd been pretty lucky that neither Sabine nor her mother had been recognized by anyone yet. He'd looked up photos from the trial and from Google and noticed that she'd changed her appearance substantially just by growing out her hair. Before, she'd kept it in a short, pixie style that was flattering to her face, but Ben loved her long, thick hair. He especially loved running his fingers through it when they were both naked in his bed. He sneaked a glance over at her.

"Are you having sexy thoughts about me?" Sabine asked.

"Maybe. It's been several days, you know. And we'll be in a bed and breakfast together. I've gotten two rooms in case we get busted by Richard, but that doesn't mean I can't check on you at bedtime, does it?"

Sabine's sexy grin made him shift uncomfortably in his seat. "I might allow a room check."

"You're killing me, sexy woman. We've got four more hours to go. Might as well talk turkey on the wires and listening devices Howard gave us." He spent the next hour sharing his newfound expertise on spy gear with Sabine.

⇒⟫⟫⟪⟪⇐

SABINE OPENED HER eyes as they were pulling in to a driveway. "Oh. Did I fall asleep?"

"Only three hours ago," Ben said.

"What? No way." She looked at the clock on the dash. It read 4:15. They'd left just after ten this morning. Ben had stopped three hours into the trip to gas up and they'd grabbed a cup of coffee and a snack. Now, her bladder was protesting. Time to find the nearest bathroom.

As they parked and climbed out of the truck, Sabine noticed an elderly couple approaching them. The woman was dressed in a colorful muumuu with leggings and a wide headband. She was a head under five feet for certain and had crackling blue eyes. "Well, Mr. B, here they are. We've been waiting for you."

Ben and Sabine looked at one another, wondering if maybe she was mistaken.

"You *are* Ben Laroux and Sabine O'Connor, are you not?" the woman asked.

"Yes. That's us."

"Well. Welcome. You come with the blessing of our dear friend, Tanner Carmichael. That means you might as well be family, isn't that right, Mr. B?"

"Eh?" The old man perked up.

"I said, 'Any friend of Tanner's is just like family to us, am I right?'" She nearly yelled at the poor guy, who clearly either was hard of hearing or was selectively so.

"Just call me Miz B, short for Bergeron, you know. We open our bed and breakfast for select guests now. Not everyone and not all the time. We've had our regulars for over fifty years."

"It's very kind of you to take our reservation. Your home is lovely," Sabine said.

And it was. It was a large, well-maintained uptown mansion. The uptown section of New Orleans on Napoleon

Avenue was graced with great, old painted historic homes that had seen a hundred years of humidity and hurricanes.

The lovely old homes were shaded by even older oak trees. The Bergeron's home had extensive porches that stretched across the front and sides on all three levels. Ceiling fans turned lazily with the breeze. Lush ferns hung from iron hooks at intervals, adding to the welcoming and cozy atmosphere. Sabine breathed a sigh of relief. This house so reminded her of the house where she grew up several blocks over in the Garden District.

Sabine looked around, her beloved city unchanged in the two years she'd been away. It had been her home since birth and, even now, the familiarity seeped into her soul. The sidewalks, uneven from the tree roots growing through them and the shifting soil. New Orleans was below sea level and, over the decades, the ground accommodated the floods and moist earth. The humidity hung around them, even though it wasn't especially hot. The mighty Mississippi River powered its way through the city, only a couple blocks from where they stood.

While Sabine recognized this as her home, she already missed the life she'd built in Alabama. How could it be that a lifetime here had been supplanted so easily? Even as she'd tried to minimize her place in Ministry, Sabine realized now that it had become her home. Falling in love with the town and its people hadn't been part of her plan. It had begun as a temporary place to hide and work while her life quieted down.

Now that she was back here, it gave her perspective and understanding. And it raised the stakes for returning to Alabama permanently. She couldn't let anyone screw it up for her or her mother. There wasn't a doubt that Mom intended to stay with Norman, and Norman was a permanent resident of Ministry. The worst possible thing to happen would be bringing their dirty laundry and past embarrassment to town.

Sabine wasn't sure what Rachel intended but, hopefully, she would also consider making her home with them. They all assumed Dad would return to New Orleans and pick up the pieces of his life. He knew plenty of people and was a very socially active man. Women clearly loved him, so he should land on his feet in no time.

Who was she kidding? Dad would be a problem for them. He would want to intrude on their quiet lives in Ministry and be in the mix. How that worked for Mom, Sabine had no idea. She figured it was a wait and see deal. People divorced after lifetimes together all the time and worked these things out. They would find a way to co-exist somehow. And Dad would have to get used to the idea that Mom had found Norman, and that Norman wasn't going away.

"Dear, can we have your luggage brought to your room?" Mrs. Bergeron's melodic voice broke into her thoughts.

"Oh. Sure." Sabine turned toward Ben, who was already

taking the bags from the truck.

"Why don't we let Clive do that? It's what we pay him for, after all," the woman said. Sabine looked beyond her and noticed a graying black man who was at least six feet tall, but probably nearing ninety.

Clive stepped up to take the bags from Ben, who appeared horrified to give the job to such an elderly gentleman. "No, sir. I can get them," Ben said in a kind voice.

But Clive wasn't to be dissuaded. "Sir, I've been a bellman for going on sixty-five years. I might look a feeble old man, but I've got the strength of an ox." He laughed then, like rocks rolling around in a tin can, his grin revealing a perfect set of dentures.

Ben stepped back, sizing up the older man and, clearly not wanting to disrespect his position, handed over the two small bags. "Yes, sir. Thanks for your assistance."

They all entered the bed and breakfast together. Mrs. B gestured for them to meet her at the small counter. "I've prepared the honeymoon suite, since it's our largest room, dears."

"Oh, we requested two rooms," Ben said.

Mrs. Bergeron wrinkled her brow. "Well, I'm sure I don't see that here on my book." But her eyes twinkled when she looked up. "It doesn't appear that I have anything else available, at the moment."

Sabine wasn't sure how to handle this woman. Clearly she was matchmaking and interfering, but why? She didn't even know them.

Sabine and Ben shared a glance. "We'll gladly take the honeymoon suite. But if it's all the same to you, we'd appreciate you not letting anyone know we're here if they come asking."

Mrs. Bergeron blinked, her large, round eyes resembling an owl. "Of course not, honey. What goes on upstairs isn't anyone's business but ours. And yours, of course."

"We appreciate your understanding. There are some, uh, delicate matters we're attending to while we're in town," Ben said.

"Ooooh. Well, believe you me, we are the souls of discretion. This isn't our first top secret rodeo, is it Mr. B?"

"Eh?" The old man tuned his hearing aid and everyone cringed at the high-pitched squeal.

Mrs. B rolled her eyes. "I'll show you to your room." As the stairs creaked under the woman's weight, and her bones creaked at the significant effort, she turned and said, "Oh, and you can pull your car around to the back of the house if you don't want anyone to see where you've gone." She winked. "That's very unusual here, you know. Most folks have to park on the street."

"I grew up here, so I can appreciate you having parking off the street. We're going to have another car to drive in town, so that will be very helpful," Sabine said.

"Our friend, Tanner, communicated that you might have some special circumstances you might need accommodation for," Mrs. B said.

"I shared with him that I was coming here and was looking for a place to stay just like yours. It seems he knew exactly what I was looking for."

Sabine shot Ben a sideways look. "Did you tell your buddy, Tanner, *everything*?"

"No. Just that we were in a sensitive situation and required a small, discreet, and out-of-the-way housing situation. He's had some real interesting cases and personal family situations, so I figured he would be our best bet for local information."

They'd made it up to the top floor and were waiting for Mrs. B to unlock the door. No keypads or beeping cards. Real keys and locks here. When the heavy door opened, the woman stood aside for them to enter. Sabine sighed appreciatively. It was lovely—gorgeous even. The honeymoon suite was a suite that extended the entire top floor of the home. The ceilings were high, and ceiling fans hung from long poles. The dark wood floors shone and smelled of beeswax. The furniture was comfortable, with several pieces covered in muted florals, stripes, and solids, if a bit oversized. There was a powder room and a sitting area, along with a tiny kitchenette.

"It's lovely," Sabine said.

"The bedroom and master bath is through here." The bed seemed gigantic, with its four posts. She'd have to take a running leap just to be able to get up there; it was so high off the floor.

The bathroom was small, but well-appointed. It still maintained the architecture of the old home, but allowed for more modern plumbing features.

"This is perfect. Thanks for allowing us to use the suite," Ben said.

"I know you'll make the best use of your time here." Mrs. Bergeron grinned. "Well, it looks like Clive has brought your things up, so I'll clear out of here and let you freshen up before dinner. Have you made plans this evening?"

"We discussed taking a walk down the street to Pascal's Manale for barbecue shrimp," Sabine said.

"I highly recommend it. They've been in business as long as we have on this street." The woman nodded her approval. "How about I give them a call and let them know you'll be along, say, around six thirty, seven?"

"That would be fantastic. Thanks so much," Ben said, and looked at Sabine, who nodded her agreement.

They'd walked to the exterior door of the suite. "Toodles, dears."

Ben shut the door behind the woman. "Toodles?"

Sabine giggled. "Remind me to send your buddy, Tanner, a fruit basket. Possibly with a snake inside. Just kidding. What a colorful couple. This place is fantastic. I can't decide if it's going to be a terrific place to stay or a nightmare. It feels a bit like a surreal horror movie on the one hand—like we've just been lured in and it's too good to be true. Very strange."

Ben laughed at her. "Watching too many weird movies lately?"

"No. Just having a hard time relaxing."

"I saw something in the room next door that might help." He took her hand and led her through to the bedroom with the Fred Flintstone bed.

"I don't think I've ever seen a bed quite this big."

"I like having a lot of surface space to work with." He picked her up before she had the chance to react, and she squealed.

Then, he dumped her on top of the very large and very soft surface space, where he joined her with his big, hard body that made her forget all the things she'd been worrying and obsessing about since they'd left Ministry.

"So, we've got a couple hours before dinner, huh?" he asked, while finding a very sensitive spot on her neck with his lips.

A tingle shot through Sabine. "Ah. Seems so. Any ideas on what to do? Should we nap?"

"Mmm. Nap? I'm not especially sleepy." He kicked off his shoes and they thudded onto the floor. "But I do like the idea of staying horizontal for awhile."

She tried to catch her breath as his magical fingers found the clasp of her bra. "I like that idea too." Sabine grinned at him. "But what shall we do for two whole hours?"

"Let me show you."

The giant bed was littered with their clothing and their bodies within seconds. Thankfully, the windows had shades, and those shades were currently in the down position.

And, even more thankfully, the bed was sturdy and didn't squeak, because Ben Laroux wasn't a small man, and he wasn't a quiet or still man. In fact, Sabine would describe his lovemaking as rather athletic in nature, which suited her fine in this particular instance. A little jungle sex between two consenting adults fit the bill today. The old house likely had thick walls. So, it was all good.

Very good. Twice.

"Shower. I need a shower," Sabine said, finally.

She was a puddle. A completely sated and sweaty puddle.

Ben was lying under the covers, grinning, as she stood. There was nothing to reach for to cover with, as they'd not even bothered to open suitcases yet.

"Don't mind me," he said, clearly fine with her crossing the room stark naked.

"You're an animal."

"But you liked it." She tossed a pillow at his self-satisfied smirk just before streaking into the adjoining bath. "Looking good." Sabine heard him say just before she closed the bathroom door.

She couldn't help smiling. He made her happy. Yes, happy. No matter how terrible Richard was on this trip, Ben would be right here with her, and it would be okay.

Richard couldn't actually *do* anything to her, could he?

No, of course he couldn't. She was safe. Sabine stepped into the shower and let the hot shower cleanse her worries away.

"You gonna leave me a little hot water?" Ben's face peeking inside the shower nearly made Sabine scream bloody murder.

She threw the bar of soap at him. "You asshole. You scared me to death."

"You've been in here twenty minutes."

"So? I'm not done yet. I'll let you know when I am." She pulled the curtain shut.

He shut the bathroom door. Sabine realized he was used to fighting for the bathroom with his sisters, so he likely did get cold showers pretty often throughout his lifetime. She smiled again. He was also just as likely used to not getting his way all the time.

⟫⟩⟨⟪

THEY ENCOUNTERED THE Bergerons once they'd arrived downstairs on their way out to dinner. "Oh, don't they look beautiful together?" Mrs. B said to Mr. B.

"Eh?" Mr. B asked, and adjusted his hearing aid.

"I said they're a nice-looking couple," she nearly yelled.

"Why, yes they are. You don't have to blow out my eardrums, dear," Mr. B answered.

"Pascal's has your reservation. It's about three blocks left out of here toward St. Charles Avenue. If you went the other way, you'd cross Magazine Street and head toward the river."

"Thanks so much, Mrs. Bergeron; we appreciate your help," Ben said.

"Oh, and dear, you might want to bring a light sweater. The air conditioning in Pascal's can be a little tricky," she said to Sabine, who wore a lightweight jersey knit dress with three-quarter length sleeves.

Sabine nodded. "I'll run up and get one." She did tend to get cold in restaurants and hotels. Sabine glanced at Ben. "I'll be right back."

"I have a quick phone call to make, so I'll meet you outside," Ben said.

He walked out the front door and headed toward the parking area the Bergerons had indicated earlier, should they need it. They would need it as a precaution. Ben dialed the number of the car rental.

He had to let them know they were in town and where to bring the car. Some of the lengths they were going to felt a little silly but, overkill or not, these precautions might make all the difference in how this trip turned out for Sabine.

"Yes. Please leave the key at the front desk in an envelope with my name on it. Thanks. You have my number; text me in case you need to reach me." Ben hung up.

Howard had contacted this company, as they'd used them locally before he'd retired when he'd had official business in the Greater New Orleans area. He said they were trustworthy and discreet.

Sabine came outside then, and he brought her around to

the parking area in back. "I wouldn't have even known this was here," she said. "It's like they have an extra lot just for parking, but it's made to look like part of the house and landscaping."

The driveway curved around back, and it appeared the house was larger on one side than it actually was. But the wall cleverly hid the parking area. It might have been added to trick the city to prevent code violations for the B&B's business. Parking in this area was so limited and sought after; this solution was nothing short of brilliant. The thick vegetation and tree coverage on the sides and in back helped to hide any odd visual imbalances from the addition of the wall extension.

"Should be a perfect place to park. I just spoke to the car service, and they will deliver while we're at dinner."

"Sounds good. Are you ready? I'm starving." As if to punctuate her words, Sabine's stomach growled noisily at that moment.

"Well, let's get you to the restaurant. I'd like to think I helped you work up that appetite." He grinned at her.

Sabine blushed. "A real gentleman wouldn't point that out, you know."

"Ah, but it's so much fun to ruffle your feathers. You always have such a perfectly intact facade. I love it when you go all human and flawed on me."

"I'm human and flawed all the time," Sabine protested.

"But you're very buttoned up and proper most of the

time. You don't let your hair down much, or let your 'freak flag' fly often. Except where sex is concerned. Then, of course, I consider myself a very lucky man."

Sabine sighed as they strolled toward the restaurant hand in hand. "Well, I guess that's true enough. I've always been a somewhat proper person, and worried about embarrassing my parents. Ha! Can you imagine? The whole family has ended up on the evening news. I guess I don't have to worry about my embarrassing family anymore—my father at least."

"I don't think you could do anything that would bring ruin on anyone."

"What if everyone in Ministry finds out who I am?" Sabine asked Ben.

Ben frowned. "I don't know. I really don't. Small towns are fickle sometimes. They judge, but mostly they protect their own. When Steve and Lisa got together, the entire town, I kid you not, pretty much shunned them. I was so hurt and angry that I was okay with that for awhile. But I realized later how unfair it was for an entire population to judge them, in favor of my hurt feelings, and make their lives miserable enough to make them leave their childhood home."

"That does sound harsh."

"To your point; I don't know if the town would judge you for keeping secrets and punish you for your father's or husband's sins, or pull you in and shun them for trying to hurt you—one of their own. And I don't know if it's worth the risk yet to try and sway public opinion to your side because it might backfire."

Ben hated to tell Sabine this now, but he'd seen Ministry do some good and do some pretty rotten deeds in mass public opinion.

"Group mentality is a tough thing. Nobody has to take individual responsibility for the actions of many," Sabine said. "So, if they hurt someone, no one has to face that alone."

"Exactly. Let's wait and see how this goes before we open all the confession cans of worms," he agreed.

Pascal's Manale, home of world famous barbecue shrimp, sat alongside the lovely homes of Napoleon Avenue. But as soon as one approached, there was no doubt they'd arrived someplace special. The rich buttery aroma likely pulled tourists off the streets day and night. It was completely impossible to resist following one's nose.

Inside the restaurant, they were shown to a cozy corner table. They laughed and talked together as if this trip were a romantic getaway instead of what it really was. It proved to be an opportunity for bonding and the two of them learning details about each other's lives.

"You did *not* let mice loose at your sisters' slumber party."

He nodded, grimacing at the memory. "I did. Emma and Maeve both have birthdays in January, and they share a lot of the same friends, so it was a tradition to celebrate together with a noisy, screamy, girl party. Of course, I was too young at the time to appreciate all that that entailed. So, I did what any irritating ten-year-old brother worth his bratty reputation might—I came up with ways to cause mayhem in the hen house."

"That was horrible." But Sabine doubled over with laughter despite her words.

"I felt sorry for the mice, quite frankly. They didn't deserve the violence directed their way. They were the true victims in the situation. But I admit I was to blame for any harm that befell them. But, really, they would have likely otherwise been food for reptiles and pet snakes had I not bought them from the pet store."

"Oh. I hadn't thought about that either. Did you have a cat in the house?" Sabine grimaced.

"Unfortunately for the poor creatures, we did." He shuddered. "An abysmally thought-out decision all around. I was grounded and put into my sisters' servitude for two weeks. My mom knew how to teach an effective lesson."

"I had cats too. James was abusive to them, so I had to keep them mostly locked in my room."

"He sounds like a real charmer."

Sabine rolled her eyes. "He's the same as when he was a child, only full-grown and good-looking enough to charm men and women into believing the things he tells them. He has zero conscience. But looking at him, you would never know. I feel sorry for anyone who gets mixed up with him."

"What's he involved in?" Ben asked.

"Who knows? Whatever he can get away with, most likely. Whatever pays the most money. Some legal and some illegal things. I know he's been on my dad's payroll since college. He doesn't really have an official job title that I know of, but then, I really try to stay as far away from James as possible. He only comes around when he wants to stir up trouble or my dad sends him as a messenger."

"Too bad. Family is important."

"He's not my family—not in any real way. He doesn't feel love or genuine emotions. He's not capable, unfortunately. He's like a cold-blooded reptile. Best not to forget that."

"Good to know. What about Rachel?"

"Rachel is great. She and I are very different, but we're close. She took our dad's fall from grace very hard. Rachel was a daddy's girl. She had blinders on when it came to him. She didn't see it coming, and didn't want to believe the charges and accusations, even when it was obvious they were legitimate."

"That makes it so much harder. The denial. I deal with it every day. Even when I'm defending a client of charges, it helps when the family understands the possibility of at least some of the charges sticking. Often, there is some wrongdoing or a degree of guilt that brings a case to court. Especially in family court. It's rare that one party is at zero fault."

"We certainly deal with two sides of the same coin don't we?" Sabine mused.

"Yep. I think it's why we understand each other so well. The burdens of others we carry affect us."

"And our own—burdens."

"Those too."

"I'm considering adopting a cat once I get settled. Do you have an issue with that?" Sabine grinned at him.

"None, whatsoever. I actually have a few feral rescue cats in my barn that I feed. They mostly handle the rats and other vermin, but they stay warm and dry. I have to warn you though; I'm a dog person. How would you feel about a big, lopey coon hound, or maybe a retriever? My sister, Emma has one named Big Al and he's the best dog ever."

"I'm familiar with Big Al and, yes, he's a love, but he's really *big*. I mean, I've seen him take Emma down, right off her high heels onto the floor."

Ben laughed. "Yep, that's Big Al for you. Emma allows him a bit too much exuberance, if you ask me but, heck, she's got to live with him. Well, I guess Matthew's got to live with him now too."

"Matthew's a good guy, and he seems to get along fine with Big Al." Sabine hadn't been around them a lot, but she'd seem them together walking the oversized blonde pup around town.

"You're welcome to come and meet my barn kitties any time," he said.

Sabine was interested in the fact that Ben housed feral cats. "Barn cats, huh? I'm not familiar with that concept, but

I guess I could go by and check them out." The idea that Ben rescued cats just added a tiny bit of soft padding to her already dopey feelings she was currently feeling during this discussion of their future animals.

"You dodged and avoided my dog question. Would you consider having a dog?"

Sabine thought for a moment on how to answer. "Dogs intimidate me just a little because they expect so much from their people *all* the time. I mean, there's no downtime with dogs. They're on a hundred percent besides when they sleep. They want to be fed, they want to play, or be held or petted."

"Uh, huh. Who else does that sound like?" Ben's expression made her face turn beet red.

Sabine was horrified that she'd just loosely described how full-time and needy children would be. "Oh. I didn't mean—well, this is embarrassing. You think I'm really afraid of putting that kind of time and effort into the commitment of having children. But I'm not, you see. I want children above all things."

"You do?" Ben's smile could have lit the entire room.

She nodded, but then her expression turned serious. "Do you?"

"More than anything. I want everyday, mundane homework, playtime at the park. I know it's what I want because I've been the outsider uncle helping out with it for a long time now. I'm ready to have it for myself. It's not especially sexy, I know, and who would have thought a single guy like me just wanted to be not single and saddled with a couple kids and a wife?"

Sabine laughed then. "I really had no idea this was your dream above all things. When I met you, I would have said you were living it then."

"Sabine, you have to know I'm crazy about you, and I want us to work so badly."

"I'm having pretty dreamy thoughts right now about you too, Ben. But, let's get through this trip before we make any life-changing decisions, okay? It's so much to think about and I don't want to hex the divorce with—" How could she say it?

"With my getting down on one knee before you're free to accept?" Ben's eyes sparkled.

She realized he was serious in his intentions then. He really wanted to make a future and have a family together. But there were issues before them. More than he even realized.

"Hold that thought. Don't change your mind, okay?"

He grabbed her hands across the table. "Sabine, I'm not changing my mind."

Chapter Fifteen

THEIR LOVEMAKING THAT night was slow and intention-al—a passionate joining of two souls who planned to make a lifetime commitment savored; quiet and unrushed, they lingered, finding the other's sweet spots and sighs.

This morning, Ben understood Sabine's nerves and her solemn demeanor. Richard once held her hopes and dreams in his hands, and he'd broken her heart. What he'd done required far more expletives, as far as Ben was concerned, but he'd leave it at that. The man was a pure asshole and Sabine deserved nothing less than a clean break. They were meeting at a local coffee shop. Sabine had refused to go to the house she shared with Richard, or his law office, for that matter. Richard hadn't liked that she was being *difficult,* but at least she would be out in public, and not on his turf.

And Sabine had insisted it be just the two of them with-out Richard's lawyers. After all, fair was fair. Since, so far as he knew, she didn't have one with her representing her interests—at his insistence. That had been one of the details Richard laid out initially for him to agree to even discuss divorce. She'd agreed, but Ben wished she hadn't. He was so relieved to have Lisa and Steve within reach.

"You ready to wire up?" Ben asked Sabine when she came out of the bathroom where she'd just brushed her teeth.

She smiled at him. "I guess so." She untied the bathrobe to reveal matching undies.

"Wow, this is going to be harder than I thought." He grinned, separating out the wires and earpieces Howard had so kindly provided.

"Are you sure he won't see this stuff through my clothes?" she asked, biting her lip.

"Not if we do it right. Howard was very specific about placement and taping things down just so." Ben gently placed the wires across her milky skin and just under her bra. They were beige, so they didn't show when she put on her blouse. She'd chosen a loose, button-up shirt that tucked into a trim skirt, so it was a perfect foil for what was going on underneath.

"Oh, that's not too bad. A little itchy, but I'll get used to it, I guess."

"Now, for the ear bud." He handed her the tiny flesh-colored ear piece. It was nearly undetectable, even without her thick hair lying on top.

"Will it fall out?" she asked.

"It shouldn't. Shake your head to be sure. There's one a bit larger if that one is too small."

"No, this one's good, I think."

They worked on getting wired up for another fifteen minutes or so. Ben had his own equipment ready. He'd stopped by Lisa and Steve's place right after the stop at Mom and Howard's house, so they should be up and running anytime now. The trick would be not answering them if Sabine was nearby. Their earpiece would be in his other ear. Tricky stuff.

"All set?" Ben asked Sabine.

"I think so. I feel much more confident knowing you'll be right there with me. I hope he buys it that you're my driver and not my sexy man candy."

"I'll do my best to stay in my place and mind my manners, ma'am."

They arrived at the Mojo Coffee House on Magazine Street at eleven sharp. Ben was dressed in basic black trousers, starched white dress shirt, black jacket, and of course, a driving cap. Sabine had agreed the more official he appeared, the more believable he'd come across. He also sported a tie pin that doubled as a camera and microphone with recorder, should it be necessary.

Ben opened the door for Sabine, took her hand, and properly helped her out of the car. He'd parked alongside the curb just across the street, which was a near-miracle since parking in this area had proven to be a hellish nightmare, especially for a car this size. He'd circled the block four times before a spot opened up.

"Do I look normal?" Sabine fussed with her hair near her ears.

"I can't see the earpiece or wires, if that's what you're asking. You look stunning, by the way. Can you hear my voice in your ear?"

"Thank you, and yes. You?"

"Loud and clear."

He helped her up onto the curb, since her shoes had a small heel, and if she wasn't careful, would get stuck in any one of the many wide cracks and craters in the old, crumbling sidewalk. Clearly, infrastructure wasn't something this city spent its tourist dollars on. Perhaps the potholes and *patina* in places where a fresh coat of paint might have prevented wood rot, was considered part of the charm.

The bells attached to the door jingled when Ben opened it for her to precede him. He entered a respectable distance behind her. The walls were papered a deep red, while the floors were a dark, scuffed oak. The coffee bar was solid wood paneling painted a dark green and topped with an ancient planked oak. It smelled of history and coffee.

Sabine looked around the mostly full establishment, and Ben noticed her go stock-still. Then, he observed a man rise from a seated position and lift his hand in greeting.

Sabine muttered. "Oh, shit. There he is."

"Easy, now. I'm right here. Don't move your mouth. We don't want to tip him off. Smile and say hello like you don't know he's the world's biggest dick."

Ben faded back toward the entrance. The help weren't supposed to be introduced to their betters. "I'll be right inside by the front door."

⟫⟫⟪⟪

SABINE HAD THOUGHT she was prepared to face Richard again. But she'd not considered the rush of emotion that flooded through her when he took her hands and kissed her cheek.

She'd thought she might feel a reminiscent affection or confused vestige of longing for her old life with him, but she hadn't been prepared to get hit with an overwhelming urge to punch him in his handsome nose. Sabine didn't despise Richard, she *loathed* him. She wanted to retch and cringe at his touch.

"Sabine." He pulled her close.

It was all she could do not to physically resist. But she mustn't.

"Richard." Her voice trembled—in sheer anger. Hopefully, he believed it was some other, less aggressive emotion.

"You're finally home. Oh, I've missed you." He motioned for her to sit across from him at the table. "I ordered your favorite skinny latte, fat-free, sugar-free."

"Thanks, but I'd prefer a cafe au lait with two sugars, please."

"Some things have changed, haven't they?" Richard laughed, though his expression clearly communicated disapproval. He held up his hand to get the approaching waiter's attention.

"A lot has changed, you'll find, Richard. I hope we can get through this as amicably and quickly as possible. I know you want me to attend the ball with you, and I'm willing if you insist, but I plan on going home with a divorce agreement in hand."

Richard's smile froze. "Home? This is home. How about you ask how I've been first? If I'm well. Inquire about my mother's health, in fact. I don't like that you think you can breeze in here and call the shots, darling. You abandoned me. I was grieving just as you were about losing our child."

It was all Sabine could do not to rake his eyes out with her nails. "As I recall, your way of *grieving* involved multiple hookers."

"You were shut off from me completely, and I needed you as much as you needed—I'm not sure what you needed, Sabine. But you're here now, and I still need you."

Sabine froze. "I'm not staying here, Richard."

"Maybe I can persuade you, if you'll give me the chance. Louisiana is a fault/no-fault state, is it not? I can claim that you abandoned me in my time of need."

"Richard, you're a lawyer. You, of all people know that we've been living apart for nearly two years and we don't have children together."

"Yes, but in a covenant marriage, the law is two years. If we reconcile, it's like you never left." There was a gleam in his eye that made Sabine go cold.

"We aren't going to reconcile." She ground the words out.

He ran a finger over her bare forearm and she recoiled before controlling the reaction. "You never know. Stranger things have happened. I remember a time when you couldn't get enough."

"I'm here for a divorce, Richard, not reconciliation. Besides, I've got proof that you were unfaithful to me. That's enough to undo the covenant marriage laws for divorce. You see, I've been reading up on the laws too. It doesn't take an attorney to understand my rights. Draw up the paperwork, Richard."

"I know you want your cozy, life with your little damaged patients and your mommy over in Mayberry, RFD, Alabama, but I counsel you to reconsider making rash choices. I need you to stand beside me during this election cycle. Reelection is all that matters. Your threats to ruin my chances for that put me in a position to take actions that I'd rather not even consider."

Knowing that Ben was listening, and likely recording the conversation made Sabine bold. "What are you suggesting, Richard? Are you threatening to hurt me?"

Richard's expression became guarded. "Of course I'm not going to hurt you. You're far too valuable to me. Plus, I love you, Sabine. You're my wife." He shifted in his chair. "I'm telling you that I can make your life in Alabama less pleasant than the one you have here. I'm certain your patients trust you. They share all their deepest, darkest secrets with you, don't they? What if they found out you were a fraud? Not legally licensed to practice as a therapist?"

Sabine's heart nearly dropped to her feet. "What are you talking about? Of course I'm licensed."

"Clerical errors happen all the time. I mean look at all the names you've gone by. If your license is a phony, for whatever reason, it's not legal. Seeds of doubt are easily planted, especially when they all find out who you really are. Your father is a pariah. Everyone will know who he is, and what he's done, even all the way over there. It's a strong Christian community, is it not? A sinner is a sinner. A liar, is a liar. The townsfolk don't take kindly to either one."

"The town knows me and they trust me." Sabine hoped he was wrong.

But a larger part of what Richard said rang loud and true in the back of her mind.

"And Sabine, don't even consider backing out of going to the ball. It's the only way you'll get your divorce without a hugely contested and nasty fight in court. I can and will drag this out. And neither of us wants that, do we?"

She shivered at his smile.

"Take a breath. I'm coming," Sabine heard Ben whisper in her ear.

"You're a horrible liar, Sabine. I'm surprised they haven't figured you out by now."

SUSAN SANDS

Sabine looked around the room, as if for a way out.

"Excuse me, Dr. O'Connor, I found your sweater in the back of the car. I wondered if you might need it?" Ben held her sweater in front of her. He'd never looked so handsome, and so official.

Richard frowned. "Who is this?"

"This is Ben, my driver and personal security while I'm in town."

Ben nodded politely.

"Could I get your last name, son?" Richard asked.

"No, you may not. He works for me, Richard. It's no longer your business whom I hire or what I do. I'm leaving now. Draw up the papers. I'll sign them Saturday at the end of the evening. That's all you'll get from me. I'll have my attorney back home handle the details."

"Ah, so you do have an attorney?" Richard's voice was smooth, but angry.

"Of course. Did you think I was stupid and trusting enough to let your attorneys see to my best interests? Everyone who divorces hires an attorney."

"I believed we could handle this between the two of us," Richard said.

"Clearly we cannot. I'm leaving." Ben gave a quick nod and pulled out Sabine's chair for her. He then coolly inclined his head at Richard. The split-second insult wasn't lost on Richard.

"I'll pick you up at your hotel tomorrow. Send me the

306

address," Richard said.

"I'll meet you there," Sabine answered. "Ben will drive me."

Richard reached down beside his chair and brought up a shopping bag. "Take this, Sabine. I like you in red," Richard said.

Ben stepped forward, taking the bag from Richard to carry.

"I'll wear what I choose." She turned her back and Ben followed, the bag dangling from his fingertips.

❯❯❯❮❮❮

THEY WERE BACK in the car and Sabine's breathing was near to hyperventilating. "How could I have ever married such a complete pile of shit?"

"People change. Richard took a hard nosedive to the dark side. Buckle up and hang on because I'm going to do some pretty slick driving in case Richard's people follow. He seemed pretty keen on finding out where you were staying, and considering his threatening tone, we can't take the chance."

Sabine clicked her seat belt into place and settled in for a bumpy ride, understanding how many potholes they would hit moving fast. "Do you think he's going to let me go without a fight? And what was all that about reconciling?"

"Doesn't sound like he's in the mood to cooperate." Ben hauled butt through a yellow light that was turning red.

307

SUSAN SANDS

Hopefully, he wouldn't get stopped by one of New Orleans's finest. Those guys didn't play when it came to meting out justice. "Watch for cops, okay? The last thing we need is for Richard to call in the cavalry to put you in jail so he can have more access to me."

Ben glanced back at her and his expression was fierce. "I didn't think of that. Does he have that kind of pull?"

Sabine rolled her eyes. "Of course he does. He can call in favors all over town. We should have checked in under aliases at the B&B."

"We did. I mean, I asked Mrs. Bergeron to put us down in her book as Mr. And Mrs. Grey Harrison if anyone asks."

"You did?" Sabine somehow missed that exchange, but was secretly impressed by his secret agent preparedness.

"I thought about it later."

"What did she say?"

"She just winked and nodded. Said we weren't the first couple staying at her place who didn't want to be found. But she trusts Tanner, so she trusts us."

"Thank God for your buddy, Tanner, once again."

Ben nodded and briefly met her eyes in the rearview mirror as he squealed tires around another curve. "Not sure if that black sedan two cars back is one of Richard's guys."

"Oh." Sabine turned to try and get a visual of the possible tail. The windows of the car in pursuit were heavily tinted, which was pretty typical of Richard's security detail. The car was nondescript, so no help there.

"I'm going to try and lose them at the next light I can run. There's still a car between us, so maybe I can shake them."

"Does Howard have any pull with the local authorities? Like from a higher authority? Maybe it would supersede any questionable, corrupted favor Richard might call in," Sabine asked.

"Worth a try." He quickly pressed a button and tossed his phone back to her. "Howard's number is in my top ten contacts. Give him a call and tell him what's shaking. See if he can help."

Sabine took his phone and dialed Howard's number. "Hello?"

"Hi, Howard, this is Sabine. We're at the corner of St. Charles Avenue and Jefferson Street uptown. We are pretty sure Richard's guys are following us and that he has influence with the local police. Do you have any available resources to help us out?"

"Are they just tailing you or are you in danger?" Howard asked, all business.

"I don't think we're in danger at this point; I think Richard wants to find out where I'm staying, but I wouldn't put it past him to have Ben stopped by police to get his information. Right now, we'd like to lose the tail."

"Got it. I'll need the license plate number of the car you're driving. It's in the glove compartment. That way, the two of you won't be bothered."

"Okay. Hang on while I get it." She kicked her shoes off and proceeded to crawl over the front seat next to Ben. Her execution wasn't exactly ladylike.

Ben raised his brows when she landed in a heap beside him, legs in the air. His lips curled in amusement. "Well, hello."

She rolled her eyes at him, then set to work finding the information for Howard. "Okay, here it is." She read off the car's info from the registration.

"Do you have a full tank of gas?" Howard asked.

Sabine leaned over to see the fuel gauge. "Yes."

"Tell Ben to keep driving safely until you hear back from me. Then, head toward the nearest police station once I've established my connection with authorities. We'll make sure your tail is detained after that so you can safely get to your hotel from there. What does the car behind you look like?"

"Black four-door sedan with heavily tinted windows. That's about all I can see."

"Okay. Should be easy to identify if they stick close."

"Thanks so much Howard," Sabine said.

"Of course. What's an old spy to do with his golden years and security clearance if not help out his family?"

"Thanks, Howard," Ben spoke loudly enough from the driver's side for Howard to hear on his end.

"Tell my stepson to drive safely or his mother will worry, and I can't have that."

"Yes, sir," Sabine said and disconnected the call.

"He said to keep driving safely until he calls back to confirm he's made his connection with the authorities. We're to head toward a police station and they'll detain the car tailing us so we can get free of them."

"I'm so glad he's my new dad," Ben said. "I mean that in so many ways."

Sabine believed him. If one was going to acquire a new father at age thirty, it might as well be one as awesome as Howard.

"Are they still following?"

"They're still a couple cars back." Sabine was now in the front seat beside Ben. He'd slowed their speed down and the car behind them didn't appear to be trying to move closer— only keep them in sight, which was a relief.

They made their way toward the mighty Mississippi and took a left hand turn on Tchoupitoulas Street that meandered along the riverfront toward the French Quarter. "I'll check to see where the nearest police station is." She pulled up her GPS map and entered the New Orleans Police Department locations. "The Port of Orleans is on our right in about a mile and a half. It might be our best bet."

"Okay. This traffic's crawling, so we're not in any danger. There isn't any place to go." Ben's phone rang then. "Hello? Hey Howard. We're on Tchoupitoulas about a mile and a quarter from the Port of Orleans on the river. Okay." Ben listened for a couple seconds. "Makes sense. Great. Thanks again. We'll check in when we get back to our hotel."

"What did he say?" Sabine asked.

"Howard says to be looking for a police presence in a few minutes. Not sure how they'll manage it, but there'll be a tie-up just long enough for us to get loose and for the cops to detain the car following us."

Sure enough, as they approached the port authority, blue lights appeared on all sides. The officer asked to see Ben's identification and then waved them through without so much as a flicker of recognition. These guys were good.

However, as Ben and Sabine stared into their side-view mirrors, they noticed the driver of the black car on their tail wasn't so lucky. He'd been made to step out of the car by the officers.

"Whew. Glad that's over. It looks like they're letting everyone else go by now. It's still likely to tie up traffic until they move the car. I feel awful about that. Most of these people are on vacation," Sabine said.

Having lived in the city, she understood how terrible traffic could bottleneck in this area.

"They'll get them moving quickly now that they've got their guys. I'm sure they'll just run a quick driver's license background check for unpaid parking tickets and fines and let them go. By then, we'll be well on our way," Ben said.

"Richard will be so angry his guys were detained, but it happens all the time here to ordinary citizens. I doubt he'll think anything was amiss. Just dumb luck. And it's likely his guys have some outstanding unpaid fines or tickets, so it will come out as their own fault in the end," Sabine said.

"True. I find it unlikely they're fine, upstanding citizens who pay their fees and fines in a timely fashion, or always park in an approved zone, for that matter," Ben agreed. "Then again, if the police constantly ignore their transgressions because they are Richard's minions, they may turn up squeaky clean."

"I kind of doubt they maintain that same deference in their personal lives. Richard wouldn't excuse or allow any bad behavior to stain his reputation if any of his people went around using his name in vain without him there," Sabine mused.

"You have a point. Their personal records could be a mess. These are guys who go around every day at work behaving like the rules don't apply to them. It's unlikely they switch that behavior off when they clock out at the end of the day."

When Ben got near the bed and breakfast, Sabine noticed that he checked his mirrors carefully. He passed the driveway and went a block, making certain they weren't being followed. "I know it seems like I'm behaving overly cautiously, but I really don't want Richard having the upper hand by knowing where you're staying."

Sabine nodded. "I understand. I don't want him to know either. He creeped me out this morning. I'm surprised you didn't pounce on him the minute he started insulting me.

Good job on your self-control."

"I hope you realize that I wanted to rip that skeezy bastard to shreds within a minute of your stepping inside that coffee shop. But I was recording his words in case he let anything slip. I know I can't use them in court without his knowledge of being recorded, but the more information we have, the better our chances of getting you unhitched from him quickly and without complications. It's a low and dirty way of handling things, but Richard is proving to be as low and dirty as they come."

"I wasn't being passive-aggressive. I know you wanted to step in and take him out. You're a hero-type and a gentleman. I could feel your protective streak kick in. I know how hard it was for you to do nothing and wait it out. Plus, I could hear you cursing under your breath in my ear and calling him names. And it kept me from tearing his eyes out with my bare hands. I was afraid when I saw him I would feel *something*. But this black cloud of anger overtook me and it was a struggle to even speak in a civil tone to him."

"I could hear it in your voice. Here I thought you'd play the good cop and make him feel like you were putty in his hands. That's why I came in with the sweater when I did. I couldn't handle any more, and I could tell you were at your limit. I was trying not to make sounds in your earpiece so you wouldn't react and make him suspect anything was off."

"He's a politician. The only thing that keeps him from even considering that I've found someone else is his huge ego. I mean, how could I possibly desire a relationship with someone else when I could have a lying, cheating slimeball for a husband?"

"He's somewhat attractive, I'll give him that," Ben admitted. "In fact, I'd go so far as to say he and I share some similar features and coloring." He pulled the car behind the house and parked in the super-secret fenced-in space that was completely undetectable from passersby.

Sabine climbed out, grabbing her shoes from the backseat. "Are you suggesting that I'm attracted to you because you look like my estranged husband?" She was having a hard time not breaking out into a gut-busting guffaw. Ben was so different in every way than Richard that she couldn't find a single similarity besides the fact they both had dark hair.

"The thought had passed through, though I'm much better looking and slightly younger."

The laughter she'd been trying to hold in came tearing out.

"What? It's not that crazy of a thought."

"Richard is a weasel. I mean, his eyes are close together, and his nose is thin, and I was thrilled to see that his hair is beginning to thin, thank the Lord, because it's such justice." She continued to laugh at that thought. "He's always believed himself so good-looking and irresistible. In fact, he pretty much let me know that I'd married up. It was a long time ago, but I'll never forget it. He was drinking at the time."

"Wait just a damn minute. *He* treated *you* like you were the lucky one? I'm going to punch him in the nose."

"Oh, stop. No nose punching. That's so tenth grade."

"I guess his hairline *is* thinning a little. But I think he more resembles a possum than a weasel."

They were both laughing as they entered the bed and breakfast.

"Oh, just look at the two of you. So sweet and happy together," Mrs. B said from the tiny desk inside the foyer. "I hope you've had a nice appointment this morning." Her bespectacled eyes were bright and curious. Perhaps she was hoping for information.

"It was productive, thanks, Mrs. Bergeron," Ben said politely but his tone brooked no further questions.

"Lovely," Mrs. B said, her voice melodious.

Ben's stomach growled then. "How about we walk a few blocks for beignets and cafe au lait?" It was still somewhat early and not quite lunchtime.

"Cafe Beignet is a bit of a walk, but it's a nice day," Mrs. B inserted.

"I'm all for getting out and enjoying some fresh air. We can go up and change. I'll definitely need some better shoes than these for walking."

"Perfect." He motioned toward the stairs and Sabine led the way.

Who knew they would have an opportunity to spend a

little quality time enjoying the city while they were fighting the forces of evil?

>>>«««

WHEN THEY'D RETURNED from their outing, full of beignets and coffee, Sabine said she'd like to lie down and rest for a bit. This was a relief to Ben. He needed to touch base with Steve and Lisa. They'd been in his ear and had heard everything Richard had said to Sabine this morning. He'd wanted them to understand the full picture of what they were dealing with. They'd also been yelling in his ear while they'd been trying to lose the car tailing them this afternoon. That hadn't been easy to hide from Sabine. And he *hated* having to propagate the lie. He wished like everything he'd been straight with her from the beginning. She'd been through enough without finding out about his duplicity.

"I'm going to head out to my truck and grab a file and make sure it's locked up. I need to make a couple phone calls, so I'll probably just sit outside in the courtyard in back while you rest." Most of that was true, but he still felt like utter shit.

He avoided conversation by putting his phone on his ear while heading through the lobby/foyer on his way outside. He raised his hand in a quick wave and smiled at their hosts.

Ben headed around back where the small fragrant courtyard was in full bloom. There were two wrought iron benches that appeared to be older than him, but he figured they'd likely withstood a few category five hurricanes, so he should be good to go.

Ben settled onto the bench. He'd grabbed a couple file folders from his truck for effect in case Sabine came outside. His subterfuge bothered him greatly, but he'd come this far and felt as if the end justified the means. In other words, better to be a little sneaky and have plenty of support to make certain Sabine came out of this situation safe and without being taken advantage of in her divorce agreement than the alternatives.

He sat and dialed Steve's number. "Where the hell have you been, man? We're dying over here wondering what happened to the two of you. You kept cutting us out while you were driving back from the café. We only heard parts of what was happening."

"Sorry my communication has to be pretty one-sided. And if Sabine and I are having a private exchange, I'm turning you off. Obviously, she doesn't know I've got y'all in my ear. All is well. She's upstairs resting. I guess you heard that Howard handled the tail that Richard put on us to find out where Sabine is staying." Ben had muted their conversation with the tiny button that peeked out the bottom of his shirt when he felt it was appropriate. He'd managed to slip a second device on when Sabine wasn't looking this morning. This was going to be trickier than he'd thought.

"We heard the parts you allowed us to. I hope that's the only reason he had you tailed," Steve said.

"I'm just going to assume that's why. Anything else would be pure speculation," Ben said.

"How's Sabine holding up? Those were some pretty awful things Richard said to her this morning. She handled it like a champ," Lisa said.

Steve had put him on speaker.

"She was a little concerned that she might feel some nostalgia at seeing him, but I think he mainly disgusted her instead, which, I have to say, relieved my mind."

"Can't say I blame her. He sounds like a real slimeball," Lisa said.

"What's the plan tomorrow night?" Steve asked.

"I'll drive her to the museum where the event is being held at seven o'clock. We'll all be wired up and Sabine will have a tiny tracker in her shoe. That was Howard's suggestion."

"I like it," Lisa said. "A little extra protection."

"Since I'm her driver, I'll be expected to stay outside the venue and out of the way. Security is tight during this event, so they'll give me a pass to stay with the car, so at least I won't have to be beyond the grounds. It's not a perfect scenario, but I should be close enough to step in should Sabine need me."

"We'll hang out at the nearest public area or coffee shop while the party is underway. Is there a public area or park nearby? We'll do some research and figure out the closest proximity to the museum where we can be available at a moment's notice, as well." Steve and Lisa were staying at a nearby boutique hotel in the uptown area not far from Ben and Sabine's location.

"I don't expect anything to go down, but I didn't like his tone or his manner with Sabine this morning. It was almost as if he had no intention of letting her leave now that she'd come home. Maybe he believes he's that persuasive," Ben said.

He heard the disgust in Lisa's tone. "Has the man never met a woman with a mind of her own? It's pretty clear just from what little I know about Sabine that she would never allow him to decide her future."

"There's no way he can keep her here or make her stay married to him. We're here to make sure that Richard doesn't even have the opportunity to try anything under-handed. And we've got the advantage because he doesn't know Sabine has that kind of support around her," Ben said.

"Neither does Sabine," Steve said.

"I'm planning to tell her after this is over and we make it back home with no trouble," Ben said, his tone slightly defensive.

"We know you will. And we'll do everything in our pow-er to persuade her that we talked you into this and that your intentions were only for her safety and concern. Oh, and that we bullied you into doing this to make us feel better about hurting you, and it's our way of making amends and evening up the score for our guilt," Steve said.

"I doubt that explanation will prevent her smarting from the fact that he shared her personal information with us without her consent—knowing she asked him not to," Lisa reminded her husband.

"Sabine is coming. I'll talk to you both tomorrow. Go to Pascal's for barbeque shrimp. You can thank me later." Ben hung up just as Sabine approached.

She'd pulled up her long, dark hair in a clip of some sort, but strands of it still hung down around her face. She had no makeup on and wore flip-flops and a long T-shirt and yoga pants. She was a knockout.

"Hey there. I just spoke to Steve." Best to keep a shred of honesty about him. "Did you get a nap?"

Sabine smiled, still looking a little sleepy. "A small one. It was very relaxing. I'm amazed at how pleasant this trip has been thus far, considering what we're doing."

"I've had the same thought. We really don't have any-where we have to be until tomorrow evening. Do you want to make a dinner reservation and head down to the French Quarter and walk around?"

Sabine grinned. "This is my town. I would love to show you around from a native's perspective. But we won't necessarily be going to the expected tourist traps."

Ben stood and opened his arms. "I'm all yours."

Chapter Sixteen

B Y THE TIME they'd fallen into bed last night, Ben could truly say he'd experienced the city of New Orleans in a way he never had before. Sabine had led him on an insider's tour of small voodoo museums, graveyards, historic homes of people he'd never heard of, and even on a twilight swamp tour just over an old, narrow bridge spanning the Mississippi that made him never ever want to cross a body of water again.

Sabine hugged the old Cajun who'd greeted them upon their arrival at what appeared to be a dilapidated pier on the edge of a swampy bayou. The old Cajun grinned at Sabine with such affection, it made Ben do a double-take. She introduced him as her parrain, which meant godfather in Cajun-speak. Ben had heard the term before, as he'd had a couple other friends from South Louisiana in college.

This raised questions but also answered a few about why she, a city girl, would consider taking them out in his tiny aluminum boat with this old man and his .410-gauge shotgun. Ben questioned if this would be enough firepower should they need to fight off the gators they got within tooth-counting range of.

There were water moccasins hanging in groups off the moss-laden trees. Ben had marveled that this place was only a half-hour outside of the city.

"We're surrounded by water on all sides. It shouldn't be such a shock," Sabine had said.

She didn't seem to be bothered by all the nature.

Ben, who'd grown up around a mountain, man-made lake with no timber, and with furry animals more than reptiles, tried hard not to behave as if he worried how far the hospital was from their location and if the tackle box in the bottom of the boat held a snake-bite kit. And if anyone would hear their cries should the creature from the black lagoon make an appearance and swallow up the boat in the approaching darkness.

They'd made it back to the bank without incident, but Ben wasn't certain if all his manhood was still intact in Sabine's eyes. He'd behaved a little squirrelly out there, he had to admit.

When she climbed out of the boat, Sabine spoke to the elderly man quietly off to the side. She handed him some bills as payment. He grasped her hands in his and placed his forehead against hers. There was clearly a deep bond between these two.

Ben shook the man's hand again and expressed his gratitude for his skilled handling of the boat. "I've never been out in the swamp. It was quite an experience."

"*Mais oui.* You'll do just fahn for our Sabine, here. You kept your screams inside, son. Had you yelled like a scaired little girl, I would have dumped you into the bayou." Then her parrain cackled, a rusty sound, like he'd been saving it up for a long time and it was struggling to make its way out.

"Parrain has a cabin not too far from here. My dad used to bring me out here when I was a little girl. He and Dad are half-brothers."

"Ah. That makes sense," Ben said.

And it did. Jean-Claude Prudhomme was native Creole all the way, from what Ben had found out when he'd done a little further research on the man. Ben had been curious about him when he'd found out he was Sabine's father.

"We should get back to the city if we want to hit the oyster house I have in mind," Sabine said.

"Ya'll go on and get across dat devil bridge before it falls down, *bien sur,*" Parrain said.

"I'll have to agree with you on that, sir. My girl sounds are more likely to come out crossing that bridge than when we passed the snakes and alligators in the swamp," Ben said.

Sabine laughed. "You'll have to close your eyes and let me drive."

"The hell I will. My truck is huge and takes up the entire lane. If you're not used to driving something that big—" He shuddered.

"Okay, big guy. Let's get out of here so you don't have to

navigate it in full dark." She turned to her godfather and her expression softened. "Thanks so much, Parrain. I'll try to get back and see you soon. Now that Dad is up for parole, hopefully, everyone's life will get back to some kind of normal again."

"How is your sister?" he asked.

"She's doing okay. Still very angry at Daddy for making such a mess of things. They were close, you know."

The man nodded, his sweat-stained straw hat appearing to be a part of his head. "Your papa changed when he got into politics. He wasn't always like that, *ma chere*."

"I know. But it's too late to fix what he's broken now. We've got to move on with our lives now."

"And your husband, the *cochon*?"

"Yes, he turned out to be a giant pig. And we're here to persuade him to sign a divorce agreement. Ben is a lawyer."

"Not a *politicien*?" The man gave Ben a suspicious look.

"No. Thank God. Not a politician."

Ben's heart sank. He'd not shared with her that politics might be in his future. The governor had mentioned throwing his support behind Ben's run for a state house seat in a couple years. He couldn't fess up to that now. At least not with the .410 within the man's grasp.

"*Bien*. I've got a bigger barrel for politicians." He held Ben's eyes.

"Parrain, stop scaring Ben. I can't imagine him as a politician. He's way too honest."

Ben died a little inside.

⋙✦⋘

REMEMBERING THEIR DAY together gave Sabine the strength to march forward on the sidewalk toward the entrance of the New Orleans Museum of Art, holding the arm of her former husband. True, he wasn't officially her ex, but in every sense of the word it was true. Ben had dropped her where Richard had been waiting with his limo just outside the fray.

Richard was wearing an Armani tux that was tailored to fit him perfectly. He appeared every inch the part of the confident senator, complete with his woman on his arm.

"I thought I requested that you wear the red." She heard the annoyance in his voice; clearly, he was irritated that she didn't heed his instructions.

"I'm very happy with my choice, thanks." She touched the gorgeous fabric of her gown, which was a crème-colored floating creation with a beaded bodice. She'd adored it the moment she'd laid eyes on it. It fit perfectly and fortunately provided enough coverage for her underlying wires. "Plus, you don't get to choose my clothing for me anymore, Richard. Or my hotel—or anything for that matter. I'm leaving tonight and I'm not coming back unless it's for a fun weekend or to visit someone of my choosing. It is my hometown, after all. I don't want to have to worry about being stalked or tailed in my own hometown." She gave him a hard look then, one that told him nothing, but hopefully caused him to question everything.

Richard's mouth tightened, but he didn't say a word. There wasn't time, because they'd made their way down the black and gold carpet, the official New Orleans Saints colors, to where the press was rabidly snapping photos and thrusting microphones toward their prey. And it seemed they'd caught the scent of Richard and Sabine. He quickly turned toward her and muttered, "Don't screw this up for me, Sabine. Follow my lead. Oh, and smile." His own phony, pasted-on smile must have been sincere enough to draw in the predators, because she barely had enough time to draw a breath before they attacked.

"Senator Habersham, we're surprised to see Mrs. Habersham here with you this evening. Does that mean the two of you have reconciled?"

"Mrs. Habersham, there are rumors you've suffered from mental illness and had a breakdown after your father's conviction. You're looking well. Do you care to comment on your absence from public life for the past two years?"

"My wife is in fantastic health. I mean, just look at her. Does she appear ill to you?" Richard spun Sabine around slowly like a ballerina as if daring anyone to suggest otherwise.

Sabine stepped forward. "I was grieving the loss of my pregnancy and, yes, my father's incarceration did take a toll on our family, but I've been taking a pause from political life to reevaluate my priorities. I'm doing very well, as you can see. Thanks for your concern, but I've suffered no mental health issues, though, as a licensed mental healthcare provider, a great deal of my time and effort is spent supporting those who are in crisis." Sabine then flashed the reporters a dazzling smile and moved forward down the carpet, not bothering to retake Richard's arm, and not caring if he caught up.

He caught up. "Nicely done, though I would have preferred that you communicate your support of my reelection."

"Don't worry, Richard. They assume as much because I'm here with you. Let's not appear that we're trying too hard. It smacks of desperation."

His brows were set in a frown. "I don't like your attitude. You've gotten very mouthy since you've been away."

"I don't see any point in controlling my mouth since I'm leaving in the morning. You don't have to deal with me anymore. Besides, I like the changes in myself." She smirked at him; she couldn't help it.

"Sabine, watch it. Don't piss him off too much. He's already a man on the edge. I can't get to you as quickly as I'd like." Ben spoke softly in her ear, and hearing his voice surprised her. She tried not to react, and it definitely was a challenge.

"Sabine, if I were you, I'd take it down a notch," Richard warned her. "And don't drink more than a glass of wine. You're a lightweight when it comes to alcohol, and I can't take the chance of your blowing it."

"Don't worry. I'll make sure to get what I need out of this farce." Sabine smiled widely when she said this, as an old acquaintance approached just then, and a waiter fortuitously offered her a glass of champagne, which she accepted it with a salute toward Richard, whose mouth tightened and hands fisted.

"Darling, Theresa. Where in the devil have you been?" It was Susan Schubert the wife of Edward Schubert, one of Richard's cronies, and someone she would have loosely called friend.

"Hi, Susan. So nice to see you. I took some time off from the rat race. How have you been?" Sabine answered without actually answering the question.

If she'd learned anything from the politicians in this room, it was to evade giving facts that could be checked out.

"Well, that is a mysterious answer, but it's a party and I won't press. But, we've missed you. I must say, I'm jealous of your little vacation from all of this. Though I don't know how you managed it with all the reporters sniffing around here all the time." Susan gestured around the room with her free hand.

The other held a stemmed glass filled with chardonnay. Sabine doubted it was Susan's first of the evening and, odds were, it wouldn't be her last. They'd attended more than a few parties together, and Sabine had to give it to the woman, Susan could drink a three-hundred-pound man under the table and remain standing in her five-inch stilettos.

"Lovely to see you, Susan. I'd better get something to eat or this champagne will go straight to my head." Sabine used the excuse to avoid any further questions.

"Tata, dear." The woman laughed and turned her back on Sabine, already moving toward a handsome and much younger man, who Susan was rumored to have had an affair with a few years ago.

Sabine shook her head slightly, trying not to judge, but marveling at the audacity of this crowd she'd called her peers for years.

"There you are. Sorry I was distracted for a moment. Didn't mean to leave you on your own." It was Richard and he was back like a bad rash.

"The speeches will begin soon. I'll have a quick opportunity to stand up and say a few words. That's when I want you to pop in front of me and tell the crowd how much you've missed seeing all of them and how excited you are to be here amongst them and with me to support my run for reelection. Got it?"

"Isn't that a little obnoxious? I mean, I'm not on the agenda as a speaker for this evening. I know for a fact they run a pretty tight agenda for this gala."

"Everyone will think you're just a little tipsy and overenthusiastic about your support of my candidacy. They'll laugh and clap and think it's adorable."

"It's disgusting."

"Sabine, I realize you're in an angry place right now, especially after your breakdown, but you might want to figure out a way to keep smiling or I'll share that you're mentally incompetent."

"What? Are you insane?" She seethed at him. "I haven't had a breakdown and you know it."

"I'm not insane, but the folks you've been treating won't like the fact that you're having identity issues. That you ran away from home, grief-stricken, and changed your name to hide out from your own problems, then you created a whole new identity in your mind to shield your brain and emotions from the pain of the truth. There's a diagnosis for that, right? I looked it up. Yes, it's called creating an alternate reality. Plus, I don't have a problem with creating a scene that will make the newspapers, and then supplying them with a headline."

Sabine laughed at him then. "You really are a monster, aren't you? And I really do have my own words to tell my story. Part of that will be the truth about my husband being a predator with underage young women, and contributing to the exploitation and abuse of girls that you've sworn an oath to help protect in your office." She downed her glass and glared at him.

"Oh, Sabine, I was afraid you were going to try and use that against me. Sadly, this means I'll have to take other measures to make sure that doesn't happen."

"Other measures? I'm a free woman. There's nothing you can say or do to suppress me. If you think the threat of revealing who I am to the people in Alabama is enough to make me stay here and live a lifetime, or even another day with you, you are sadly mistaken. I would rather live two lifetimes alone and miserable than a week with—with you." Sabine stumbled. She realized now, that as she'd spoken her passionate words, Richard had moved them toward a back exit.

"Maybe you just need a little air," Richard suggested.

"Sabine don't go anywhere with him. I'm coming." A voice seemed to come from heaven.

"O-okay."

Sabine wanted to fight Richard, but found herself suddenly unable to make sense of anything happening. They were outside and the air was cool. A long, black car pulled up and Richard opened the door. She was swaying on her feet now. Richard picked her up and stuffed her inside. She tried to fight him, but her attempts were weak, as if she were moving underwater.

"What's going on?" she mumbled.

"What's this?" Richard demanded.

And before she could figure out what he meant, he was pulling at her dress and pulling at the taped wires.

The wires. "Ben—help—" The world went dark.

⋙⋘

THE ONLY SOUNDS Ben heard now, since the struggle, were of cars passing. Richard had obviously found the wires taped to Sabine's body and removed them. What had he done to her? Where had he taken her? He spoke to Steve and Lisa. "He's taken her. Can you access the tracker in her shoe?"

"Working on it. We didn't have it up on the screen because we already knew her location. Wait, here it is. Looks like they're headed toward the Garden District."

"Okay. I'm headed your way with the car now to pick you up. We'll follow the signal. Let me call Howard and see who our best bet for help will be." Ben dialed Howard's number.

He picked up on the first ring. "What's going on over there, son?" Howard asked.

"The son of a bitch has taken Sabine from the ball and I believe he put something in her drink. He found the wire and disabled communication, but we're tracking her location now. Which law enforcement should I call?"

"I'll handle law enforcement. I can bring the tracker online from here. Y'all go to Sabine. Wait for backup, son. We don't know what his plan is."

"Thanks, Howard. Just knowing you've got our backs helps."

Ben hung up and nearly squealed tires as he pulled up to the curb where Steve and Lisa were waiting. They'd been stationed at a set of benches nearest to the museum. It wasn't far from where Ben had to wait with the car.

Lisa climbed in back with the laptop and Steve rode shotgun beside Ben. "Tell me where to go." Ben took off as soon as Steve shut the door.

"Turn right up here on North Carrollton and then hit I-10 East. It looks like they just exited onto St. Charles Avenue," Lisa said. She was navigating on the computer from the backseat.

"Where could he be taking her?" Steve asked Ben.

"I'm getting a bad feeling about this. I believe Sabine lived on St. Charles Avenue with Richard."

"You think he's taking her home?"

"Remember when he said he believed they should reconcile?" Bile rose in Ben's stomach and he pressed down harder on the accelerator.

"Easy, man. Howard's got her tracked and is in touch with the police, right? They should be able to get there quickly. You can't swing a cat in New Orleans without hitting a cop," Steve said.

"Surely, he won't try to force himself on Sabine and call that a reconciliation?" Lisa sounded horrified.

"We've confirmed that he's a sexual predator. If he believes she's not cooperating with his plans, I'm not certain how far he might go to meet his objective of bringing her to heel," Ben said.

"How does he think he can control a wife who doesn't want to be with him? Is he deluded enough to believe she'll just shut up and do as he says?" Lisa asked, not for the first time questioning Richard's reasoning where Sabine's free will was concerned. "This guy's obviously got a few loose screws and likely isn't thinking clearly. Do you know if he uses drugs? Because if we're dealing with a drug addict in addition to an irrational thinker, we definitely should wait for the police before confronting him."

"Sabine didn't mention drugs." Ben didn't want to talk anymore.

He needed to get to Sabine. *Now.*

>>><<<

BEN WAS CARRYING her. That was nice. She was super tired. *Wait.* That wasn't right. This person was huffing and puffing. Ben didn't struggle. He carried her without breaking his stride. *Richard.* Sabine tried to struggle, but couldn't move her arms and legs. What the hell was wrong with her?

She tried to control her fuzzy thoughts without panicking. Her mind was groggy and her body was almost completely paralyzed. She could still breathe, thankfully. Drugged; she'd been drugged.

Richard opened a door and nearly dropped her. It was all Sabine could do not to make a panicked sound. He hadn't yet realized she was conscious. He shut the door behind them and it penetrated Sabine's still-confused brain that she was at their Garden District home—the one she'd shared for almost eight years with Richard. Why did he bring her here? Why had he taken her from the ball? *Oh, God.* What was Richard planning?

He must have found the wire she was wearing. And her

earpiece. Where was Ben?

She lost her bearings as Richard tossed her none-too-gently onto a bed. This caused the breath to inadvertently whoosh from her lungs. Needless to say, she made noise then, which alerted Richard to her now-wakened state.

"Now, let's get that dress off you. Wouldn't want to ruin it, would we?"

Without warning, he flipped her over and pulled down the zipper from the base of her neck to her hips. Her outraged gasp must have amused him. "Are we shy, dear? Or merely eager? Yes, me too. Don't worry, it won't be long. I'll just let Mrs. Jones know we've arrived, that you're home with me from the party, and that we don't want to be disturbed."

Sabine planned to scream then, to lambast Richard for this insanity. But it was as if her mouth was filled with cotton and wouldn't work properly, even though she was beginning to think more clearly. Still, her arms and legs would only move slightly, even with the greatest of effort.

"Yeah. Sorry about that. It's a bitch, huh? The doc that gave me the drug said you'd be fine in a couple hours. But damn it, Sabine, this is all your fault. You should have just come home and done as I asked. It really wouldn't have come to this. Excuse me a moment; I'll just call Mrs. Jones." He wrestled her out of the dress.

She was left in her skimpy bra and panties. She might as well have been naked—Sabine wanted to harm him now.

She grunted her anger and frustration at him. Because grunting was all she could do at the moment.

"Hello, Mrs. Jones, Mrs. Habersham and I are home from the party. I know how much you've missed her and thought you would want to know that she's home safe and sound." Richard's voice was pure honey as he paused for the woman to speak. "We're both pretty eager to celebrate our reunion, so you'll understand if we say goodnight. Yes, I'll tell her. We'll see you at breakfast in the morning. Yes, I'll set the house alarm shortly."

Sabine knew Mrs. Jones would be thrilled she was back. They'd been close despite being employer/employee. Sabine tried again to scream. A guttural sound passed her lips.

Richard crossed over to the A/V receiver on the shelf powered by a digital music player, and suddenly, the speakers filled the room with Michael Buble's smooth, rich voice. Any other time, it would have calmed her.

"Now, let's finish what we started here, shall we? In case there was any doubt in your pretty head, we're about to *reconcile* in the eyes of the law, my darling."

Sabine's eyes opened widely in horror. He was planning to actually *rape* her to prevent her from divorcing him. That was insane. The act itself was grounds for his arrest and for her gaining immediate divorce. He truly believed himself untouchable. Her father's arrest, conviction, and incarceration should have taught Richard better. If anyone had been an untouchable, it had been her dad.

Sabine seemed to be gaining back some control of her limbs. Of course, even if she could scream now, Mrs. Jones wouldn't hear, considering how loud Richard had cranked the crooner. Not tipping him off just yet, Sabine stayed still while Richard undressed. She would wait until she got the opportunity and figure out how to avoid his advances. The prospect of her being able to hop off the bed and outrun Richard with her still-weak, and likely wobbly, legs was highly improbable.

He approached, in his underwear, and leered at her. She would rather fight him to the death than let him lay a hand on her body. She screamed then.

⇛⇚

THEY ARRIVED AT the house to find one of Sabine's shoes on the front step. "Shit." There wasn't any sign of the police yet, so Ben kicked the door, nearly breaking his foot. "Aahhh. What the hell?" What kind of rescuer was he?

"Let's do this together," Steve suggested then.

They both backed up and attacked the front door. It gave way, the wood splintering at the deadbolt. A woman screamed from someplace and they followed the sound. An older woman appeared in their path, a baseball bat in hand.

"Ma'am, we're here to save someone, not here to hurt anyone." Lisa assured the terrified woman, who didn't appear convinced.

"Who are you people?" The bat-wielding woman asked,

her voice shaking.

Ben stopped explaining then and went to find Sabine.

He kicked in the closed door, possibly finishing off the fracture he'd begun while trying to break the front door. "Sabine?" he yelled, terrified of what he might find.

"I think I killed him." Sabine's face was pale and she was crouching over Richard's still form on the bed, and she was holding a candlestick with what appeared to be a substantial amount of blood on it.

"Sabine—oh, thank God. The police are on their way." He was careful not to touch anything. He picked up a blanket from the end of the bed and wrapped it around her shoulders.

"Is he dead?" she asked.

But Richard moved then and moaned.

"Not dead," Ben said.

And then he put his arms around her. She was shaking. Richard tried to sit up then.

"Lay down, Richard. The police are on the way," Ben said.

Richard reached up to grab his head where Sabine had clearly knocked him cold. "You hit me, you crazy bitch." He made a move toward Sabine.

Ben really couldn't allow that.

He pushed Richard back down on the bed. "Not today, asshole." Richard stayed down, holding his head.

"I'm dizzy," he complained. "I'm not feeling well."

"Do you think you feel worse than I did when you drugged me where I couldn't move, and worse than when you tried to rape me?" Sabine demanded.

"You left me no choice," Richard defended.

Steve and Lisa came inside the room then. "Everything okay?" Lisa asked, but directed her concern toward Sabine.

Sabine's expression reflected complete confusion. "I'm okay now." She turned toward Ben in question.

But there was a loud ruckus then, and the police burst into the home. Steve and Ben went out to show them inside the room.

The officers had their guns drawn and insisted that everyone step back and identify themselves. There were four officers and five people already inside the bedroom, so it was getting a little tight. Lisa and Steve stated their names and let the officers know they'd come to aid Sabine, so two of the officers accompanied them outside the room for the moment, which left Richard, Sabine, and Ben with the other two.

"I'm officer Taggert. Would anyone care to start?" Taggert asked.

"He drugged me with something that paralyzed my arms and legs and told me we were going to *reconcile* against my will. I haven't lived here in over two years. I came back to divorce him," Sabine said with little emotion.

"Darling, that's nonsense. You don't appear paralyzed to me. Anyone else?" Richard smirked.

"Senator, I assure you this is no joke. You've been accused of serious crimes," Taggert said.

"And I'm a state senator and can have your badges like that." Richard snapped his fingers for effect.

The officer ignored Richard's threat. "How did you get the head injury?" he asked Richard.

"She hit me over the head with that candlestick."

"Ma'am?" Taggert raised his brows at Sabine and she nodded.

"I did when he tried to lay his hands on me against my will. The drugs were wearing off and I was uncertain if I'd be able to get up and run, so when he—I hit him over the head with it."

"How do you know he drugged you?" Officer Taggert asked.

"He even said the doctor who gave him the drugs told him the effects lasted a couple of hours," Sabine said. "I guess he slipped it in my glass of champagne at the governor's ball."

The cop looked toward Richard for his response. "So she says. I have a right to an attorney, don't I?" he asked.

"Yes, you do. But we're taking you both to the station. Please get dressed," the officer said to them both.

"Can I go find something besides this ball gown to put on?" Sabine asked.

"Yes, ma'am. But one of us will need to accompany you," Taggert said.

"I'll go too. I'm Ben Laroux, Mrs. Habersham's attorney. I was here to negotiate her divorce terms."

"Fine. Suit yourself."

"Sabine said you were her measly driver." He'd sat up now and turned on Sabine. "I should've realized how underhanded you were. I was so trusting."

They all just stared at Richard as if he'd grown another head. What a ranting fool he was.

Ben and Officer Taggert followed Sabine to her very large walk-in closet, which was pretty full still, considering she'd been away for two years.

She pulled out a pair of jeans and a lightweight cream-colored sweater. There were rows of shoes on racks. She chose a pair of slip-on canvas flats with a rubber bottom. Ben hadn't really thought about her life before Alabama, but he realized now the wealth and privilege she'd been accustomed to before she'd broken free of Richard and her marriage.

"Okay. I'll just go into the bathroom alone to change, if that's alright." Taggert stepped inside before Sabine to check and make certain there wasn't anything or anyone hidden that might somehow sabotage the investigation.

"You'll need to dress where we can see you. I'll turn my back, but since we'll need to run a tox screen on you for possible drugs in your system, I can't take the chance of your ingesting anything without my knowledge. Sorry."

"Okay. Fine. I'm already stripped down to my under-wear," Sabine said. The men turned their backs while she slipped off the blanket Ben had placed around her shoulders. She pulled on the jeans, top, and shoes. "Okay. Done. Let's go stick it to this asshole once and for all. I'm ready to go home. Home, as in Alabama."

Ben's heart nearly beat out of his chest. "I can't wait to get you as far away from here as possible and to take you home. Are you okay?" he asked, hoping she would really look at him, because thus far, she'd avoided meeting his eyes directly.

Since she'd seen Lisa and Steve come into the room. She didn't. But she did glance momentarily his way and give him a slight smile. At least that was something. He had a lot of explaining to do.

"Okay. Let's go," Taggert said. "I'm sorry, but until we sort this out, you'll have to ride in the squad car."

"Can I ride with her?" Ben asked.

"You're her attorney, so I guess that's okay."

The paramedics had arrived while Sabine was changing and were now having a look at Richard's head wound. "Will I need stitches?" He sounded fearful.

"Nah, we'll clean this up and put a little glue on the cut. You'll be fine." The paramedic was a capable woman in her mid-thirties.

And she likely recognized a clear case of self-defense when she saw it, so it was obvious Richard's whining didn't resonate with her.

"But it really hurts. Are you sure I don't need to be

checked out at the hospital?" The other tech tried to control his snort of what might have been laughter.

Ben thought he might have whispered the word pussy under his breath, which wasn't especially professional, but apt.

"Sir, are you alright?" Ben realized the female paramedic was speaking to him.

"Huh?"

"I noticed when you came into the room, you were limping. Did you hurt yourself during this evening's events?"

It was then Ben realized how badly his foot and ankle were throbbing. "Oh. My foot. I kicked the door. Twice, actually."

"Why don't you let us have a look while we're still here?" Then she smiled at him.

A winky-blinky smile. Her name badge said Jennifer Tarpley.

Dear Lord. But his foot really did hurt. "Thanks, Jennifer. I might need an ice pack."

He sat down on the chair in the corner of the bedroom, and elevated his leg on the ottoman, allowing the professionals to evaluate his injury.

Richard had changed into business casual, but still looked like hell. "I want to call my attorney since no one has placed me under arrest."

"Fine. Use your phone." Richard, afforded no privacy, only communicated to his lawyer that he required his services immediately at the sixth district police station.

It was determined that Ben's lower ankle was badly sprained, with a possible fracture. He was given a pair of crutches and the foot was splinted and wrapped with Ace bandages and an ice pack. He hated that his injury took more time and care than the possibility that Sabine was drugged, kidnapped, and nearly raped.

Sabine and Ben were led to one of the police cruisers while Richard was placed in the other.

⫸⫷

SABINE'S TRAUMA AND fear caused by Richard was over, thank God. She had enough witnesses on her side and plenty of hard evidence to prove to the police and the world what he was. But what she couldn't understand was the presence of Lisa and Steve.

She turned toward Ben in the police cruiser and asked the obvious. "What are Steve and Lisa doing here?"

Ben's expression was telling. "I was worried about you. Steve came into my office to offer an olive branch after he and Lisa had started working at the firm. I let it slip that I was researching Louisiana divorce law on your behalf. Steve did a law thesis on Napoleonic Code in law school and is somewhat of an expert on the subject. Anyway, Lisa walked in while we were discussing it."

"And you didn't think I would mind your discussing my very private and delicate business with them? Before you asked me?" Sabine really couldn't believe how insensitive he'd behaved.

And how out of character this seemed compared to what she'd thought of him.

"I know, Sabine. In fact, Lisa was incredibly insulted on your behalf. But once they understood the situation, it couldn't be untold. So, they offered to help. Lisa insisted we inform you as soon as the opportunity presented itself. They were our backup in case things went sideways with the divorce stuff—in case Richard tried anything funny with his attorneys. They figured Steve's knowledge would be helpful. They *were* helpful, and I *was* going to tell you. And I knew they couldn't tell anyone because our client business stays within the bounds of our firm's privilege agreement."

"But I'm not a client. And I didn't agree to anything—least of all your sharing my whole sordid life's story and lies with your ex-girlfriend and your buddy. I appreciate Lisa's sisterhood, but the whole thing is humiliating. The fewer people who knew about this the better. You understood that. In fact, I insisted we keep this only between only those who needed to know."

"You're a hundred percent right. My only defense is my feelings for you. I'm a problem solver, Sabine. I wanted to be certain Richard couldn't hurt you more than he had already. I saw a way to ensure that. I'm so used to fixing situations for clients and my family that I didn't weigh the outcome of your feelings before I opened my stupid mouth to Steve."

"You know, my father was a problem solver like that. He did everything in his power to make certain to gain the best outcome no matter who got hurt. He even had good intentions most of the time. And he really loved us all. But he made decisions that tore our family apart. Richard also made rotten decisions and told me they were in my best interest. Is that the kind of man you are, Ben? Because I'm all done with men who make choices with the noble grandiosity of doing what's best for me, despite what I tell them." She glared at him.

As angry as Sabine was, she realized this wasn't really the time or setting for this discussion.

Ben's expression was grave, but there was fierce light in his eyes. "I only want to love you. I want to marry you and keep you safe and have babies together. I screwed up. In my need to protect you, I overstepped and I blew your trust."

Something twisted inside her heart. Love. She did love him. This wasn't anything like what she'd felt for Richard. It was so solid and real. Ben wasn't Richard and he wasn't her father. That, she was certain of.

She placed her hand in his overturned one. "I'm ready to go home."

⟫⟩⟨⟨

WHEN THEY REACHED the police station, Ben accompanied Sabine and a detective into one room and officers took Richard into another, where he waited for his lawyer. Lisa and Steve waited in the main area, where they were questioned as well.

Ben was able to make a quick call to Howard to let him know that Sabine was safe and the threat was over. "I'll make certain to secure things on my end," Howard said.

Ben had no idea what that meant, but he assumed Howard would secure what needed securing and that it would benefit his people. "Thanks for everything, Howard."

"Of course. And, Ben, I haven't had the chance to give the dirt on Richard. He's being investigated by the higher-ups for some pretty nasty things. Of course, I can't compromise their investigation, but suffice to say, he's already in really hot water and it's all about to blow wide open. The more distance you can put between him and Sabine quickly, the better. Let me know when you're back at the bed and breakfast."

Ben felt suddenly sick. "Got it. Thanks."

The detective came in just as Ben disconnected the call. "Hello, Mrs. Habersham. I'm Detective Bouttee." It sounded like Boo-tay.

"Sabine, please," she corrected.

"And you're her attorney?" the detective asked.

Ben nodded. "Ben Laroux."

"Tell me what happened." He allowed Sabine to speak without interrupting.

She was calm and confident. Her therapist training doing her proud.

There was a knock on the door. Detective Boutte stood and opened it. The paramedic, Jennifer, who'd attended to Ben's foot, which was now propped up on a chair, entered the room. She carried a small plastic carrying case with vials and other paraphernalia.

"How's the foot, slick?" She grinned at Ben.

Sabine just shook her head and laughed, so absurd was this woman hitting on him in this situation.

"Much better now, thank you."

"I was asked to get urine, blood, and hair samples from the victim," the woman said and gestured toward Sabine.

Good thing they were viewing Sabine as the victim, as Richard had the obvious injury and wore the actual bloody wound.

"We're going to run a tox screen to check for the paralytic drug Sabine accused the senator of administering to her," the detective said. "You'll need to head to the facilities with Ms. Tarpley here."

Sabine nodded, and Ben was hopeful the drug had a long half-life, seeing how she seemed pretty normal now. He was relieved they were taking a hair sample because often when a drug didn't show up in blood or urine, it still showed in the hair follicle. Sometimes, not right away, but later.

"I'll accompany them," Ben said, but winced as he struggled with the crutches.

"Up to you and your client."

Sabine nodded her consent. "How's your foot?" Sabine

asked as they made their way down the hallway together.

"This is where you wait outside, slick," Ms. Tarpley said.

"Of course."

The paramedic handed Sabine a sealed cup, but showed it to him as well, because the whole point of his being present was to make certain all protocol was followed and, therefore, all results admissible in court. "Just give us a urine sample and place the lid back on the cup. There's already a label with your name and what we're testing for."

Ben nodded his agreement, and the women went inside the restroom while he waited in the corridor.

He felt pretty confident Sabine was in good hands, so Ben decided to wander down the hall where Richard was being questioned. Richard happened to be outside the room with his attorney waiting to be fingerprinted.

"What do *you* want?" Richard sneered the question at Ben.

"I have an offer to make." Ben had an idea.

And he knew for a fact it was something Sabine would be on board with.

Richard's attorney, sensing an opportunity to possibly save face for his client, stepped forward and stuck out his hand. "Joe LeBlanc. What do you have in mind?"

"Could we speak after my client wraps up the drug testing? It might behoove us all to have a sit-down before any formal charges are filed," Ben suggested, and then pulled Joe to the side. "We have video evidence of the senator's involvement with underage girls. And I've received extremely reliable information from my source in a far higher division of law enforcement that there's an ongoing investigation of a similar sort that will yield devastating charges shortly. My offer might prevent your client's reputation from complete ruin, and it might preserve your career if you've any knowledge of his previous activities that might have endangered minors."

Joe spared Richard a quick glance, which, in Ben's opinion, displayed a very narrow thread of deference to his client.

"See to your client and we'll be here when you return," the attorney said.

Ben heard a somewhat explosive response from Richard as he walked away. The attorney would save his own skin if possible. No way would he go down with Richard's sinking ship. And it was going down fast in a ball of flames. The knowledge in the man's eyes told Ben all he needed to know.

>>>«««

"SABINE WILL HAVE her divorce with absolutely no contest. She will distance herself from you so that her reputation will not be stained by your heinous actions. Period. In turn, she won't tell everyone you tried to force yourself on her teen sister, or testify against you in court regarding your drugging her and trying to rape her to force reconciliation. Sabine will retain the evidence in her possession of your encounters with underage girls unless asked specifically for it by law enforcement. She will simply say that your divorce was the result of irreconcilable differences. Whatever happens to you in the future will not be by her hand, unless you refuse to cooperate." Ben laid the situation out in front of Richard and his attorney.

"We'll take the deal," Joe LeBlanc said.

"What? No, we won't. Are you crazy? She's not going anywhere. I'm not going to jail. I'm a senator, for God's sake. As long as she's my wife, she can't testify against me anyway," Richard's face was almost purple, he was so angry.

Joe turned to Richard and said very calmly, "You are a screaming buffoon. Your housekeeper knows what you did because of the front door camera. It shows you carrying Sabine inside like a lifeless sack of potatoes. Did you forget about that? She'd already called my cell phone to tell me about it. She was scared by the police bursting inside and was worried about Sabine. Do you think your staffers don't know what you've been doing? Everyone has scrambled to cover your ass for the last few years, Richard. You'll be lucky if you don't get sentenced hard labor in Angola."

Richard appeared puzzled. "I don't understand. I have immunity."

His attorney laughed. "Immunity? Do you think you're that special or untouchable? You're a corrupt predator of young women, you asshole. You're not immune to shit. Take the deal and hope the feds go light on you when all this blows up—and it will. Because the more evidence and testimony against you will be years added on to your sentence, and I don't see you faring well as Big Bubba's bitch in the pen." He looked over at Sabine and Ben. "Sorry for the profanity. I've been waiting years for that opportunity. He's been blackmailing me over a minor drug arrest he helped me out with for years so that I wouldn't quit."

Richard glared at his attorney. "You're fired."

"How about we sign this paperwork first?" Ben reached inside the folder he'd been carrying with him. He'd apparently added a few additional items to amend the original circumstances and initialed them. Sabine noticed the handwritten line items.

Joe LeBlanc spared Richard a glanced as he spoke. "What do you say, Richard? You want to let this nice lady go on about her business and keep your secrets or take your chances with Big Bubba for more years than you choose to count?" He smiled then. "And then, I'll quit."

"I also added a small codicil declaring your attorney noncomplicit and unaware of your extra-curricular activities," Ben said.

Joe held up his hands. "I don't know exactly what he's done. I've never actually seen it. Only hearsay."

"Bunch of sons-a-bitches. I get railroaded while the lot of you whistle off into the sunset. Now, how am I supposed to get reelected?" Richard nearly shrieked.

Sabine blinked. He still believed there was a shred of opportunity for reelection. Sabine had been quiet, but as she'd listened to her soon-to-be-ex-husband rant like a lunatic, she realized how far out of his way Ben had gone to prepare for just such a bizarre situation such as this one.

She'd never guessed any of this might have happened. Ben had arranged for spy devices, backup lawyers, and friends, should they need them, and he'd come along to support and protect her. And she'd needed every bit of it and more. She'd been followed, drugged, and nearly raped by her husband. But Ben hadn't taken a single chance with her safety or her life. And he'd had paperwork ready to finish this thing by protecting her reputation and severing her ties with Richard and his nefarious actions.

Sabine stood and approached Richard, her voice even and reasonable. "So, you might get reelected, Richard. Sign the papers or you'll never know. Because I guarantee you won't if you don't."

He appeared sullen and resigned at her words. "Fine." He picked up the pen and scrawled his signature.

She smiled at him, realizing he had no clue what kind of fantasy world he was living in if he believed he would walk out of here and remain a free man, much less be elected to an office where he would be entrusted to serve the people of the state.

Ben signed as her attorney, and Joe as the witness and attorney for Richard. This was a legal document. An agreement between parties that ensured Sabine's freedom from this odious criminal. No matter what he'd done, she would be free. And she would have Ben Laroux in her corner. She'd misjudged Richard, but not Ben.

They'd been allowed to have their meeting in private. Now, as Ben hobbled to standing and Sabine opened the door, there were two uniformed officers waiting outside. Were they going to arrest her for assault?

"What's going on?" she asked the officer closest to them.

He winked at Sabine. "Not to worry, ma'am."

They moved closer to Richard, who had yet to stand. "Richard Habersham, by order of the State of Louisiana, and the New Orleans District Attorney's Office, we're placing you under arrest for engaging in prostitution with a minor and contributing to the delinquency of a minor child, and felony sexual exploitation of a minor. You have the right to an attorney."

"He's my attorney." Richard pointed to Joe, looking like a caged animal.

"Nope, sorry, Richard. I just did my last task as your minion. You are officially without the representation of me or my firm." Joe appeared relieved not to have to take this as Richard's representative. He'd dodged a bullet, thanks to Ben. "Nice meeting you, Ben. Best of luck to you, Sabine."

Joe exited the room a free man.

"Bye, Richard. Good luck," Ben said. "I'll file this paperwork first thing Monday morning."

Sabine took a final look at Richard. She didn't hate him. It was pity that took up the space inside her where other emotions previously resided. "Goodbye, Richard."

She expected a cry for help, since Richard had never lost at anything in his life.

He just stared at her in silence. Silence, and maybe acceptance. He wasn't a stupid man, just incredibly filled with his own self-importance and denial of responsibility. Tonight, he'd been taken down. He'd been humbled. Now he would face the dire consequences of the sum of his actions.

Chapter Seventeen

"**I**T'S FINALLY OVER," Sabine said.

They were in his bed. They'd had to wait until Monday morning to file the legal paperwork. Since Sabine and Richard's divorce would be dissolved in Louisiana, it had to be done there. They also were asked by police to stop by the station to fill out more paperwork to finalize the reports from Saturday evening's events. So, they'd not been able to leave right away.

Plus, the DA had subpoenaed the video evidence in Sabine's possession on the spot, so she'd turned it over. It was a good thing they'd brought it with them in case Richard wanted proof it existed, or that she had it.

"Finally. Hopefully, they won't ask you to testify at his trial. Since you provided a statement that you would give up the evidence in your possession but had had no other or prior evidence of his crimes. But we'll face that if and when we have to. He likely wouldn't go to trial for at least a couple years, as slowly as the system works."

"Sure makes it easy to get a divorce when your spouse

has been charged with a felony and proved to be an adulterer, along with living apart for two years." Sabine was granted a divorce on those grounds on the spot.

"Free woman, huh? I like the sound of that." He kissed her on the head.

She was lying in the crook of his shoulder, and they were both rested and sated. And happy.

"Yep. And home in Alabama. Seems my worries are few now." Sabine had shed the mantle of Richard and all he'd represented in her life. She was free to embrace her future now.

"Oh, by the way, my mom wanted to know if we could stop by this evening for dinner. And she included Rachel, your mom, and Norman in the invitation. You free?"

"Um, sure. I'll let the others know. It'll be around six before I can get free since I'm making up a couple sessions from yesterday." She'd had to cancel her Monday patients since their return was delayed.

"I'll let Mom know to expect us around seven?"

"That should work. It'll give me time to go home and freshen up first."

They'd also stopped by Touro Hospital before leaving New Orleans and had Ben's foot x-rayed, and thankfully, it wasn't broken, only badly sprained. So, he was put in a boot for the next couple weeks, and would see a local orthopedist. Sabine drove them home, since he'd injured the right foot.

"HONEY, ARE YOU sure she's ready for the whole family descending on her like this?" Emma asked. "We aren't exactly an easy pill to swallow all at once. I mean she's met us all at one time or another, but a family dinner? With all the kids and animals?"

"Gotta be sure she can handle us, you know?" Ben grinned at his older sister.

"Ooohh. You slick devil, you. I'm so happy for you. Don't you worry. We've got that other thing all handled. She's going to love it! We've all been involved, even the children. We're thrilled you realized Sabine was the girl for you. We all knew it right away. You're different with her. She brings out the best in you—happiness."

Ben had a surprise for Sabine. The obvious one and the not-so-obvious one. He'd set the sister brigade on a mission that none could resist.

He'd left the office an hour early to make sure everything was on schedule, so he ignored a call from the office landline and let it go to voice mail. He would check it later. There wasn't anything urgent on his schedule.

Ben entered the kitchen at Evangeline House and inhaled. "Cammie, that smells amazing."

"Of course it does, Brother. I've earned my queen of Southern cooking crown. The crawfish pies will be out shortly. The gumbo is simmering on the stove. I'm using Papa Bean's recipe. I can't wait to see what Sabine and her mom think of it. I know they're amazing Louisiana cooks, so

I just had to do Cajun tonight. I've got bread pudding in the oven with pecan praline sauce."

"I'm dying here," Ben said. He loved Cajun food, and his sister knew it. "Thanks for doing this."

"Are you kidding? I'm finally feeling a hundred percent now that I'm in my second trimester. I have the energy of a freight train. Just try and stop me."

"I wouldn't even attempt it, if I were you," Grey Harrison said. He'd entered the kitchen, and slid up behind Cammie, covering her very slightly rounded tummy with his big hands. He was obviously a very happy man.

Ben's heart warmed seeing his sister and Grey so happy after all the turmoil they'd gone through not so long ago.

Two screaming preteens burst in the kitchen like a tornado. "She's here, Uncle Ben. Can we bring them out yet?" Samantha and Lucy were so excited, they were about to burst with it.

"Not yet. Wait for my signal, okay? I want the surprise to be just right," Ben said.

"Ooooohh. Okay. But, hurrrrrry." The girls ran back out to their post.

Ben followed, albeit a little limpy, to greet Sabine. Rachel, Elizabeth, and Norman were with her, so his greeting was a little less obvious and enthusiastic than it might have been if they'd had a moment of privacy. He really couldn't seem to get enough of her. Seeing her after a long day apart was like a lifetime of separation. What kind of romantic fool had he become? Who cared? He was in seriously big love and the happiest he'd ever been.

"Hi there. Wow, there's quite a crowd. I didn't realize the whole family would be here." She didn't seem upset, only mildly surprised. "How's your foot today?"

"The foot's okay, but you'll need to understand the true nature of my family. Sometimes you get the whole bunch when you least expect to." As he finished the statement, JoJo, Beau, Suzie, and Dirk came in the front door.

"Hey there, Sabine," JoJo hugged her, and Sabine greeted the children. Suzie was five, and grinned up at Sabine, obviously happy to have the attention of the pretty lady. Then, she spotted her uncle Ben and shrieked as she threw herself into his arms. As was their custom, and despite his gimpiness, he carefully spun her around until she was dizzy and he set her down so she could walk like a drunken sailor while Ben made certain she didn't get the business end of anything hard or sharp until she regained her equilibrium.

Ben then turned to Dirk and gave a fist bump to the gangly fifteen-year-old, who grinned at him with the adoration of one who hoped to walk in the same shoes someday. "Hey, buddy."

"Hi, Uncle B. Sorry to hear about your foot."

Beau, the quietest of the whole gang, shook Ben's hand. Ben liked his brother-in-law, and appreciated how Beau supported his family as a strong male role model and a person of great character. He never swore in front of his children or drank to excess. Ben had learned what kind of husband and father he wanted to be someday by watching Beau over the years.

"Happy for you, man."

"Thanks, Beau."

Sabine was speaking with JoJo and Cammie, and Ben enjoyed simply watching how well she meshed with his people. It mattered so much to him that they got along.

There was a bit of activity at the front door, as the group had moved toward the main living area. Since the Evangeline House was an event business inside a large mansion, it was set up perfectly to welcome groups large and small. It seemed that his oldest sister, Maeve and her husband, Junior had arrived. Their daughter, Lucy was already here and assisting with the plans.

So, the group was all here and dinner was ready, according to Cammie and Mom, who'd come out of the kitchen and announced that everyone should move toward the dining room. Eat first, was the family motto. The Laroux family had a lot of family mottos, but that was one of his favorites.

There were place cards, so no one got confused as to where they were to sit. It wasn't at all formal, but knowing where to sit saved chaos with a family this large, especially when someone had a goal and an agenda like Ben did this evening.

A bell sounded to quiet everyone and Mom announced,

"Serve your plates and find your places, everyone, and we'll get started." Howard helped herd the crowd toward the serving board on the side of the dining room. They'd already carried out the dishes filled with food, it seemed. He certainly would've helped with that if he'd known they needed it.

>>><<<

SABINE HAD TO admit that she was a bit overwhelmed at the sheer number of people at a regular dinner with Ben's immediate family. But none of them seemed even slightly fazed by it.

As they sat down to eat, she felt as ease, as if she and her mother belonged with this zany, fun group, and they fully accepted her and her past. Sabine knew that at least half, if not all, were in the loop about what had gone down in New Orleans. She'd given Ben the okay to inform them. She didn't want to live a lie, wondering when, or if, her bubble of belonging and happiness would burst. Her true identity would spread around town; it would be gossip, and there would be talk. She intended to share the news during her patient sessions as soon as possible, where she could control how they received the information.

Howard stood and said grace over the food, once everyone had managed to serve their plate and was seated. His prayer was touching, and not limited to the food. He thanked God for bringing them together and asked for continued safety for his family and friends. This came from a heart full of love for his new family, and after a lifetime of being alone. The words were simple but the sentiment far deeper and more meaningful, which caused everyone at the table to join hands in silent understanding for their own blessings. They were healthy, together, and held a deep abiding love for one another.

Sabine teared up, looking around. She missed her dad. Yes, he'd screwed up, but he was her father, and her family. She also realized her mother and father's relationship couldn't be repaired. Mom had moved on and was happy. They would go to the hearing Thursday and support him for real. Hopefully, he would be released. Sabine knew that deep down he wasn't a bad person, only a man who'd weakened and lost his way.

Just as they were saying their amens to Howard's heart-felt prayer, the doorbell rang. "I'll get it," Ben jumped up, nearly forgetting about his injured foot, and went to answer it.

When he came back inside, his expression was confused and somewhat disturbed. He cleared his throat and everyone looked up. "Um, say hello to Governor Grumby. Apparently, he stopped by my office and I wasn't there, so someone told him he could find me here."

"Greetings, Laroux family. I'm sorry to interrupt your family dinner. I was on my way from Huntsville to Birmingham and thought I'd swing by and make my announcement. But there are a few folks outside who might also want to hear what I have to say."

"Well, hello, Governor Grumby. Who's outside?" Howard asked, his tone protective.

"About half the town, I figure, and several reporters. It seems once word got around that my security detail was spotted, folks came out to see what the ruckus was about. Looks as if they've followed us here."

Everyone got up from the table to look outside then. "What sort of announcement do you plan to make, sir?"

The governor smiled. "Son, it's a surprise, so why don't we go on outside and we can get on with it? I'd like to get home before midnight."

Ben looked like he wanted to argue with the governor but thought better of it because it was foolish to do so. But Sabine knew him, and he appeared worried.

The entire family headed out, confused, but somewhat excited.

Sabine stood next to Ben, who stood next to the governor once they were outside on the large porch, which acted as a stage, as it was elevated above the crowd by the set of steps leading up to it. The family stood on both sides.

And sure enough, it did seem as if half the town was there. Good thing the Evangeline House was set back from the road and had a large lovely front yard for just this kind of gathering.

Governor Grumby began, his deep, booming voice carrying across the crowd. "What a fantastic impromptu gathering we've got here today. I've come to town to honor one of you own today. Many of you know Ben Laroux as a local attorney, but he's far more—he's a hero. He's recently been appointed to my special board to help identify corruption and waste in our great state, and he's doing a fine job. But just this past weekend, he managed to play a major role in bringing down a high-profile criminal who's been under surveillance for quite some time."

The crowd murmured its surprise, and Ben turned a shocked stare toward Sabine. He had no idea this was coming.

"While Ben here managed to help bring down the felon, Senator Richard Habersham, his wife, Theresa Prudhomme Habersham, who has been estranged from him and living a covert life here in Ministry, was especially key in this arrest." The governor nodded toward Sabine.

Sabine closed her eyes, understanding the gravity of what had just happened. As she opened them, she looked over the crowed and measured their reaction. Shock. Hurt. Anger. "Dr. O'Connor isn't a therapist?" one of her patients asked aloud. "Wait, Prudhomme? Isn't that the corrupt New Orleans's DA who got sent to prison? Are you his daughter? Wait, I saw that on TV. It *is* you. Your hair is different."

"No. I'm a therapist. I'm just using my given name. My other name. Oh, I'd like a chance to explain—" Sabine began.

"Sabine isn't Sabine?" another asked, and an angry mur-

mur spread into a few shouts. "Lying must run in the family."

Governor Grumby held up his hands for silence. "I'll let you work out your beef with Mrs. Habersham, but I wanted to honor them both with a governor's certificate. *And* I want to offer my endorsement for Ben's run for next term's state house of representative of this district."

Sabine's eyes filled and her heart plummeted. Of all that had just gone sideways in her life within the past five minutes, this was the worst. He planned to run for public office? How could she not know this? He'd never mentioned it.

She couldn't/wouldn't marry a politician, no matter how much she loved him. Politics had ruined her life. She felt someone at her elbow, supporting her. It was Rachel.

She whispered into Sabine's ear, "Smile. You can fall apart later. Appear confident. Say thank you. We'll sort this out later."

Ben tried to place his arm around her shoulders. She couldn't allow it. She felt so betrayed. Surely he understood she couldn't be with a high-profile political figure.

The crowd was casting angry glances her way. They'd been betrayed too.

Then, someone said, "Dr. O'Connor saved my marriage. I don't care what her real name is." A few folks nodded in agreement.

Another patient stepped forward. "Sabine was there for

me when my ex-husband left me and she counseled me through my fight for custody this past year. I couldn't have survived it without her." This was a very private thing, and Sabine was shocked this woman had spoken out.

"Thank you." Sabine had tears in her eyes now.

"She persuaded me to come to marriage counseling and get help with my drinking problem." One of her male patients stepped forward, shocking Sabine. "We owe her our marriage and my life. I don't care what her name is."

Then, what capped it off was Judith Jameson, who had pretty much driven Sabine crazy as a patient this past year, came forward, stepped up onto the porch, and addressed the crowd. "Good people, it seems that Sabine here has had some misfortune of her own, and she came to this town for refuge. In her time here, she's managed to do many of us a great deal of good. For me, she's changed my outlook about how I see my relationships with my loved ones. I still think a lot of you are wannabees and suck up to me to get into the Junior League and get Kappa Delta reference letters for your girls at Alabama, but I've made *personal* progress because of Sabine."

Judith placed her hands on her hips in a power stance. "Y'all need to think about what I've said and look inside yourselves and decide if our town has been better since she's arrived. Our Ben here certainly seems to think so."

The crowd made the turn and began applauding wildly. Judith turned and winked broadly at Sabine. Sabine had never been so touched by a gesture.

The town chose her.

The governor stepped up and presented the framed certificates to Ben and Sabine. They accepted, and the reporters took photos. Then, one of them asked Ben, "So, Ben, will you make a run for the state house next year?"

Ben looked over at Sabine and shook his head. "Nope. I've got enough going on here with my law practice, and hopefully will be planning a wedding." The crowd oohed and aahed.

Sabine grinned at him as he struggled just a bit to get down on one knee. "Theresa Sabine O'Connor Prudhomme, will you marry me?"

He left off the Habersham, she noticed.

"What? No ring?" someone shouted.

"I'm going to let her pick it out. But until then, I've got something to keep us busy." Ben gave a cue to his two young nieces.

They giggled and ran to get something inside.

"Thank God. We've been waiting all day for this," Emma said.

The girls were back in an instant hiding something behind each of them.

Sabine couldn't have been more shocked and thrilled when each of them presented her with a furry creature. Lucy held a squirmy puppy of about six weeks, which looked to be a golden or Labrador retriever mix, and Samantha held a tiny golden kitten with large blue eyes. Sabine nearly melted right there. The crowd went wild, which caused the kitten to bury its claws in her arm while she tried to hold onto it.

Ben took the puppy, and asked again, "So, will you marry me?"

Sabine laughed and slid into his arms, along with their new family. "I will marry you, gladly, Ben Laroux."

More cheers from the crowd.

Someone shouted above the din. "Ben, would you consider being the mayor? We're in need of one, you know?"

Since Ben had helped rid the town of Tad Beaumont, the town's former mayor, for his corruption last year, they'd had an elderly interim mayor, who'd made it clear he had no interest in a permanent career.

Ben looked at Sabine, who smiled and said, "Mayor Ben Laroux. I like the sound of it. It's not like they don't already treat you like their public servant already. We wouldn't have to go to Washington D.C., would we?"

He laughed then. "Um, no. But are you sure you want to be a mayor's wife? I mean, you might have to judge a pie contest or cut a ribbon from time to time, and then there's the Ministry Christmas Parade. How do you feel about riding on the back of a convertible?"

"Sounds like great fun compared to my past as a politician's wife. Just don't let it go to your head, okay?"

"Me? Let popularity go to my head? Never."

Surrounded by family and friends and most of the town

by now, they turned toward the crowd, puppy and kitten in one arm each, Sabine held up Ben's empty hand between them. "Ben Laroux for mayor of Ministry!"

Of course, the crowd went wild.

The governor, not to be ignored, added, "I support this candidacy!"

Epilogue

One Year Later

"CAN YOU HOLD her for a second? I need to feed Ala and Bama before we go." Sabine handed their little nine-month old nugget, Janie, over to her daddy, who took the wiggly, giggly baby with open arms.

"How about we go wrestle you into that devil car seat? 'Kay?" Ben carried his daughter out to the SUV they'd purchased several months before Janie's birth. The past year had been the busiest, craziest, and most fun of Ben's life. He'd become mayor of the town, which had been a whole new kind of insanity he'd only imagined, married his beautiful wife, gained two codependent pets, and become a father. It was everything. All the best things he'd wished for such a long time.

Wrestling his cooing, gurgling baby girl into her car seat wasn't an easy feat. Ever. She was a handful, and never static. "Be still, you little mess. But first, I must blow on your belly!" He raised her little dress and make loud raspberries on her chubby tummy, which sent her into peals of screaming giggles.

He looked up to see Sabine watching them, such love and happiness in her gaze that it humbled him.

"So, it's the first time your dad is meeting Norman, huh?" Ben asked.

"Yeah. I hope it goes well. Mom and Dad have done pretty well as friends so far, but it's taken him a while to get used to the idea that she's found someone else."

"What about Rachel?" Ben didn't see Rachel that much. She did a lot of wedding photography for Evangeline House clients and had been taking on a lot of magazine shoots, but their schedules hadn't meshed much lately. But he got the impression she planned to stick around.

"Rachel's starting to get her bearings here. I think she likes the town, and that's saying a lot for her. She's such a free spirit; I'm surprised at how much she's been in one place lately."

"We all get to a point in our lives where the future begins to weigh on us," Ben said.

"Maybe. She and Dad seemed to have made peace, for the most part, now that he's out of prison. His decision to stay away from Louisiana was surprising, since his history was there. But he says his family is here, so he wanted to be closer to us." Jean-Claude had bought a home on the coast at Orange Beach a few hours away. It was a beautiful area with white sands and crystal waters. He told Sabine he wanted to have a place for them to come with their children on vacation and to visit their grandfather. It was close enough and far enough away.

Her brother, James, had crawled back to New Orleans and had gone to work for an ambulance-chasing law firm that advertised on huge billboards and on television. At least he was keeping busy and staying away.

Richard was well ensconced in prison for the foreseeable future. The evidence against him was overwhelming and his new attorneys had strongly advised him to save the taxpayers the time and expense, and himself the humiliation of a long trial. His sentence reflected the disgust the judge held for those who'd been elected by the people to serve and protect, but had broken that trust in a terrible fashion.

Cammie had also given birth to a bouncing baby girl, Stephie, who was now fifteen months old and teaching their little Janie, all the tricks. Lucy and Samantha were in baby heaven as the designated babysitters. Emma had worried she and Matthew wouldn't ever be able to have children because they'd been trying to get pregnant from day one. Since Emma's biological clock was ticking away, she'd been more and more stressed. They'd just gotten word that twins were in their immediate future.

Ben and Sabine, despite their rocky beginning and misunderstandings, had overcome their many challenges. The world kept turning, and even when awful things happened, they'd come together and done what family did—stuck together. And they always would. With family like theirs, how could they not? Ben continued his therapy with Sabine and worked his way through his list to make amends with anyone he felt a need to apologize to or have a conversation with regarding a past indelicate situation where he might have misunderstood signals.

Sabine made him a better man. And she still made the ground shake—every single day. Just as she had from the moment he'd met her.

The End

More by Susan Sands

The Alabama series

If you loved Forever, Alabama,
don't miss the rest of the Alabama stories.

Again, Alabama
Cammie Laroux and Grey Harrison's story

Love, Alabama
Emma Laroux and Matthew Pope's story

Forever, Alabama
Sabine O'Connor and Ben Laroux's story

Available now at your favorite online retailer!

About the Author

Susan Sands grew up in a real life Southern Footloose town, complete with her senior class hosting the first ever prom in the history of their tiny public school. Is it any wonder she writes Southern small town stories full of porch swings, fun and romance?

Susan lives in suburban Atlanta surrounded by her husband, three young adult kiddos and lots of material for her next book.

Visit her website at SusanSands.com

Thank you for reading

Forever, Alabama

If you enjoyed this book, you can find more from all our great authors at TulePublishing.com, or from your favorite online retailer.

TULE
PUBLISHING

34529108R00236

Made in the USA
Lexington, KY
24 March 2019